WEIGHING THE SCALES

SCALES

Dragonsigns – Book Two

Ken Hughes

Windward Road Press

LOS ANGELES, CA

Windward Road Press
11923 NE Sumner St Ste 879426
Portland, OR 97250-9601

Publisher's Note: This is a work of fiction. Names, characters, places, and incidents are a product of the author's imagination. Locales and public names are sometimes used for atmospheric purposes. Any resemblance to actual people, living or dead, or to businesses, companies, events, institutions, or locales is completely coincidental.

ISBN paperback: 978-1-7350002-6-8
ISBN ebook: 978-1-7350002-5-1

Book Layout © 2017 BookDesignTemplates.com
Cover © 2021 by Sleepy Fox Studio

Weighing the Scales/ Ken Hughes -- 1st ed.

To Scott

— I never know what you'll summon up next

CONTENTS

CHAPTER ONE

GUARDED

Miss nothing. He could be anywhere.

Colin crept down the broad, bright corridor, searching the walls for that one faint mirage-blur in the fluorescent glow that could be Eric's outline. If the bastard tried again, he had to spot him.

Colin's sister was out of sight ahead. They'd wheeled Terri out of surgery, but he had to move softly and hang back or crouch down in hopes none of the doctors noticed the faint shape of him—all while keeping his concentration on controlling the "skein" that covered him.

Eric's had more practice with invisibility, and everything else this magical substance does. And he was here trying to take Terri back just minutes ago.

Colin slowed his tired feet, stared through the gauzy haze over his eyes at the junction of corridors ahead. Two, no, three nurses stood talking with a doctor at some kind of station: "watch for any reaction—" "if those cops get in your way—"

And two uniformed police stood behind them. Of course they did, just when Colin felt the urge to reappear and simply talk to them, take his chances to work *with* someone again.

Bea wasn't stationed among the cops. She wouldn't be, anymore.

Instead Colin edged around the intersection—his foot scraped on the floor once and he saw a cop glance up, but he froze and the cop looked away again. There was nothing but "a trick of the light" to see, if they had no idea his glimmer could be more.

Colin moved up the corridor to the side, away around the staff. The hospital's mix of sounds and stillness in the night sounded almost peaceful, so there had to be a way to work around the crowds and catch up with Terri.

Make no sound. Keep in the corner of every eye that could notice me. Hold onto the concentration twist *that makes light blur around me, and spot any outline that could be Eric...* Bea had used skein to help her *see* their hidden enemy, but Colin could only search every pattern of light he saw.

The next intersection was clear, free to let him turn back toward where Terri had gone—

Something twitched at the intersection beyond it, at the edge of a corner. Colin blinked, started on the wider circuit toward that. It looked like simply a shadow, but he couldn't ignore it.

And how many shadows and detours would it take? Did he have to check every inch on Terri's floor, and then check it again, just because Eric could be here? Tiredness blurred at his vision.

A doctor stepped into view at the junction, then another. Colin pulled back, back toward the more direct way around. He had a sudden image of his sister lying alone in some room and Eric simply coming in through her window. The skein's strength could tear right through glass, or iron bars.

Even the intersection he'd passed up had a nurse standing in it now. But she stood off at the corner staring at her tablet, easy for Colin to slip past her and her cart and on toward where Terri should be.

A foot scuffed on the floor behind him, where no person had been.

He whirled. A *motion,* a huge skein-bulked blur lunged at him.

He flung himself clear, far as the skein could let him leap. In midair came one thought: Eric should be faster, staying invisible was slowing him down too—

Colin slammed against the wall, glanced off it and crashed down against some clattering shape—the nurse's cart.

And even that impact didn't cover the *crunch* of Eric's fist gouging into the wall.

Colin looked up, saw the nurse whirling toward him. *Can't let go, have to keep the skein hiding me from light.*

Eric sidestepped her. That blur took a slow pace to move out of the nurse's line of sight, and began stalking toward her.

No! Colin sprang up and advanced on his enemy. Eric hadn't lunged yet, she wasn't his real target...

Footsteps raced up in the corridor. A woman charged into view, short blonde hair and watchful eyes and no fear at rushing into the scene. Bea wasn't really a cop anymore, *and* she'd lost her skein, but she was still here.

Two uniforms pounded up behind her, and a doctor at their heels. Colin froze, watching Eric—the blurred shape was already crouching down, letting their gazes pass over him.

"Ma'am? You alright?" one cop said the nurse.

"That son of a bitch trying to get to his sister?" the other growled.

They still think it could be me... oh. These two were the same cops that had walked into Colin's last fight with Eric, the ones he'd attacked in the confusion...

They all looked right past them both now, staring around and missing the two mirage-shapes. All except Bea looking in Eric's direction, no doubt watching his every move.

Eric edged back, away. Colin let out a hushed breath; of course Eric wouldn't risk so many witnesses seeing the not-quite-hidden outlines they ought to be watching for. And Bea let him go.

A motion up the other way caught his eye. Another uniform stepped out from a doorway, with Colin's mother behind him.

If Zara—she was always Zara, to everyone—had just been in that room, then Colin had found Terri. He moved toward them.

"So you just knocked the damn cart over?" one cop was saying behind him.

"No! I wasn't anywhere near it—"

Colin edged away, smooth and silent as he could move. One officer up ahead walked a few steps towards him but never glanced over as he slipped by.

Zara stayed at the doorway. Colin heard his foot scrape on the floor now, and she blinked and stared at the approaching shape.

"It's just me." Somehow his whisper was enough to distinguish his blur from Eric's, and the hardness that had been tightening on her face eased away.

He slipped into the room.

The space was small, too small. But it had room for the unconscious Terri da Costa.

His sister looked odder than ever, as pale and wasted away as when he'd found her, but now surrounded by medical tubes and wires instead of the skein she'd been encased in. She'd survived the Rayo Hill Earthquake, and Eric had kept her prisoner for three years with the skein to keep her alive... and then he'd ripped the stuff away when Colin rescued her.

And he still wants her back. To take her away, or prove he's right, or something.

"The guy's long gone." Words from one of the cops drifted up from outside. "We *all* going to stay here all night?"

"Eric Rowe has already killed four cops," Bea said. "Any time you want to look away, you keep that in mind."

"I get it. But look, you shouldn't even be here, *Miss* Simms."

Colin shook his head. If the police did pull out, if he had to keep watch for Eric all alone—and they forced Bea away too...

He looked at Terri again, so still. Hours ago she could barely crawl, even when she was coated in skein, and then Eric had taken that and she'd still defied him. The doctors must have stabilized her, but they'd just gotten her back.

Soft feet behind him showed Zara stepping into the room. Her gaze went right to him; his control over the skein must have slipped, but she didn't even blink at the silver-green-sheathed figure of her son.

Instead he stepped into her hug.

One warm, sheltering moment after so many hours chasing Eric and trying to keep Terri—and Zara herself—out of his claws... For one moment Colin wondered how she'd talked the hospital into letting her stay this late with her long-lost daughter. But then, saying no to the heart of the Hillside community had never been easy.

"They say they've sewed her all up," Zara said. "As best they understand all her half-healed injuries. They think she's good. Or, alive."

Zara was doing it again. Refusing to show her fears for her children's sake, and almost succeeding.

But Terri had a whole church collapse on her...

"Don't forget, she spent years wrapped up in what has to be the perfect bandage." Colin forced a smile, though she wouldn't see it behind her shoulder. "And I've got plenty of skein to give her—but wait, it's no good until she wakes up to control it."

And she *had* to wake up. This was just the anesthetic, not some sign that she'd bled out the last of her strength. It had to be.

The door moved.

He'd forgotten the police out there. Now he had one instant to clutch at the skein's power and step out of Zara's hug, before the cop looked in.

"Looks like it's nothing, ma'am—'Zara,' sorry." The man looked at her, frowned, but made no real reaction to whatever faint silhouette he saw behind her. "And... when we find your son, we'll try not to hurt him. We just need his whole story on how he found your daughter, and all the rest of it."

You mean lock me up while you bury me in questions, Colin thought. He held his breath until the cop had stepped outside again. *And I let my guard down, stupid!*

The door was closing, but it halted and Bea stepped in.

When she'd shut it fully behind her, he let himself reappear.

She didn't even blink at that. She only said "I'm sorry, Zara. I keep telling them Eric's still a threat. I suppose it's hard to believe."

Colin slipped forward a step to her, enough to keep his voice from the cops outside. "And you're so sure you can't tell them what they're up against."

Bea only looked back at him. That same controlled face, really almost as young as his, that he'd been just learning to get a smile from... She'd taught him to hunt Eric, tracked down Terri beside him, but she'd always been so certain they had to hide the skein from her superiors.

And now Terri was here, helpless, and the police still had no idea what they were guarding her from. Was it really a surprise they were talking about reducing her protection, or ready to suspect Colin himself?

He glanced at Zara. His mother stood so *quiet* now, when it should be her fire and insight pushing them and making every step ahead clear. That she kept still meant that they'd reached a point with little left to say—or no choices at all.

But we survived. He looked between Zara and Terri again, both alive. Except Eric could be stalking back toward them right now, or else watching for some time tomorrow or later, simply waiting for the police to let their guard down. A few of those voices rattled out in the corridor, dry, scattered sounds that felt as restless as drumming fingertips.

While Eric was... something cold slid up Colin's spine. Eric was far enough gone to lash out at anything, and now they knew the price for making even more skein was simply *human flesh*. Did Eric even have limits now, to how far he could build up his strength or what lives he could toss to it?

He was our friend. *But he blames the family and the whole town and its history for Terri and more—*

Colin looked down to see his hands trembling, shaking with rage and just too tired to hold it in.

Bea broke the silence, with a sudden, confident "I'll stop him. The whole department's looking for him now, and I can still use that. It has to be done."

"I hope you're right." Zara barely stirred as she spoke.

"And while you're searching?" Colin said. If the police let their guard down watching Terri...

A voice pushed through the sounds outside. Calm, soft, and stilling the fragmented noises from the police: "What happened here?"

"False alarm, sir," one of them said.

That voice. Colin whispered to Bea, "Who's that cop there?"

"Lieutenant Hoyle. He's running this now."

"He spotted me when I first got to the hospital, and he let me go. And we need someone to get how serious this is."

" 'Get' what?" Bea's voice dropped lower, and fiercer. "Invisibility, bulletproofing, and now using that 'protection spell' to make more skein by feeding people to it? —Oh yes, Zara told me what Eric tried doing to her," she added. "You know once you tell them about the skein, this'll never be about protecting you, or stopping Eric."

It can't mean you have to shoot someone when they're helpless, or risk your badge over it. Even Eric.

Colin stepped past her, toward the door.

"Wait!" Zara snapped. "You heard how the police spoke about you. It's not safe."

"It's not getting any safer." Not for Terri, trapped by her injuries and waiting for Eric to come after her again, with Colin afraid to step away or sleep at all. They needed that police protection.

Colin reached up to the crown of his head. His fingers dragged the skein back, and a *thought* magnified the motion to make the stuff split and peel away, down his head and on down his body.

Zara's breath caught when his face appeared. He'd only had a glimpse himself, of the raw scars on his face and arms, from trying to control what the spell did to the skein. Now just pulling the stuff away from the gashes stung worse than any bandage—

He kept his eyes looking past her, and kept his features steady as he flattened the skein to slide in under his shirt. At least she didn't have to see his pain too.

It's either keeping a full police watch here, or Eric wins.

He opened the door.

"Hey!" "That's him, what the hell—"

The two nearest uniforms closed in on him. One scruffy beard, the stocky build on the other—of *course* those were still the two that had broken up his fight with Eric in the church, the two he'd lashed out at. He looked around for Hoyle, but the lean older man he remembered was nowhere in sight.

The bigger cop grabbed him and wrenched him around in an arm lock. "Don't you move!"

"If he was going to fight," Bea said, "why would he be here? Think."

"Sure you'd say that," the other said. "We know about you and your boyfriend."

They just go right to that, when Bea and I never let it happen.

Colin gritted his teeth. "Where's Lieutenant Hoyle?"

The cop's grip tightened. "What's it matter? You hit my partner, da Costa."

"So hit me!" Colin flung back. "You want us even, fine. But I'm telling you, it's the same man who's been attacking all of us."

"Hit you? You think I'm stupid?" The cop shoved Colin a step, toward Zara watching it all. Her lips were clenched white to keep silent.

The two cops pushed him down the corridor. Colin tried to move with them, to keep pace and walk with some dignity. Sure, enough concentration could spread out the skein under his shirt sleeves and give his arms the strength to fling the cops off, but he needed them to *listen.*

"That's enough."

Hoyle stepped into view. Colin knew him by his calm voice—and the way the officer's grip went slack—more than the lean build and the wisps of red hair that he'd glimpsed in his first minutes here.

"Lieutenant." Bea's voice came from behind them. "Colin has come forward to explain his side of the last few hours—"

Hoyle held up a hand to cut her off. "Thank you, Simms. We'll discuss your suspension later." He turned to Colin. "Now, let's talk, the two of us."

"Just tell him the truth," Bea said. "That Eric Rowe actually is that stealthy—"

"Coaching a witness?" Hoyle warned. "Now, this way."

"Sir?" That was the cop who had Colin's arm.

Hoyle waved them to back off. The cop let go, and Colin stepped clear and followed the lieutenant away.

For a moment they could have stepped into normalcy, no officers watching them or need to hide from anyone, only the quick stride of the man in front, and the doctors and nurses they passed. Except for the glances Colin caught from some of them, at the marks on his face.

Hoyle stopped them at a simple junction, where stepping around the corner gave them a hint of privacy. He gazed over their surroundings, and turned to Colin. "All right now…"

"*Can* you help Bea?" Colin found the words gushing out. "She's a cop who chased down a murderer—"

"And tried to shoot that murderer when he was captured."

Shooting to wound *him!* Colin wanted to say. But Hoyle probably knew that too.

And the lieutenant went on "It's only the fact that Eric Rowe is still such an obvious threat that's kept charges from being filed so far." He let out a sigh. "Her sergeant and I are doing what we can. But, did you really come here to defend your friend?"

"No." Colin squared his shoulders. "I came to defend my *family.* You've got witnesses now that prove Eric held my sister prisoner, and he grabbed my mother trying to get her back. He's still trying."

Two doctors in white walked by in the corridor. Hoyle let their footsteps pass, then said "Is that why you're here? Go on."

"Alright. Look... I know Detective Simms was bending the rules when she let me near the case at all. But I know a bit about Eric. I was the first one to recognize it was him, and I was right."

Hoyle's eyebrows rose, slow and thoughtful. "How'd you manage that?"

"His voice." Colin drew himself up taller, sloughing off the weight of the last day's fighting, anything to make the truth credible. "Eric Rowe used to be our friend; he was *engaged* to Terri. Not that we had a clue he'd been all twisted up by finding she'd survived the earthquake. But he'd been holding her prisoner for all three years, and when we found where he kept her..."

He looked at the floor a moment, until he forced out the next words.

"Then I rushed in ahead of the cops, and pulled her out myself. I know, it would have been cleaner if I'd let all of you do that."

"Awkward, but understandable after so long," Hoyle nodded.

"Thanks. But the next minute was when it went south: Eric caught us in the street and attacked. I'm sorry I left Bea and the others there, but I did get Terri away from Eric for a while. Then tonight he set a trap—"

"Never mind that now." Hoyle's eyes locked onto Colin's. "Several of our officers tried to bring you back, but you got away from them all in broad daylight, carrying your sister. You want to tell me just how you pulled that off?"

"Well, the Hillside's my home turf, I guess more than for the officers there." Colin frowned; one mention of *how* from Hoyle and he turned evasive? But he went on "And I only had to make it to the top of the hill, above the streets—"

"You make it sound easy." Hoyle waved that aside. "I know a bit about you, Colin da Costa. Some martial arts, but mostly you've been a workhorse for your mother's community efforts since you left school."

"Because we lost Terri." It sounded defensive, even to Colin's own ears. "I guess that's me. What are you saying?"

"That being able to throw a punch doesn't tell me how you left Rayo Hill's Finest in the dust. Not that morning or when Rowe escaped tonight, and then a third time with me here." He leaned forward, gaze boring into Colin. "We have a four-time cop-killer out there. But you, you bring your sister and then your mother out of danger, and you come back with those scars..."

He waved at Colin's face.

"I need to know how that's possible."

"You need to know it *is* possible, or Eric will just keep killing," Colin flung back. *I'm stalling again*—but he felt his fists clenching, ready to push back the more Hoyle leaned on him. "You can't stop him with ordinary guards."

"I asked you how *you* got past us."

"Too easily. I mean, can your cops be ready for the smallest little sign that someone's creeping up on them? Can you keep them in pairs as if any moment could be the one someone gets hit?" At least that kind of protection might make Eric back off. He waved around the corridor; any corner of that space could be Eric creeping in if they turned their backs on it.

"You're explaining security to me?" Hoyle scowled. "How is that different from how I'd protect any victim?"

"It has to be better! Eric's already lured Zara out and grabbed her once, to get Terri back. He'll try again if you can't stop him." He leaned in to meet Hoyle's gaze. "That is the real goal, right? Bringing him down?"

"Four. Dead. Cops. Of *course* bringing him down is the goal."

"Glad to hear it." Colin stopped to let his breathing ease. "I just don't think your protection here will do it."

"The security is fine." Hoyle took a step into the main corridor, and waved. Two uniformed cops marched into view.

Colin stared—they couldn't be *arresting* him now, could they? But the two men held back, still a few paces away.

Holding his voice even, he told Hoyle "I hope you're right. One other thing: when Bea shot Eric, he was reaching for a weapon. And even then he was strong enough to break away from your cops, and me. And take Zara."

"That's still hard to believe," Hoyle said. "Even the way this case has gone, the more you claim, the harder it is to swallow."

Does that mean... "If you believed it, would you let Bea off the hook?"

"This isn't a negotiation," and Hoyle glanced at the two cops. Like they might have overheard that, like he couldn't make promises in front of them, but...

But, what would Bea want? Colin felt the extra glimmer of hope in his mind turn harsh and ugly. Bea was the one still fighting to keep the skein's secret to themselves; trading it for her badge would be a betrayal.

And... did he need to give the whole story right now, if he could just make them open their eyes?

"I asked you a question," Hoyle said. "Tell me how you keep dodging us, and I *might* look the other way for tripping over our investigation."

A bluff. It had to be.

But Colin's teeth clenched. Threatening to take him away, with Eric still out there?

Through his teeth he said "But, you *are* hunting Eric, and watching for when he makes his next move here, right? Like he was more dangerous and more tricky than anyone you've chased, ever?"

"What are you saying?" Hoyle said. "We've tracked cop-killers before."

"You think you're ready for him?"

Colin stole one more glance past Hoyle and the two cops, down into the corridor. Then he said,

"Prove it."

and dove past them down the wide hallway.

His first running steps flung him almost into a nurse with a tray, but he twisted aside. Another long moment later he heard the shout that tore open his head start: *"Grab him!"*

They took the bait. *Good. I think.*

Colin charged down the corridor, flinging and wringing all the strength his worn-out muscles had into clawing for another inch of speed. It was still his own strength, with no chance to shift the skein to around his legs yet. Voices rang out ahead of him, closing him behind him. He threaded past another pair of nurses, twisted up one side that looked more empty, then one more...

Far enough.

Out of sight for a moment he flattened himself against the wall, and willed the skein to come flooding out. The silver-green substance surged out from under his clothes and encased him again, and another thought *twisted* light around him. He gasped for breath, clenched his lungs still against their ragged sound...

The two cops barreled by him, too fast to glance at some discoloration against the wall. An intern charged after them, shouting warnings.

Before they got too far, Colin dashed the other way, still blurred against sight. The skein casing his legs drove him forward in long—loud—steps, and he heard the cops behind him react to the noise. For five long steps he darted by, too quick for anyone to focus on the passing blur.

Then he ducked around another corner and slowed, and slipped behind a counter. He could hear them searching, shouting their confusion—and determination. The determination they'd need, to slow Eric down.

I could have told them. Showing them the whole thing would be so much easier... but Lieutenant Hoyle's prodding had just been too much. Bea knew them better, and she might be right.

Right now, putting the police on guard had to be enough.

CHAPTER TWO

A REST

Summer nights in Rayo Hill were warm, easy things. Even for someone napping out on a corner of the grass by the wall.

The Novato Hospital buildings and the bits of brush around the parking lot made enough pockets of concealment for Colin to stay near Terri's room, as the night sank down and stirred itself up into morning. Colin waited, watching what he could guess at about the police protection through the windows and number of cars. He had to believe he'd put them on alert enough to make Eric think twice about trying again… enough to grab a little sleep, at least.

His stomach gnawed and churned in him, the hunger from so many hours working the skein. Worse was looking up past the wall behind him and wishing for his own tiny, "temporary" apartment, that he'd lived in for years and Eric had already invaded once. All those days of working with the community, speaking and hauling and hoping he'd made enough difference here to leave for the Army, for a bigger purpose and an adventure… *hah.*

And the Vargas House itself that they worked out of was gone, rubble. How much did they even have to go back to?

Again and again, he tried to force his thoughts back to Lieutenant Hoyle and the other cops. *If I have to sit here worrying, at least worry about Terri's protection and if I can risk walking in there again, about what comes next. Did my secrets and my 'dare' change that, or could I risk walking in after all?* Bea hadn't answered his calls.

What phone contact he had gotten was a few moments with Zara. And now he could only wait for her before he made his next move.

He kept the skein hidden under his clothes. But when he walked by some of the cars in the lot, he caught glimpses of his face in the windows, and refused to let his eyes stare any harder at those uneasy reflections. Getting some rest folded the numbing exhaustion back, and the pain across his flesh stood out now, as if he'd run through a forest of thorns.

I got stares just yesterday, after the first time I'd set the skein off. Maybe those looks are all I'll ever see on another face again...

He'd *earned* those battle-scars, he kept telling himself. Terri lost so much more, and he'd earned his in fighting Eric and learning the skein. Part of its magic was feeding on flesh, when anyone said the spell and touched it. He'd been lucky.

All part of the fight, the purpose.

Protect Terri and Zara. Stop Eric, somehow.

It had to be worth it...

The curtains at Terri's window edged back, and Zara's hand waved.

Colin drew the skein out around him and faded away. He crept out to the wall below the window, and went to work.

Small, sharp hooks pushed out from the skein at his palms and knees. His thoughts forced them into shape: each an inch long, but needle-sharp, and as stone-piercing-strong as he could make them. He stabbed them into the wall and heaved himself up, one grip at a time. Finally he reached the second floor and the window.

The hospital glass was bolted shut, of course, but he'd looked at the design. He concentrated on the skein until a tendril of it worked through the cracks and into the latching mechanism—a slow, fumbling process to work by sight alone, when he couldn't feel the skein move like actual fingers. *That* would be one step too unsettling.

Then the probe reached the bolt, and he wrestled it to turn and slide back. The window pried open to let him heave himself inside.

Zara stood over at the door, holding it shut and watching him with fascinated eyes. Out beyond that he heard voices and footsteps rolling by. A blaze of white flowers and another set of blue ones stood on the table, when Terri had only been brought in last night.

And Terri... she lay asleep in her bed, covered in a gaudy yellow blanket—why would they use that too-bright color?

Zara pressed a kiss on Terri's forehead, and watched Colin shut the window. "Is there anything that skein doesn't do?" she said softly.

"Not *so* much. It takes all the practice I have to give it that kind of control." He held up his hand and drew the probe back into his "glove," and added "You were reshaping it yourself last night, on your first try."

Zara's hand—a hand with a broad, pale bandage across the back, he realized—touched her pocket. That must be where she kept the sliver of skein she'd used to cut herself free, when Eric had begun feeding her to it.

He went on "Most of the skein's tricks come from making it move. It worked better than a cast for Terri, and it can push us around with more force than we can move on our own. Eric uses that—he's fast, strong, deadly. And some of its shapes work as armor, or blades. Strong ones."

"I saw that too." Zara's voice dropped to a whisper. "I don't know how you could fight Eric off at all, when he's got so much more of it."

"Skill, I guess. It seems like that still counts."

Except I've only had the skein for a few days, I've just been fighting *longer. That's the only thing Eric's not used to, people who can fight back...*

He said "Its only use that doesn't come from its shape is how it can bend light and makes us disappear. I've got no idea why it can do that—but it's how Eric can hit us anywhere. And then, Bea used hers to help her *see* him, but I never figured that trick out."

And he was still wearing the skein over his head, ready to duck from sight. He reached up and peeled it back.

Zara winced. She reached a hand toward his face, and drew it back. "I can't believe you did that to yourself. You saw what a bit of it did to me, and you still…"

He forced a smile. "Like you said, Eric had more of it, so I tried to match that. Sometimes skill isn't enough."

She stared at him. "Don't you laugh, Colin! Tell me, how much does it hurt?"

He widened the grin. "It's not so bad."

"Liar," whispered a voice.

He swung around to look at Terri, at her pale face and her body stretched flat on the bed. Her hair looked shorter, or just cleaner now, pulled back above the monitor wires that spread from her throat. And her voice—he'd barely heard it, it was so wispy and weak.

"Awake again." Zara's voice had only a hint of strain in it, like Terri had been in and out before, and he'd missed it.

Colin shuffled toward her. "How do you…" *How do you even move* now? *Will you ever?* "You're…"

"I'm here," and Terri's lips curved.

She is. That should be what matters. But I've seen this before, she only has the strength to say that much—

His eyes clenched shut. He swayed on his feet, a lump the size of a baseball caught in his throat.

"Here." He stumbled to her, and pulled off a chunk of skein to lay it over her arm, over one of the smaller bandages on her.

Terri's eyes settled on the scrap of green. And it stirred, stretched under the gauze to her wound. Colin tried not to think of what kind of half-healed, reopened damage the doctors had been patching up there.

At least the skein obeyed. Terri's body might be shattered, but her concentration was strong, and she'd spent years wrapped in the stuff.

Her arm shook. It stirred, lifted from the bed—the monitor beside her gave a single squeal and calmed. Zara gasped and moved back to where she'd been holding the door.

Then Terri moaned, one soft sound. Her arm dropped to the bed.

"What's wrong?" Zara said. "Can't it heal her? Eric said enough if it could…"

Terri sighed "Won't last."

And the bit of skein slid out and dropped away from her, green against the blanket's yellow. She'd pushed it out again.

"I think I get it." Colin patted her hand, and scooped up the skein and joined Zara at the door where they could keep their voices lower.

"What's wrong?" she whispered.

"It doesn't… *heal,*" he said. "It can work more like a bandage or a powered prosthetic, but it can't restore anything itself. I guess the skein can't help her any more than it already has." At least with a full suit of it she could crawl a bit, but now—

"Then try harder!" Zara pulled the bit of skein from Colin's grasp and stepped to the bed.

Colin took her place holding the door shut. Just outside, feet tromped by, and voices melded into each other, everyone intent on their own missions.

Zara laid a hand on her daughter's shoulder, and pressed the skein on the bandage again.

"You know we thought you were gone, Terri. And we've got so much to show you. And we'll keep you safe, Eric will never hurt you again—"

Terri's face twitched, from what looked deeper than pain.

Zara motioned to the flowers behind her. "Our friends are just starting to hear about you. They need to know you're doing better, you know."

Terri breathed "Yes… but…"

The skein on her arm stayed still. She *could* move it, but…

"Sandy's baby is growing up, running around. *Everywhere,*" and Zara gave a brittle laugh. "You haven't seen the town after the quake, have you? It's all rebuilding, slowly. We've had a chance to see who cares about the Hillside... I know, you used to say there were never enough of us left here, but wait till you see how we pull together." She gripped Terri's hand.

She's not mentioning how the Vargas House itself, that we looked after for years, collapsed after one minute of Eric and his claws.

"They all want to see you. How after all this, you've come back to us alive. It's a miracle—"

Her voice broke.

Terri's hand stirred to squeeze back.

The skein slid from her arm, abandoned.

* * *

Too soon, Colin felt the door he stood against moving. Zara called "Sorry!" and he had a moment to wrench at the skein's power before they let the nurse in.

He slipped into the hall soon after the nurse left. But at least he got to scoop up a fistful of breakfast bars Zara had brought, and tuck them under his skein out of sight.

He worked his way outward from the room. The more police were on watch, and the more patients and staff crowded in this morning, the more it would slow down anyone trying to slide through between one gaze and the next. *Yes, I got in, but if Eric wants to* take *Terri then anything that makes her a harder target will help.* Of course Eric could still slash his way through all of them, but...

The hospital entrance loomed up ahead. He'd gone all the way out.

And the bustling, blind crowds had thickened behind him.

Colin eyed the gaps along the walls, the best chances to slip back—he should be with his family, and stay where Eric might strike, but how long could he just *sit* there? He ground his teeth.

But what else was there he could do? Go back to predicting where Eric might search for more skein, from the hints about where Matt Vargas had left it? Useless—now that Colin had let Eric learn the spell for *making* skein.

Making it from people. *He's tried using Zara, but he could make it from the flesh of anyone else, anywhere. God, we* have *to catch him.*

Colin let the crowds push him away outside the building. When he'd slipped far enough away from the voices and behind a parked car's cover, he tucked his skein under his clothes and walked out into the crowd, to let him take out his phone.

Bea didn't answer. And any message he left her might be found if the police went through her account.

If he could risk calling her at all. Instead he attacked the food, gulping down nut-rich mouthfuls and imagining he could feel the energy trying to fill the skein-hunger and the long hours. He was tearing at the corner of the last bar's wrapping before he felt his stomach protesting, and shoved the last snack away for later.

There *could* be clues about Eric at his home or his work, but would Colin even know them if he saw them? Instead he drew the skein out again and held back outside the hospital, keeping watch.

He counted three police cars around the lot. He watched the entrance—two more cops drove up and walked toward it, and he crept along behind them to study how well they kept watch. No casual chatting, good, they seemed alert.

One glanced halfway back toward him, and Colin had to freeze and let them walk on inside. These cops had their eyes open, even without him trusting them to know the real danger.

Or were they watching to arrest him too? He hadn't even had a chance to watch Hoyle again, to see how the lieutenant had really learned from his vanishing trick.

And none of it would stop Eric simply slipping in and killing…

The next time he stepped back from the crowd and into sight, he called Bea again. Still no answer.

Is she keeping me at a distance now? That cop's "boyfriend" crack last night wouldn't help—Bea had taken a lot of heat for letting him in on the case, and he'd heard her snap at her own sergeant for saying her reasons might be anything she felt for him.

Except for the moments when that might be true.

Colin shook his head. Bea was also the woman who'd shot a captured Eric, and she'd probably never be a cop again—

Oh.

The morning air suddenly felt ice cold.

Bea had wounded Eric, and then she'd lost her own skein when the police almost found it on her. All the power Colin wore now came from leaving Bea unprotected, the obvious target...

Leo Tozier used to bully Eric, and Eric had hunted him down and terrorized him, then killed him. What would he do about the woman who put a bullet in his hand?

Colin glared at the hospital entrance. The police were in there, he could march in and *demand* they check on Bea, and deal with the consequences later. No, better to call her sergeant, Jordan had been trying to help her—

His phone buzzed.

He grabbed it out, saw *Bea Simms* on the screen. A hitch in his breath eased away.

"You okay?" Was that shaken, hungry voice his own?

"Fine." Bea must have heard his tone, but she gave no sign of it. "I missed your calls, and you weren't answering."

"Well, I had to turn the phone all the way off whenever..."

Whenever he crept around the hospital. All that time he spent invisible, when he couldn't risk a sound vibrating in thin air...

He found himself laughing. "I'm an idiot. Of course I missed your calls, guess I'm still trying to figure out how juggling all this works. But look—"

The laughter faded from his voice.

"Promise me, you won't forget Eric is out there. Hidden, wounded, and we've seen how he likes his revenge. Don't you forget that for a second."

"Why would I forget?"

Bea's clear voice sounded *surprised.* But she would be, she was the professional here.

"Still," and her tone went quieter, "thank you for the thought. Now, I've got news."

"What's that?" Finally, maybe something to *do.*

"I hear they've got a warrant for Eric's home. The search could start any minute."

"Got it. You think they'll find much on—"

On how Eric learned so much about the skein? No, Eric wouldn't leave answers like that just lying around his home.

Probably.

He said "I guess there could be something there. Hell, Eric could try to protect it—like he showed up at Terri's prison. I'll come keep an eye on the cops. And, um…" He glanced around the lot, the buffer space that had been keeping him back from the crowds and the police. "Do you know if it's even safe for them to see me?"

"I haven't heard about a push to arrest you. But, they could be keeping me out of that loop. They already think I've bent so many rules it took Jordan to shield us."

"I guess." And the sergeant could be a target himself, in his wheelchair. But Ed Jordan already had the kind of home security that would make Eric keep his distance.

"I'll send you the address."

"No need. This is Eric, my old *friend.*" He swallowed the bitterness in that word. "So… see you there?"

"Right."

He glanced up at Terri's window again. He could still plant himself up there ready for the worst. But this was a chance, to find some clue at Eric's, or even save some police from a trap. Staying away was more than he could do.

* * *

Walking invisibly outside would never have worked; Colin knew that after the first block. Even a few people on the sidewalk made too many chances their gaze would catch on his outline, when he walked in open space in full sunlight. Or someone might have bumped into him.

The last thing Rayo Hill needed was rumors about ghosts, after the last few days' killings.

Instead he marched openly down the street, not even using the skein to help him jog. Twice he saw police cars roll into view, and both passed on by, a good sign. He also saw eyes turning and lingering on him, on his scars.

The blocks he passed looked dirtier than he remembered. Up on the Hillside, the original Rayo Hill neighborhoods, empty buildings would get a certain basic cleaning up—not always repaired from the quake, but the people looked after them. Down here... it could be Eric's rants last night about Terri being trapped in a doomed town, but...

But down here in the more urban streets, he saw fewer gaps. Instead of places waiting to be used again, there were full blocks of shops and apartments and all, and so many of them looked *rushed.* Sign after sign promised a quick, shady deal on fixing cars, or sent out the smell of greasy food that made him wolf down his last scrap of breakfast.

This was the more active part of Rayo Hill, and how it had patched the quake over after three years. And Eric's home was down here, because he'd left the Hillside long ago.

When Colin reached the corner of Eric's block, he stepped out of view and shifted out of sight. The buildings here were small chunky houses crammed together, without enough plants or fences to slow him down as he crept along with his back to the walls.

Two police cars stood in front of Eric's door. One officer stepped from the building, heading to a car with an armful of boxes. A handful of people stood around the street observing—Colin looked around those for Bea, hoping the police would at least let her in the area.

He waited for his moment and slipped across the street to watch from the opposite side, still keeping his outline clear of people's notice. Another cop carried out a box of what looked like papers, more and more potential clues being taken away from Colin and anyone who might know how to read it.

As Colin edged along he squinted and glared at the space around the house, for any faint shape that might be Eric lurking there. *Could I even see him from across the street, or move in time if he attacked?*

At the far corner of the block stood Bea. Standing next to two neighbors, watching the show together.

There she is at last. He knew he should move away to watch a different angle of the search, but instead he shifted toward her.

Step by slow step, he edged behind one onlooker and then another. Just a quick whisper with Bea would be enough, for now. Enough to meet her soon, and give her back some of her skein so she wouldn't be walking around unarmed.

The neighbors mostly kept their eyes on the police across the street. A cop brought another box of evidence out to the cars. Colin eyed the several scraggly trees around the house, wondering if he'd even spot Eric blending in behind one.

A car pulled up the street beside the black-and-whites, a midsized, upper-middle-end model that reminded him of Bea's car even before Hoyle stepped out.

The lieutenant marched up to the nearest uniform and exchanged a few low words. The cop trotted to Hoyle's car to unload his boxes, faster than before.

Colin eyed the box of evidence as it vanished into the car. *Probably nothing in there,* he knew. Eric wouldn't leave clues at his home or need to defend anything there. *I came here to see Bea too. But I'll keep an eye on the police while they're here.* Eric was still the enemy who'd killed a man in a crowd with one invisible shove.

He watched the street, the crowd, weighing his chances of slipping across again and moving nearer the cops—

"Mommy? What's that glowy thing?"

A little girl in a sparkling shirt looked right at him and pulled on her mother's hand.

Colin dropped flat onto the grass. A faint shimmer along the ground wouldn't be a telltale humanoid shape—but the girl tugged again and pulled closer. *Stupid, standing around this close to them, what was I thinking?*

Another head turned toward them, as that hint of curiosity began spreading in the crowd. Colin gathered his knees under him. He *had* to dash away before they got a closer look, before someone accepted that there could be a near-invisible human being in their midst. Just let the mother look away for a second...

"Hey there."

Bea was walking toward the two, drawing their attention. Of course she'd spotted his situation.

"Look, what's that?" the girl began, as Colin bolted away.

Fast as the skein could fling him, he dove onto the street, away and out of their view.

A car growled up in the street—but still safely up the block, and he was already crossing the far pavement and catching hold of a knobby tree trunk to halt and crouch beside it. A glance around showed faces along the block still watching the police near him. Even his few footsteps must have been swallowed in the general murmur.

The car he'd heard settled in to park in front of Hoyle's. It was painted a pale green, one of the Gardner Development company cars.

Colin crouched lower behind the tree. Eric's old employers, here?

A man and a woman in suits swept out of the car, charging straight at Hoyle.

"What are you people doing? Invading Eric Rowe's home, hounding him like an animal?" The man's voice bellowed around the street, and raised a rustle of curiosity from the onlookers, like a breeze brushing leaves.

Colin held his place, eyes still on the shapes and spaces around the cops. Eric couldn't make a move against them here, but why were Gardner people here defending him at all?

The two accusers' voices dropped lower, but from their waving arms they were still trying to pressure Hoyle, while he stood unmoved.

Another man emerged from the green car, thin and Asian. Dennis Fields, Eric's own boss—and the one who'd started to see how unhinged Eric had become. He hung back from the others, a worried look on his face.

"This kind of persecution will not stand!" the woman flung at Hoyle. "We demand that you put Mr. Rowe's possessions back, this minute!" She shouted it, openly playing to the crowd again.

Among those faces, reaction still looked more intrigued than joining in sympathy, good. A glint of light moved—

"You want to defend Eric Rowe?" Hoyle snapped. "That's a known cop-killer you're talking about. We have a full search warrant for here. And Gardner wouldn't be helping a fugitive, would they?"

The shape moved again.

A faint, faint glimmer against a wall across the street, that could only be Eric.

And he moved toward Bea, along the back of the same yard she stood in. Colin's fingers tightened on the tree bark. *I should never have kept her skein.*

"Not hiding him, no," the Gardner man was saying to Hoyle. "But we see this company as a family, and we're fighting every step of the way to see that Eric gets real justice. What evidence are you basing your charges on?"

There—that flick of motion had to be Eric sliding over the house's door, halfway to Bea now. Colin locked his eyes on that wall. *Eric might not try it right out here, but I have to move...*

"If you want to know about our evidence, talk to the DA," Hoyle said.

"You mean besides one rabble-rousing da Costa woman with a grudge against us, and—"

Bea moved. She strolled away from the knot of people near her, across the grass and away from the house and Eric. As she did, she took a sidelong look behind her.

Watching Eric. Ready.

"And right there, there's the 'detective' that assaulted Eric when he was helpless!" the Gardner man shouted. "And this is your idea of justice?" He swung a finger toward Bea, and heads up and down the street turned to follow.

Bea froze. Even across the street, Colin saw her face go blank, her step falter. Bea lived for her job, and now to have all these people confront her with the choice she'd made, trying to protect them all...

Colin forced his eyes away from her, to Eric. If the bastard made just one move now...

"And you still bring *this* woman here, as part of your persecution? Do you people have any shame at all?"

Bea stepped toward her accusers. "You're talking about events you know nothing about." Her voice was clear, firm. "The one thing that's certain is that Eric Rowe is a murderer."

She said it without a glance back at the man himself, as if all that mattered was that the words be said.

And that answering the challenge let her walk farther away from Eric and into everyone's view. She's using this to guard herself. Colin grinned, watched their enemy for even one first sign of him chasing her.

"How dare you come here?" the woman in the suit said. "How are you even still free?"

"That is enough." Hoyle's voice was the lowest there, but it still carried. "We have a warrant for our search, and for our suspect's arrest. If you want to argue with either of them, take it to the judge. But—"

His voice went softer, and Colin could just make out what he said:

"We're going to have words, if I find you're protecting that killer."

This time the two had no answer. Colin saw Fields behind them, gaze fixed on the sidewalk. That man had had a glimpse of what Eric had become, of course he'd be mortified to see the company still tying itself to him...

Across the street, Eric crept away alongside that house and out of view. Colin watched the walls and the yard for any flicker of movement that might be him slipping back.

Three police walked out from Eric's house, with just two bags between them, the last of their collection. They set them in the cars, with no more interference from the Gardner people.

Hoyle waved Bea to his side. His words to her were far too low to hear, but Colin could see how still she stood and how little she answered. She'd embarrassed them all, even on suspension—because she kept taking every last step she knew that would keep them safe from Eric. No matter what it cost her.

CHAPTER THREE

CLEAR TO SEE

It only took a minute for them to break up and drive away. The group from Gardner pulled out, taking Fields and any explanations he might have about their interest away with them. Hoyle and his cops headed off, the crowd began dispersing.

But Bea herself… after whatever Hoyle had said to her, she was left walking along the sidewalk. A car that looked like her modest black machine waited up on the next block, but she trudged along as if she were facing a much longer journey.

Colin walked up beside her. She glanced toward him—still a faceless blur—and he said "You're not alone."

Her clenching fists relaxed as she heard his voice. "I know I'm not," she whispered back. "Jordan and now Hoyle are the reasons I'm not up on charges already." Her face showed only its usual calm, but did her voice have the smallest catch in it now?

"Already? You mean you're going to *jail* soon—"

He cut off, as an older woman up ahead on the sidewalk glanced toward them. He'd been whispering right to Bea, the bystander couldn't have overheard, but still she looked right at his outline.

Then the woman blinked, looked at Bea, and walked on past them.

Because what could she say? "Do I need my eyes checked, or is that a ghost beside you?" Lucky.

Colin looked around the street—just more quiet houses and sleepy streets, nobody else was within earshot of a soft voice. And Bea was still walking, not replying.

"You think they'll lock you up?" he whispered. "You can't let that happen! Hell, if you do, how are we going to find out why Gardner is standing up for Eric instead of cutting him loose..." The challenge sounded awkward even to his own ears, but he kept feeling that Bea was about to just walk to her car and leave him behind. "We can't let them do this to you!"

Bea smiled, faintly, still only looking at the path ahead. "So that's up to you?"

"Eric was going for his skein." Colin could still see her pulling the trigger, but now he pushed past his own shock at that moment. "I mean, just moments after you shot him he still stomped over us all, and he got away with Zara. I *saw* it!"

"And you think they'll listen?" The sharp, sad irony in her voice stabbed at him.

"They have to! Eric's proved what a danger he is, every time. They need to know what we're up against!"

"Hold on..." Bea slowed, finally glanced toward him. "Is that what it sounds like? Tell them the whole story, for *me?*"

"Of course for—"

A door opened at the house just ahead, and a couple walked out. Colin choked off his words and slipped around behind a parked car, out of sight from anyone in front.

And the street behind him looked empty enough—*screw this*—

He released his grip on the skein and reappeared. Another moment stripped it clear of his head, his shoes, then his hands as he stood up. Let people take the rest of it for some shiny green jogging suit.

He trotted up beside Bea.

She opened her mouth, but he said "This is what I'm talking about! How do we keep stopping to hide *all this* when we need every second and everybody to run Eric down? We shouldn't even be out here, we're the only ones who can stop Eric if he goes after Terri again. Because the cops don't even know what they're keeping watch for! We have to tell Hoyle about the skein."

Bea's face went still. He could feel her gaze pressing at him, with not one flicker to hint what was behind those eyes.

Then she said "We can't. Are you forgetting what that would do if word got out?"

"I know. But you've *seen* what happens when we keep our mouths shut. Listen, what did I say when I started with you—that I couldn't let Eric kill anyone else? He's killed Leo and four cops since then."

This time she flinched. He jabbed a finger at her, leaned closer.

"Bea, I trusted you about the secret. But you can't go to prison to hide what this is. Or let Eric get the drop on any more police. They have to know."

"It still doesn't work that way." Bea didn't raise her voice, she stepped in nearer, eyes steady and certain. "Invisible weapons? And now it's prosthetic parts that anyone can grow by letting the stuff *eat someone's flesh*—don't you look away," she added. "Of course we have to do this ourselves. You just keep protecting your family, and let me dig up what I can. And stay away from me, I'm the one who's got too much attention to be around."

"You're putting *me* in danger?" He scowled back at her, searching for any doubt in those fierce eyes. *She was protecting* him, *by burying the secret and taking all the blame?* Of course she would.

"You wouldn't know what we're risking if we broke our silence," she added. "If I'm right, there are more risks in letting Hoyle know any—

"Look out!"

She twisted, he pivoted and ducked away, as a man behind them broke from a jog and charged right at them, lashing out with skein gathering on his fist.

Colin dodged back and deflected, let the blow glance off his armored arm. A wrecking ball of force flung him back, sent him stumbling and crashing over.

I thought Eric was gone, or I thought he'd be invisible.

Instead a figure in mismatched, oversized jogging clothes loomed over him, still Eric under that cap hiding in plain sight. All his mass of skein seethed in motion under those clothes.

And Bea had no armor.

Colin kicked off the ground and drove at the killer. He rained punches, kicks, fast as he could twist from one move through the two it led into.

Eric flinched back. His arms flew up to guard his face, and green skein tried to creep up from his collar to shield him. Colin struck faster, with his own still-bare hands, anything to keep the pressure from slackening for one instant.

The skein slid over Eric's head. His guard lowered an inch, and slackened, unconcerned. Unhurt.

Colin saw the punch coming. He twisted away and blocked, trying to break the monstrous force of all that skein on Eric's arms. He grabbed for Eric's arm, the swollen gauntlet that must still have a wounded hand under it. His own weak fingers slipped and missed the hold.

He lashed out at Eric again. Behind him, a young man stared at them, ignoring Bea's shoves to run away—

Can't glance away! Colin rained blows on his enemy from every angle he knew, breath roaring. *It's my fault Bea's unprotected here.*

Eric surged forward. Simple, brutal, his bulked-up body ploughed into Colin and forced him back, hands grabbing at him. Colin leaned away for a throw.

His back crashed into something metal-solid. He'd been herded right into a parked car.

Eric bent him back over the car, iron strength and invulnerable body. Colin scrabbled to hook a leg out from under him, but Eric's balance and power were flawless.

The hand holding his arm shifted. Colin saw claws sprouting on those fingers, *to rip my skein off me,* again. *Or tear my throat out.*

"Hey, look out!" That was the man who'd wandered in, more like a kid with his voice still breaking.

"Stay back—" The gasp cost Colin more of his leverage, and Eric still turned to look toward Bea and the kid.

No! Colin wrenched under the grip, tried to poke a finger around at the thin material over those eyes.

Eric turned his face out of reach, and his force crashed down with new strength. Colin's sight blurred, went gray.

I need the spell. I need a breath, to say the three words that turn both of the skeins I'm touching against us... He hammered his will into the stuff around his limbs, straining to squirm just one inch out from under the pressure. To squeeze out from one pain and trigger what would be so much worse...

He hesitated.

The grip slammed down and crushed the breath from him. His sight grayed, his ears rang.

A voice broke out from beyond them.

"Gratshay ko—"

Something whirled him around, sent him flying. His eyes opened to catch one glimpse of Bea diving clear—Eric had *thrown* him at her—and she swung a punch straight at Eric's injured hand.

He struck the ground just as he heard Eric shriek. He tried to roll up, and Bea started the spell again. *"Gratshay kodo—"*

Eric dove away. He leaped clear of her touch that would have completed the spell, clearing two and then five paces away in one blurred moment, still clutching his hand.

Colin gained his feet and tensed to chase after him. But Eric was racing on, faster every moment.

So we won, didn't we? Nobody died this time, we drove him off.
Until we let our guard down again.

"You okay?"

The kid, a gangly kid of sixteen, stared at him and Bea both. He twitched and squirmed from one foot to the other.

"Yeah." Colin flexed his fingers, then his toes. That they all worked was a good sign nothing was broken—and those were the parts he'd left unarmored. He drew in a breath, stiff but whole.

"That guy just jumped you… what was that, he dressed up to mug joggers?"

"I guess." As long as he didn't match Colin's silver-green "jogging suit" to Eric's gloves and mask.

"You going to call a cop?"

"One's already here," Bea said. "Me. I'll call this in."

The kid looked at her, stepped back a pace. "You? Okay… listen, the guy had a mask so I couldn't see him, you don't need me for any-thing… Okay?"

He backed away. Then turned and walked off, quick as he could.

Bea sighed "Typical. Everyone thinks hiding their own secrets is more important than a criminal on the street. But, sometimes it makes it easier."

"You… you saved me again." Colin let the words ease out of him, trying to wash some of the tension out of his muscles. The fact brought a prickle of embarrassment too, when he'd fought so hard to keep Eric focused on himself.

Bea turned up the sidewalk again, and he moved along with her, steps steadying as he went.

He added "Eric went after me. I thought he'd hate you more, now."

"Could be that he saw the skein on you. If he wants to disarm his enemies, you were the visible target."

"But you could have used some yourself. I only wanted to borrow yours—"

Her hand rose to cut him off.

"You don't see it, do you?" she said. "You're the one protecting Terri now, and hunting Eric—I should never have brought you out here for this. And I'm the one Hoyle has to treat as a rogue cop.

"So I use the time I have to look for what Eric's up to, and just take steps that he doesn't track me down again. I face the shooting review board, and whatever that leads to. You hang onto all the power you can get to do your job, and that means keeping enough for full invisibility. And we both keep that secret."

"What? No!" The balance he'd seen before Eric's attack snapped back into his head, clearer than ever. He waved a hand up the street. "That kid, did you already forget what you said about him? That it's people holding back what they know that stops the police from doing their job. And you want to leave them to fight an enemy they don't even *know* they can't see?"

"We just chased that enemy off. You and me and the spell. You and Zara can hold the line without me now."

"You think Eric's beaten? Did you *see* that fight? And since when are you not the one saying to be ready for anything!" he added ruefully. "You know he can keep coming at us, any moment he wants. We need reinforcements that actually know what Eric does, and we need you! That means they need to know why you shot him."

But did *she have to shoot their prisoner...* Colin wrenched his thoughts away from that doubt and locked his eyes on Bea's.

Something at the corner of her mouth trembled.

A hint of fear, guilt, something they had to push past to help her face this—

"No," she said. "And not when it's Anthony Hoyle."

"What?" He blinked. Hadn't she been saying that when Eric struck? "Why not, what about Hoyle?"

"I'm not sure," she said. "Call them rumors that a cop hears. He's a good commander, but his loyalties could be..." She shook her head. "You need to keep your secrets, and watch him."

"Me? You just drop that on me? Why, give me something!"

Lieutenant Hoyle. *He pushed me for full answers last night, and he pissed me off—was that really me picking up something wrong about him?* He seemed like a good cop.

"Just keep your eyes open," Bea said. "I wish I had something more to tell you now. But since it's you I'm asking… I'd get further if I just ask you to trust me."

"Oh."

What did that mean, that she knew him that well? But any flicker of doubt on her face was gone now.

"I'll try," he said. "No promises."

* * *

Bea dropped him off at the hospital and drove off. Whatever plans she had now, she wouldn't say. At least a quick call to Zara had confirmed Eric hadn't rushed right back to get at Terri.

Colin faded from sight and eyed the hospital entrance. There'd be police on watch inside, reporting to someone Bea said not to trust, and they still might grab him on sight. But today he'd had a *child* show him how easily his "invisibility" could fail.

Caught between those two… *I guess I just have to do this better.*

He chose his moment and ducked in through the entrance. The late morning visitors and staff churned along on their ways, at least more distracted than people on the street.

At the entrance to Terri's wing, there had been a uniform watching the main elevators and stairs, but the spot was empty now. Colin made his way slowly in, and around the cop outside Terri's door. When that woman glanced the other way, he simply slipped the door open.

They made it easy for him. It would be easier still for Eric.

Terri lay asleep in her bed. Zara looked up as the door moved, where she sat beside a stack of their record books, but she also swung her laptop shut. Before it closed, he saw the blue logo of an insurance company.

Right. *Someone has to cover the costs for keeping Terri—she's alive but she's still had half her bones shattered and half-healed while she had skein holding them together. If they can ever be right again.*

Bills for Terri, Bea facing down prison, Hoyle maybe keeping his own secrets, *and Eric's still out there...* The weight of it all pressed in and made him sway on his feet, lean back against the wall.

Zara was still watching him, computer clenched in front of her. She might not even be certain it was him yet.

He pulled off the skein mask, and forced confidence into his voice. "Problem?" he asked.

She sighed. Then she glanced over at her sleeping daughter, avoiding Colin's eyes for a moment. Zara had a thousand expressions, but none of them hid secrets as well as Bea's control.

"Simply looking at some options," she said. "Where did you go? Are you hurt?" and her eyes narrowed to study him.

Colin drew himself up, hiding aches and stiffness. "Just watching the police at work, with Bea—"

No. Suddenly, trading denials and grins with his mother felt like only poking at the wounds. "We fought off Eric again, barely, and it'll always be easy for him to hit us again. Gardner Development is making noise about defending him. And Bea says she'll be up on charges for *attacking* him." His voice cracked on the last.

"She did shoot a defenseless man. 'Defenseless' enough to kidnap me a minute later," Zara added with a scowl. "But, I'm sorry she's facing that."

Colin nodded, slowly. He met his mother's gaze, let the pain mirror between them for one long moment...

Only a moment. He pushed himself clear of that gaze, to lean back and slide down with his back to the door. "I'm sorry I left you unprotected."

The words dragged against the momentum he'd started, so he reached up and slid a thin layer of skein over his face again, just enough to lie across his eyes. A thought thinned that skein "blindfold" down to its most filmy, to let him see the world in a gauzy green haze.

"What is that?" Zara settled down beside him.

Colin held up his hand and faded it from sight. "Trying to *see* the... invisible," he finished in a whisper. Something else Bea could do, and he never had enough time with her.

He spread his fingers—right in front of him, he could feel them and the cool shift around them, but to his sight they were only a glassy shadow. *Think. The skein on my eyes can make me* see *differently, see the light that's bending around my hand...*

"All right." Zara opened her laptop again, and the insurance screen vanished. "If you aren't getting the trick of it, maybe splitting your attention will shake something loose.

"I've been looking at messages from Jessie, and Clarence too— they both heard their neighbors worrying about the future of the Hillside this morning. After the latest round of everything." She let out a small, patient sigh.

"Losing Leo. And the Vargas House. And now what's happened to the three of us." His hand was still less than a blur. He strained his will at the stuff—Bea had already proven someone could see through this.

"We can turn that around. You brought Terri back. Who could have doubts after that?"

"Thanks." Sure, talk about the neighborhood, but nothing would be normal until they ran Eric down. He said "I really saw some Gardner people shouting that Eric was innocent. Hard to believe."

"To put it mildly. Dennis Fields was starting to see what a danger Eric was. And he made a fair case that when Gardner buys up property they at least want to improve people's lives."

"He had me believing it too. Today I saw him stand back and let the others defend Eric—" Colin heard a harshness in his voice. That came out sounding like a betrayal, and Fields wasn't like Eric.

He still couldn't see his hand right.

Zara said "Did you know the Gardners had a connection to Matt Vargas?"

"What?"

"There was a reference…" She reached over and pulled one of the archive books in.

Colin watched, uneasy. A connection between the other man who knew about the skein, and Eric's employers? The great promoter of Rayo Hill history and the developers who tried to reshape it? *How did I not know this?*

"Here." Zara pointed to a line in the book, one of the pages bound from Vargas's notes. " *'Meeting with Gardner Bro.s Investors.'* That's the only mention."

Of course Zara remembered a single line in their archives. "Doesn't sound like much." Except that there were Gardners in town generations ago.

And the page's date was *1977*. Something… something about that time…

"Was that near the Beast Killings?" he asked.

From up on the bed a voice croaked *"What?"*

Terri's eyes were open, staring over at them both. Colin grinned— there was still a rush of comfort, each time he had his big sister back with him.

Zara crouched at her side. "How are you feeling? Did we wake you?"

"Fine." Then, carefully and firmly, she said " 'Beast?' "

"Beast Killings was just a name they gave to a pair of murders." Zara shook her head. "It could happen anywhere. Two people were killed with knives, and the media tried to make it bigger than it was."

"If that's all," Colin said. "What if there was more involved?"

"More what?" Zara said.

"Well, back then *someone* might have had the…" He flicked his hand into sight and out again—still nothing his eyes could penetrate. "What if they used it, and it looked like simple stabbings?"

"You could ask that about any moment of violence. These were simply two tragic moments."

"Savage ones, and never really solved, I remember that much. What if there were more, and nobody wanted to connect them if the picture they made looked too scary? The same way you just—" He cut off.

Terri added "Waved them away."

That's my sister, still the one who can see our town's glass as half-empty.

Zara nodded. "You got me. And if violence could be the skein in use... it's possible. But I don't remember any Vargas notes about past crimes or incidents like that."

"None? Not even to downplay them?" Colin felt a smile twitching. "That's *not* like him..."

Zara began tapping on her laptop. Terri watched her, both of them, with a smile.

Colin sat back in his place against the door, to give them that moment's warning if someone entered—nurses or cops or Eric himself. He grabbed the nearest archive book and began skimming through it for any mention of attacks, or the Gardners either.

A low mutter came from Zara: "I spend half my life supporting our heritage and community, and you remember two murders. Boys."

Colin smiled back. "You're welcome."

Page, page, page... the first volume was almost all Vargas's architecture notes, and he set it aside and opened the next. It was only a thin hope, but still a fresh chance to learn something about the skein or Eric, instead of simply waiting...

The door thumped against his back.

A woman outside called "Ma'am?"

Zara answered "Oh! I'm sorry—" and stepped over to the door "she'd" been blocking. Colin slid aside into the corner and pulled his skein up to fade from sight.

A woman cop walked in. She smiled at Zara, but she also took one long step past her and glanced behind Terri's bed for any obvious intruders.

Then she turned to Zara and Terri. "Sorry to interrupt. Zara, do you want me to get you a snack? The lieutenant's pulling me out soon."

"Thank you for thinking of me. I'm fine, though."

"I hope you'll be alright." The officer's gaze dipped to the floor. "He's stripping your protection down to one officer."

Colin froze where he crouched. They *couldn't*...

"Is he?" Zara's lips tightened. "You think that's appropriate, to hold off a murderer who held Terri prisoner for *three years?*"

The cop kept her gaze low. "I understand that."

"And his answer is to all but abandon us, and assume Eric won't come after us again?"

"Zara, we'll *get* him. We're putting all our resources into hunting him down."

"Really." Zara shook her head. "You mentioned Lieutenant Hoyle. He wouldn't happen to be here now, would he?"

"At the nurses' station." She edged back a step. "Please, you don't want to—"

"We'll just see about that, won't we?"

Zara stepped toward the door, and the cop fell back and then fell into step behind her as she swept out. As they left, Zara flashed one sharp gesture toward Colin's corner, a small *stay-here*. Then their quick footsteps faded down the hall.

"Hoyle's in for it now." Even with her reedy breath, Terri managed to chuckle.

Colin smiled back, wishing he was as sure. He sank down against the door again and went back to the archive books.

Or he tried to. The room felt smaller now, if the guards really were leaving and he'd be trapped here as pretty much Terri's only protector. He stared at the pages.

Searching for old murders, while we're sitting in the crosshairs for new ones.

"Taking a while," Terri said.

"I guess. But I'm right here if anything happens."

The pages slid between his fingers, protective plastic against the tight latex feel of the skein. Sounds drifted and circled out in the corridors at his back—any of those footsteps could be Eric walking right up to them.

He kept his eyes away from Terri. Eric could pick any moment to strike—they'd pushed their luck once, leaving to watch the search, and now they were losing most of their support here.

Bea had said... she'd told him to watch for Eric here, and leave the manhunt to the rest of them. As if they *could* catch Eric—and without proper security here, Colin would be leaving Terri vulnerable every moment he left this room.

How long had Zara been gone? Bea thought Hoyle could be up to something himself. *But he won't need to be; he can be just a stubborn cop, and we really think Zara can change his mind?*

One book finished, and he slammed it down and scrabbled for the next. Their last chance was slipping away. He glanced at the door.

"Go," Terri said.

"Thanks."

He swung the door wide and slipped out, invisible. The corridor was close to empty, no guards or anyone to watch Terri.

And he was leaving her alone. For his last chance at changing that.

He marched toward the nurses' station, unseen and unnoticed by what people he passed.

Zara came in view first. She walked back toward their room, face downturned and steps slow with defeat. The woman cop and two other uniforms stood up ahead.

"Hang in there," he whispered to his mother. She glanced up, then nodded and walked on.

At the corridor's end he saw the nurses' station. Its counter seemed cleared out of medical personnel for now. Instead the three officers stood around, and Lieutenant Hoyle hunched over a laptop, in quiet talk with Sergeant Jordan in his wheelchair—Bea's mentor and the one other person she showed the skein to.

Colin eyed the five cops. They could still mean to lock him up for evading them, the last thing Terri needed.

And Bea could be right about Hoyle. *But I could have more leverage if I stayed hidden and listened in... if I could sneak up that close...*

No.

They needed real help, they all did.

Colin slipped back around a corner. He let one doctor move on out of sight, then reappeared and pulled the skein clear of his head. And from his shoes, all the changes he needed to reduce it to a shiny green "jogging suit" again, this time leaving "gloves" as part of it. He took one deep breath, and walked toward the police.

The three uniforms noticed him first. The woman made a low whisper, and the three moved toward him—no shouts or commands, but edging up to surround him.

He walked forward, letting them close behind him.

Jordan watched him, showing nothing on his face. As if the sergeant hadn't been in on their secret from the start.

Hoyle moved to meet Colin, crossing his arms with his laptop still tucked under an arm. "So there you are. The 'witness' who'd rather play tag than answer questions."

"Look..." Was that weak, shaky voice his? Colin kept his gaze on Hoyle's, and his mind on his reason for meeting him. "I wanted to show you, how hard you'll have to work to chase Eric. And now I'm advising you... asking you... don't leave Terri alone. And don't punish Bea for not taking chances with a murderer."

"Detective Simms," and Hoyle's voice sharpened a fraction, "is under a legitimate investigation for shooting a suspect."

Jordan added "If you can call it that. We both saw the scene findings so far—she wounded him, but it left him enough of an imminent threat to break free from every cop in the room."

Colin fought the urge to nod. Jordan had made his point without mentioning the skein, still covering for Bea.

One of the uniforms muttered "Or da Costa decked them himself. I hear he was the only civilian left there who was tough enough."

"And then I *kidnapped my mother?*" Colin snapped at the cop, louder than he wanted to.

"What we know is that Eric Rowe did escape," came Hoyle's even voice. "With two bullets in him. It could happen... but it makes me think of how the doctors can't give a good description of how your sister survived the earthquake either."

He took another step forward, and Colin heard the three officers shuffling at his back.

"Well, what I know," and Jordan twisted his wheelchair around from behind Hoyle, "is that if someone had given Rowe a few more rounds last night, we'd have two cops still alive."

And if they'd shot him even sooner, Jordan would still be on his feet. Jordan didn't mention that, but he didn't have to.

Hoyle said "But Rowe did escape. Yes, we have statements from Terri and Zara da Costa that it was him. But when I asked you *how,*" and he jabbed a finger at Colin, "you said he was just that fast."

"And I *showed* you too. So your response is to decide one guard can keep him away?" He fought to keep his voice controlled. No accusations, he'd stick to the reasons and remember they were on the same side.

"Then there's this." And Hoyle swung his laptop open.

A familiar video image was frozen there. *Of course Hoyle has it, we sent it to the police lab.*

One of the moments the camera captured before one Gardner-sponsored street fair... Eric standing in the corner with his previous boss behind him, toppling away into traffic... But the distant shot still couldn't capture the faint blur of the invisible shove that Eric had used to kill him.

"Eric Rowe is a menace," Hoyle said. "We still don't know how he set that up, but we're taking no chances with him. We're using our full resources to hunt him down—not to look babysit you, but to *get him.*"

Colin's eyes widened. So Hoyle didn't need to know, he'd already made his decision?

"You and your family just hold on a while longer." His hand settled on Colin's shoulder, *so reasonable.* "I promise, you'll be safe soon—"

"No."

"Excuse me—" Hoyle pulled back a step.

"You can't leave us out, you have to cover us *and* chase him." Colin pressed in after him.

Sorry, Bea.

"You won't see how Eric pushed his victim there. Because…"

Colin raised his gloved hand, held close enough that his back hid it from the cops behind him. He saw Hoyle's eyes spark—was that *anticipation*?

Colin blurred his hand from sight.

The lieutenant's eyes rounded, swelled, his jaw sagged…

He snapped it closed, and his eyes darted to glance at the other cops. Colin hadn't caught one gasp from them, they'd all missed it.

Hoyle said "We… we have to talk."

CHAPTER FOUR

MENDING

Two cops at one end of the corridor—good. Colin walked past them, noting how their eyes flicked around to watch each doctor, nurse, and visitor that passed. Their sharpest looks went to the visitors, and anyone hidden in a surgical mask, but they stood taut and alert in the quieter moments too.

He passed the officer stationed at Terri's door itself, and the two officers at the hall's other end. A couple of them gave him cold or sidelong glances as he passed. But then, he was just the outsider who'd somehow gotten their lieutenant's ear.

Hoyle hasn't told them what they're watching for—"yet," he says. And I haven't told him all the skein's tricks, or how there's a magic spell that makes more of it out of human flesh. Or how Bea had been hiding some of those secrets all along.

As he turned back toward the room, an aging doctor in white shot a scowl at the guards. Still, Hoyle had made the staff accept their presence, and at some point they could shift enough patients to put Terri in an empty wing, or all the way to some safe house.

He headed into her room.

"How does it look?" Zara asked.

"Okay." He stepped over to the window and eyed the new bolt they'd slapped onto it. "This would at least force Eric to break through, and make noise. Anything that makes him hesitate is a win for us."

Zara only smiled—a bit wide, what was that for? He marched back outside again.

The corridor looked about the same, quiet but rarely empty. The two cops were in place at the far end.

As he approached them, the older cop turned to the younger one. "You see anything yet?"

"Just some kid who thinks we're off eating donuts," the other said.

"Well, he's alive. Lucky streak, I guess."

"Someone goes through all that, you bet they're jumping at shadows."

Sure. Until the shadows jump at you...

Hoyle said he had reasons for only telling them so much. And Colin kept walking, eyes straight ahead, feeling a flush move on his face. As long as the cops were *there.*

He turned the corner for one more look around the approaches anyway. Sergeant Jordan rolled up toward him.

"You didn't give those two any pushback. Good," Jordan said.

"I keep telling myself how it looks to them. I'm still just a stranger that their boss listened to." Those cops hadn't raised their voices—but Jordan still guessed what must have happened.

"Can't help you there," Jordan said. "I'm supposed to be on leave, ever since I landed in the chair. I was pushing it staying in the loop with Bea, and pulling strings for her."

"I see, sorry. About a lot," he added.

"Hoyle brought me up here because he thought I was holding out on him." Jordan's voice lowered, and the bustle of the hospital around them almost swallowed his next words: "Then he got his answers from you anyway."

"Yeah." That didn't sound like thanks, for taking the pressure off of him and Bea... "Oh."

Of course, Jordan had the same doubts about trusting Hoyle that Bea did, or worse.

Colin swallowed. The softer they spoke, the more the footsteps and voices around them cut into their voices, and Jordan being down in the wheelchair didn't help. Colin crouched down, and he saw several heads around them turn at the confidential motion.

"So you think—" Colin couldn't even whisper the details here, just— "you think I opened up something worse?"

"I *think,*" and Jordan's teeth flashed, "you saved the whole operation when it was hanging by a thread. You can sleep better now, and we'll find Rowe, whatever it takes. Worry over who reports what after this animal is put down."

Colin felt a tension ease from his stomach. "Thanks. Any word on Bea's hearing?"

Jordan didn't answer.

"Or the hunt for Eric?"

"Don't push it," Jordan said. "And I mean that: don't start asking for more than you've earned here. Let us handle this, and you stay with your sister as last line of defense. Anything else, you pass along to us."

"I'll… keep that in mind." Maybe it could work. At least he could stop and sort out which ideas would just make trouble if he followed them up alone.

He turned back to Terri's room again. The two cops still eyed him, and he caught a private glance passing between them.

This is their profession, and I'm not one of them. I could have been a cop myself, or fought harder to get to the army even after we lost Terri. But if I had…

Zara and Terri looked up at him. "So, did you find anything else?" Zara asked.

"I found the experts are finally paying attention to us, and I have no business telling them how to keep watch. Yet," he added.

Zara smiled and gave a faint nod. The kind she used when she thought he'd learned a lesson.

Then she motioned him to the chair beside her. "I've been looking at those Beast Killings again, and there might be something in your idea. But so far I've only found the two killings themselves."

"Oh?" Something else to tell Bea and Jordan, or Hoyle himself, if it led anywhere.

"I'm afraid it's really just the amount of violence in them." She passed her laptop over to him, hands moving slowly. "Does this... look familiar?"

Two pictures were on the screen.

Some description had to be written underneath them, but it was the bodies that filled his sight. Enough blood spattered them that he guessed the number of wounds as much from their torn clothes as the slashed... meat. Sharon Russ, Silas Strickland. One lying on a street and the other on grass...

Two different people, both lost to... *something.*

"I don't *know,*" he said, too fast. "It could be a knife, or skein blade. I can't tell."

She snapped the laptop closed. "If you could, what would we be looking for? That some sad moment in our history showed how the skein was used then? This would be 1977, so that might be before Vargas got involved with it."

"Probably. Or..."

He hated to ask it with Zara here, but she had to be thinking it herself.

"Terri?" He moved over to crouch by her, Zara behind him. He whispered "Last night, Eric said Vargas must have been... feeding people to the skein, to have so much of it. Do you know why he'd think that?"

"No," Terri answered at once. "Just overheard bits from him."

Zara let out a sigh of relief. Colin wanted to join her; of course Eric would assume their founder was as twisted as Eric was himself.

He asked "Did Eric know the spell made skein out of people?"

"Knew there was a spell. Made it from something. I think," Terri added.

And I showed him the rest—

No. I've let guilt slow me down too many times lately.

"So how did he learn that much? Could it be something he dug up at his job at Gardner? Did you find any more ties between the Gardners and Vargas?" he asked Zara.

"No. And still no clue why they'd start defending Eric."

Colin's phone chimed.

He pulled back to grab it out, glanced at the name.

"Bea? You alright?"

For one instant he heard a chuckle from Zara beside him. *Of course I want to hear from Bea, Eric could still be targeting her!*

"Fine," she said. "The shooting review's going okay so far."

"Fingers crossed." As long as none of the cops there said how beaten Eric looked before she shot him—it was more in hindsight that it looked like a good call. "Are they taking all your time, or did you dig up anything else?"

"I asked a few questions, checked some reports. There's been no sign of Eric anywhere. It's as if he's invisible," she added, and she made it sound like just another word.

"Or something." Was that the most she could say on the phone?

"As for Gardner Development and Eric now, nothing. I can't reach Fields so far."

"I could try that myself. I might be more mobile than you right now." Maybe just to check with Fields and pass it on to her, maybe...

"Is that why you did it? To get away again?" Bea's voice was suddenly quiet.

He frowned. "Why I did what?"

"Colin. I asked you to watch yourself, and to trust me. You didn't."

"Yeah." He closed his eyes a moment. "I'm sorry. But we needed Hoyle's help, and all you had was rumors about him. Isn't it innocent until proven guilty?"

"That's for juries. My job is to find that proof, or see that there's nothing to find. I don't get to 'presume' someone is innocent."

"I know." *I'm not a cop—or a jury either. What* does *that make me?* "I'll be careful, we all will. Anything else?"

There had to be some clue or next step, or something. Colin shifted his grip on the phone, ready for whatever else she'd share.

A knock sounded at the door.

He paused, and Zara moved to answer it.

He stepped in front of her. *There's a cop right outside, so this can't be* him *here, but...* His skein was ready under his shirt.

Behind the door was a nurse—a plump, smiling-eyed woman in blue, with a tray full of varied medical instruments. "Sorry to break in, but Terri is due for a few tests. How are you feeling, sweetie?" she added to the patient.

"Been worse," Terri said.

They stepped back and she breezed in.

Zara's voice warmed and reached out to welcome her. "How does it look for us, Nurse…"

"It's a little early to tell." The nurse smiled back, but she only held Zara's gaze for an instant before looking away and setting her tray on the table.

And I'm still on the line. Colin turned away to say. "Guess we're done?"

"Later, then." And Bea simply hung up.

The nurse readied a blood-pressure cuff, eyes still looking only at her tools. Her voice was gentle, though: "I have a whole list of tests and exercises for Terri here. If you two want to stretch your legs, this is the time."

"We could do that." Zara knelt down at the other side of her daughter's bed. "Terri? Remember, this is your first step toward you taking everything back."

"And a good attitude always helps." This time the nurse's words sounded flat, insincere, as she began puffing up the cuff around Terri's arm.

"I can fight," Terri said. "Got this far... it means I'm all set for..."

The cuff's inflation halted, already at the limit of Terri's strength, and air began seeping from it again.

"...more fights," Terri finished with a sigh.

Was that a joke? Colin leaned in behind Zara. Terri had faced down Eric right beside him—but now she had no job, her best friend had left town years ago, her fiancé was terrorizing them all. And how much would she ever be able to recover—

"Every moment is a win," he tried.

The pressure cuff took that moment to finish its second-stage test and deflate with a *whoosh*.

Make it calm, confident. He went on "Every moment. All they ever tell us is that we're facing something new, different, that they've never seen. And we keep beating those odds."

He let it stop there. Not much of a speech, but the best he could come up with now.

The nurse pulled the cuff off, and her eyes flicked from that to a page of records on her tray, still avoiding their gazes. "Um. We can understand more after we finish this round of tests. Then that might be the time to work on some short-term goals..."

Short-term? That soft voice meant they had to lower their expectations, and she couldn't find a way to say it—

Zara leaned in to take Terri's hand. "We'll work this out. Together. Every step of this will be the three of us, and the best doctors, and a whole world of our friends too. We'll relearn how everything is possible, and we'll always be with you. And right now Colin and I will get some dinner and let our friend here work, but you understand we're *always* with you. Remember that?"

"Of course." Terri's hand gripped her mother's, and her pale knuckles went white.

Colin couldn't simply smirk at seeing that nurse's defeatism shown up, so he caught up Zara's laptop and led the way outside.

When the door shut behind them, the woman cop there shot Zara a smile. "Finally taking a break?"

Zara had *slumped*—just a fraction, only enough for Colin to notice it from the hair's breadth that she drew herself up now, as she grinned " 'Finally,' Wendy?"

The cop laughed softly. Then she turned to Colin. "And yes, I did check Nurse Setter's face and her ID before I let her in." Her smile lingered to soften the rebuke.

"I'm sure you did," Colin said.

He started to turn away, but he caught himself and looked back to meet her gaze.

"I hope you don't think I keep second-guessing all of you here. I admit it, Eric Rowe on the attack is the scariest thing I've ever seen, and more people keep dying around him. But watching all of you here, protecting us... mostly I'm just grateful."

"That's our job, that's all." She glanced around the corridor, and the two police on each end. "You really think we need this many of us, for the chance that Rowe will try something here? I know he's obsessed, but he has to know he can't steal your sister out of here. Not in her condition—hate to say it," she added.

"Yeah. But he could try, or come for revenge, or something." *And Hoyle says they can't know about the skein yet...* "Anyway, I had to say I appreciate you out here, not taking chances."

"And we won't." Her voice cooled a degree.

He'd let those last words slip out, like he was still cautioning her, doubting them after all. No way to take that back—Colin had to nod and leave it at that, walking away.

He and Zara passed the two cops at the intersection, and he saw them glaring at him too.

Once they left them behind, he told Zara "Guess I have a long way before I can put 'Wendy' at ease like you. You probably made a friend for life."

"I suppose," Zara sighed.

She sounded drained, worn out, and too tired to care who saw it. Zara da Costa was *never* that tired.

Colin led the way to the cafeteria. A large room with too little to vary the off-white walls, and too few people at what had to be pre-dinner hours. The empty tables and subdued hospital talk left the space silent and hollow.

But the food... Colin felt it just from the *sight* of it waiting on those counters: the gut-punch of hunger after hours of working the skein. He rushed into the ragged line and filled his plate with chicken and a heap of rice.

Zara fell back behind him, so far back that one old man joined the line between her and Colin. She was saving her strength, he tried to tell himself.

He led her to the back corner, past row after row of empty tables. They settled in against the wall, next to a small row of plastic long-leafed plants that had seen better days too.

Then they dug in.

At the back of Colin's mind lingered the thought that the jokes about hospital food were wrong—but it wouldn't have mattered if the fare was bland or mushy anyway. Now he tore into it and reveled in the feeling of *something* in his stomach again. The hardest struggle was to slow down and not stuff himself sick.

Zara only poked at hers.

When he found his plate half empty and forced himself to put the fork down, hers was still barely touched. Instead it was her eyes that engaged most with it, avoiding his gaze and the world.

Colin drew in a deep, steadying breath.

"Something about what you said to Terri…" he tried. "Maybe the next step is to bring in more visitors that she knows. They have to be amazed that she's back with us."

Zara looked up, but her fork only went on toying with the food. "I tried calling people this morning. Everyone was so, *so,* happy to hear she's alive, but both her best friends moved out of town years ago. Or someone's delighted but they can't make it a priority just now. And some say they're thinking over whether they can stay in a town where the police and everyone keep getting cut up."

That can't be what's weighing on her, not just the town. But he could start there. "There's always someone saying that. How often do they really leave?"

"But it's *Jessie!*"

A pain flashed through her eyes, and she looked away, down at the plate again to stab the fork at it.

"Who am I going to argue points of history with now? And I've got bills, bills, bills, to reset Terri's bones if we even think about her walking again. And I'm going to pay them as what, the curator of a destroyed museum?

"And my *son* sits there and talks to me, after rescuing Terri from three years with a maniac and almost getting arrested for that—and you'll still have to look in the mirror every day and see those scars for what you've been through…"

Her gaze swung up, haunted eyes staring at him now. Her hand reached slowly toward his face.

He edged back, away from the desperate, trembling thing before him. *Mirror?* You and Terri *are my mirrors, you can't show me cracks like this now.*

Her hand dropped, her gaze took refuge in her meal again.

This time she started eating.

Colin watched her, tried his own bite of the suddenly tasteless food. How could she be this broken, *now?*

How can any of us not be?

He picked at his food and tried to find words, something. At last he said "We have Terri back. The first thing now is to finish up seeing that Eric never touches her again, and we've got all the help we need there. After that...

"Well, we've *got Terri back,* of course she's an inspiration. With her, with all of us, we can bring everyone together and start rebuilding. We came back from an earthquake, we can do this."

Please, just look up and be yourself again—

He added "What was it you said then, after the quake? Some bit of our history you used to get them moving?"

"I said *Lightning strikes twice, and that's still not enough to beat us.* The best I could think of then, the story of the town losing the last mining camp. Thank you." Zara's voice had a bit of warmth to it, finally. "But right now, can we..."

Her gaze stayed down, but he saw a flicker of a smile on her lips. She settled in to eating, one regular mouthful at a time, and Colin went back to his own meal.

While they finished, the cafeteria began to fill a few more of its tables, and the layered murmur of the people's voices pushed back against the stillness. Finally the two stood up and started back.

As they drew near the elevator, Zara's footsteps behind him fell back a step in the crowd. He turned, saw her looking at him, mouth opening to speak.

"Can you give me a minute here? Just... a minute alone?" she said.

"Alone? You think that's safe?" The words came out on their own, not caring about the lax, drained look on his mother's face.

The corner of her lips twitched. "I might be safer than you. I'm free to use the..."

The spell, since she didn't have skein on her. But the last time, Eric had simply gagged her before she could touch him—

No, she needs this time. "Sure."

He stepped to the corridor's side and watched her walk away among the crowd. Just the way she moved, was that a slow, measured glide or were her steps shuffling against the floor? She stopped by a wide window, half hidden by the shifting currents of people.

Zara was stronger than this. She had to be.

Because it's so easy for her? She's the one facing all the helplessness, and the hundred tasks of keeping us together, and dealing with a wider world than us too. I just have to hunt Eric, and at least I get to share that with Bea.

He reached for his phone, but pulled his hand back. He and Terri leaned on their mother, and now Zara needed his support, and his first thought was to dump that on Bea? No—right now, he had to be the strong one.

Zara still stood by the window, far off and alone behind the crowd.

He took a step toward her, caught himself, turned back on the way toward Terri and stopped again. No, he couldn't leave Zara alone or rush her either, he had to wait for her... and later he'd catch Eric and help her and... they had to...

Zara crumpled against the glass, staring at her phone. Her hand pressed to her face, her *sobbing* face.

He dove through the crowd. One doctor stepped in his path, a herd of children pressed him toward the wall, but he dodged and twisted and flung himself toward that hunched shape ahead.

She glanced up as he reached him. "Look," and she held out her phone.

A text, from a nurse "Setter," showing lines from medical files—
Prognosis for limited recovery, six years—
Mobility percentage—
Five-year survival chance—

And the message at the top: *There is still some chance. But please, don't disturb me while I'm with your daughter.*

"It's not true," Zara moaned. "It's not!" She cradled the phone in shaking hands, her finger hesitating over the callback button. "Wait, no, she said to let her work."

"She's wrong," he said. "They're all wrong." They had skein, they had Terri's strength, it had to be wrong…

Zara stabbed at the phone and brought it to her ear. Long moments later she choked "Still no answer."

No answer.

Colin's gut twisted. This *was* wrong, even *that* nurse wouldn't dump that kind of news on them by phone.

"Try again." His voice came out a fierce whisper.

Zara tapped at the call, the text, and her eyes went wider. "What are you—"

"Maybe that was her," he said. "Or maybe it's all just to keep us away." While Eric made his move.

He spun around and dashed for the stairs, leaving Zara behind shaking the phone. Doctors and patients and visitors sifted through his path—he wove through them and dove up the steps.

He *wanted* it to be Eric. Eric had used fake texts before, to cover one real one Terri had sent and try to distract him. This had to be him, someone to *hate*, the same monster who'd preyed on their losses before.

But use them for what? What did Wendy say, Eric knew he couldn't drag Terri away in her condition? Whatever he wanted had to be quick—quick as a claw, maybe—

The door swung open and he charged onto Terri's floor.

The two cops stood at the outer end of her corridor, good. But they leaned against the wall, slumping like they were only half awake. Even with the coffee cup at their feet.

Damn them! He stopped, opened his mouth—

"Hey!" The cop at the door, Wendy, was waving him over to her side. He spun and marched toward her, and he heard a muzzy chuckle from one of the men behind him.

Wendy stepped out to meet him. "Shh!" she whispered. "I'm still covering the door. It'll just make trouble if you call those two on it now."

"What? You knew?" He locked his gaze on her, fighting to make the pieces fit in his head.

"Look, I saw them fumble around, I know they're not really fit for duty. I don't know what's up with them, but I called for replacements. And I haven't left the door since I spotted them."

Since. So there'd been one moment she was away—and of course Eric must have done something to those two, maybe that coffee cup—

Colin moved softly toward the door.

"Hold on," she said. "The nurse said they'd be a while... but I haven't heard from her since..."

He pushed past her and cracked the door open.

A voice stirred inside, soft and dark like ripples in tainted water. Intense, *filled* with its own purpose. Colin leaned a fraction further in.

The silver-green shape hunched beside Terri's bed, all his attention fixed on her as he whispered. Too close, that two feet's distance from her would be only a thought if Eric's temper twisted into a blade. Terri only stared numbly back.

His head was bare, showing his pale face contorting as the emotions passed through him into words. Only some of those mutterings reached the door:

"...spared your mother... could have grabbed... sure to draw the attention away from us, but I... so there's less blood, for you..."

The nurse lay curled in a corner, unwounded but huddled tight and shaking in blind terror. And Eric said he was *holding back?*

Something brushed at Colin's shoulder—he swallowed a gasp and shoved the hand away. At least Eric seemed lost in his own world now.

"They said you were broken. Can't they see?" His voice was louder now. "But you look at yourself... covered in wires, flowers on the table like they want to bury you... You really think you'll get better? Do you?"

The room fell still. Colin held his breath for Terri to answer, but she lay silent.

"I can heal you. I'm sorry, *sorry* I took it away, but you attacked me! You made me forget, how much it hurts without it…"

Far back at Colin's side, a voice whispered "Crazy." The softest whisper, one pressure against Eric's whirlpool of obsessions.

Colin crouched, gathered his legs under him. His skein stirred as a hidden layer under his clothes, ready to power his lunge. But Eric was still just one motion away from Terri.

"I can give you more of it. Much more, soon, enough to make everything better. You tell me now, you think any of them can put you back on your feet, ever? Ever?"

"No…"

Terri's voice was so weak it was more the tone and the meaning that filled in the sounds. She went on:

"I…"

Eric leaned closer. Too close, too close.

"Gratshay ko—" Her hand lashed out at him in a squeal of wires. Eric flung himself back, the touch slipped off him with the spell incomplete, and he fell against the back wall.

He staggered up, staring at her.

"Why?"

"I can't get better," Terri hissed. "All I've got left is knowing I'll *never* take help from you, not knowing who you steal it from."

Colin shook himself, gripped the door ready to charge.

"You will! I'll show you. I'll show you both," and Eric turned to look straight at Colin.

Of course he saw me, I just sat there listening.

Colin swung the door open and stepped in, fists raised. He heard, felt, an emptiness at his back—Wendy must have pulled away to bring in reinforcements.

"You'll see." Eric's eyes blazed. "You have to take it, Terri— you're the only one who knows this town is worthless, you always knew. I'll show you, none of them are worth your life—"

Colin lunged. A skein-powered leap flung him at the space between Terri and Eric, feet shifting as he landed to sweep out a kick.

Eric wasn't there. He'd sprung away to slide along the wall, too fast. Colin twisted to follow up.

Eric landed beside the crumpled nurse. His hand swung down above her face and froze, claws bursting out of his fingers' skein. Colin slammed to a stop.

The nurse, Nurse Setter, whimpered where she lay.

Skein slid up over Eric's head. Any human expressions slipped from sight—the claws flexed as if Eric had sealed away his last regrets along with his face.

Colin tensed, opened his mouth to plead.

A voice from the door boomed "You're trapped, Rowe."

Lieutenant Hoyle stood there, gun leveled at Eric.

"Trapped. What good does hurting anyone now do? Either way you've got no way out—"

Eric chuckled. For one single moment.

Then he whirled, and flung the nurse at Colin. Colin scrabbled for footing, caught at her and tumbled back—he got one glimpse past her as Eric dove at Hoyle, disappearing in mid-leap—

A *crash* of bodies—*did he use his claws or not*—

Colin twisted free of the nurse and lunged at the doorway. Hoyle lay on the floor, groaning. Wendy rushed in, gun up, staring around: "He won't get through, he won't—"

Colin had to swerve around her to dive into the corridor. No sign of Eric, no shimmer or bodies, or anything.

He did all that, to offer Terri his kind of healing. And promise to "show" us something...

Down the corridor Colin ran, staring around for any chance at Eric's trail. Hopeless as it was, he'd still fight for *any* chance of stopping him now.

CHAPTER FIVE

TARGETS

By the time Colin headed back, the corridors were all but empty—
only an orderly here and there shooing people into rooms as they
waited for word that the threat was over. He rushed past those.

Lieutenant Hoyle stood outside the door itself, and Colin saw his
steps stumble as he paced between his officers. There was no tremor
in his voice: "Da Costa! Get over here!"

Nurse Setter sat in the middle of the group of cops, still huddled in
around herself and shaking. "Is he gone? Is he really gone?"

"Yes—" Colin began, soft as he could, but Hoyle waved to one of
his men to lead her away.

Zara trotted up from the corridor behind Colin. She swept a glance
around the scene, and clenched her jaw shut.

Hoyle looked at her, then back to him. "Explain this. In here—"

The lieutenant took a step toward Terri's door, then halted, and he
frowned at Zara. He shook his head, like trying to throw off the last of
Eric's punch.

Colin said "You need her, and Terri. They've been part of this
since it started."

"Alright then." Hoyle turned to his cops. "Nobody, *nobody,* comes
in here," he grunted, and he waved Colin and Zara into the room.

Nothing in the small, familiar space looked the same now, knowing Eric had stood there. The table beside the bed was knocked sideways where Eric had raced past it. Flowers lay over the floor.

"You okay?" At least Terri sounded unshaken.

Colin nodded. His ears buzzed, his steps wobbled. *Adrenaline catching up to me now.*

Hoyle stepped in near him, speaking in a hush. "So, invisible means... *invisible?* That thing can walk in here any time he wants?"

"Almost—"

"Wait, wait." Hoyle held up his hands and stared at them until the shaking left them. "Rowe still stopped to drug two of my officers, just enough to make them clumsy, and then he exploited that opening. Right? He's got limits?"

"Seems like it. And he texted the two of us from the nurse's phone to delay us," Colin added.

"But once he made his chance... nothing we had ready slowed him down. This is going to take everything we've got."

"That's what I've been telling you!" Colin waved at the overturned table. Finally, finally they'd get police who knew what they were hunting for.

Hoyle looked over to Terri. "I keep hearing he's obsessed with you. Why is that?"

"I thought he loved me. Now it's all about 'healing' me." Terri held her voice level all through her sentences—that had to be costing her. "All seen through the grudges he has."

Zara said "He's convinced this town and this family pushed her into her accident."

Colin added "So, revenge. Tangled up with exposing how everything we did was wrong. And... right before he ran, he said he'd *show us.*" The words made the room feel a fraction colder. Hoyle had to listen, he had to.

"But you're alright?" the cop said. "All three of you?"

"Sure. This time."

He motioned to the scattered flowers around their feet. *Time to say it.*

"I'm sorry, Lieutenant. But you have to see, setting out a few cops that don't know what they're watching for just won't do the job."

"Of course not." Hoyle's voice went softer. "We need more men, and we need to keep full control of that information, before 'invisible attacker' sets off a panic."

Colin froze. After all this, Hoyle wanted *more* secrets?

Bea didn't trust Hoyle, he remembered. She could be right, that had to be why he'd do this—

Zara said "But… Eric just outmaneuvered all of you. Because your officers didn't know what he's capable of."

"He can hide in plain sight, I *showed* you that!" Colin said. "You can't go after him without all of your cops knowing that."

"I can't do it *with* them knowing." Hoyle looked back and forth between them. "I'd have officers refusing to come in, or the ones that did could start shooting at every little creak they hear. Or word gets out and someone higher up replaces me, and you're back at Square One making *them* understand it…

"Believe me, I'll work on how to brief them, and how to get support soon. But all that's later, once I get this back in order."

"Later?" Colin said. "You mean, after he kills more of your people because *you didn't warn them* what was sneaking up on them?"

While we can stop him with words and a touch, the same way Eric can make more skein by melting people… we never trusted Hoyle with that one…

But Colin's voice had throttled back, following Hoyle's lead even when he wanted to scream a warning to every cop on the floor. *I hate that I can fold like this.*

"I, I know," Hoyle sighed. "But I know how command works too. Managing this is the only way."

"Is it?" Zara folded her arms. "You expect us to cover up the knowledge that could defend Terri. And you think we can feel safe?"

"You'll have more protection—Rowe still needed to make a gap in the security first."

Hoyle held up his fingers and began ticking points off as he spoke, gathering speed.

"I'll work on what to brief them. Get them some rifles... Jordan said six times the power in a pistol might crack Rowe's armor... find some way to scan for him... We'll transfer you to a safe house, as soon as they can clear your daughter to be moved. And... I'm counting on your cooperation to narrow down where Rowe might have gone."

"Of course." Zara leaned down and scooped up an armful of the Vargas books. "You could start by letting us see the evidence you took from Eric's home."

Hoyle pulled out his phone. He gave the screen only three taps and a flick before he looked up. "There. That's the summary of our findings. You want any details, you ask me later. And, I trust you'll all keep this confidential."

"We understand," she nodded. "And we appreciate your accepting our help. Nothing about this seems to be easy, is it?"

Hoyle turned toward the door.

Colin called out "Something else: can you get Bea cleared? I mean, you just saw how unstoppable Eric can be, and he *was* going for his skein when she shot him. Who's to say that was the wrong move?"

"It's... not that simple now," Hoyle said. "But I'll work on it. I'll be back soon."

And he stepped around them and slipped out the door.

Colin sagged back against the wall. The little room felt suddenly still.

Terri whispered "Rifles. Now I feel safe... er."

Zara slid in and leaned down to lay a gentle hug over her. "We take what we can, and build on that," she said. "Now more than ever, I think."

They sank down in their chairs, and Colin breathed slowly and let the rest of the tension ease out of his nerves.

We faced Eric down, and we're all okay. We could have some real help now, if Hoyle makes this work.

Except I just chased Eric and I lost him. But that may have saved my life—he only gets stronger and more practiced each time we meet.

He drew out his phone and began looking through the list of Eric's captured possessions. All ordinary things, that only told of a young man losing himself in his work instead of brooding over a secret... Colin read slowly, forcing his pumped-up thoughts to linger on each line and take time for any ideas. Too fast and he'd be done soon and start climbing the walls with frustration, too slow and he'd go crazy anyway.

Minutes passed, ten, twenty, thirty. Voices gathered outside, sharp, low sounds that had to be more guards gathering.

Then Hoyle strode back in, steady and certain as if any exhaustion has been washed away in a cup of coffee. He dropped into a chair. "Alright. Ready to take this from the top?"

"We are," Zara said. She gave her phone one quick flick—

She froze, staring at the screen.

"Oh God." She glanced at Colin. "What did Eric say, that he was going to 'show us' he was right?"

"He did." Colin's breath caught. Something was starting.

"I just got a message from a friend. His father... it sounds like the honest word would be *vanished.*"

* * *

Riding with the two cops was its own silent challenge. Instead of Bea or Hoyle or anyone he knew, Colin sat behind two men who looked more alike than not: lean, sharp-eyed older men who might have had their features ground down to go with their uniforms. They never told him their names.

Instead they watched him coldly, from the moment Hoyle told them to take him along with no explanation. And Colin couldn't even offer a guess yet, why Eric would target this man, or if it was him at all.

The streets out the window looked familiar. Something about this part of the Hillside, something he should know…

They pulled up at the Martins' home. The little house looked bare and simple in the lowering sun. The young man out front, that had to be Joe Martin Jr., was pacing up and down the yard, and ran to meet their car.

"You're here, this fast? Everyone said you'd need more time—I mean, thank you." He stared through his glasses, and his hands shook as if they couldn't settle at his sides.

"We're, um, always concerned, sir," and the shorter cop made the excuse almost smooth, but he laid it out calmly as if it made no difference if Martin doubted him or not.

Colin added "I'm sure your dad's alright."

The two cops edged ahead of Colin, cutting him off from Martin. *I should have said "I hope," not downplaying the risk.* But he couldn't hold that lifeline back now.

He added "Zara wanted to know if there's any way we could help."

"Ah, okay…" Martin eyed him uneasily.

Sure, what should he think when he reached out to a friend and wound up with the police plus a community leader's son tagging along? Joe Martin Junior and Senior weren't even that tied to the Hillside community… Zara could do this so much better in person.

The taller cop said "Can you walk us through what happened?"

"Yes!" Martin motioned back to his house. "We were sitting inside talking about where to get dinner—we had to, you know…"

"Go on." The officer's voice was bland.

"Then Dad goes out to the car. Said he'd left something in it. Then nothing—no sound, no motor, no traces, nothing. He's just gone!"

Colin saw the fear rising in Martin's eyes as he relived it, and how his gaze darted around the street. Looking for some way his father could have gone, some *sense* somewhere around him.

Eric could strike that fast.

The cop said "And then you…"

"I looked around. I called friends—"

"How far? What friends?"

"All of them! I ran blocks up and down everywhere, I called everyone we'd seen today. None of them knew a damn thing!" His voice tensed, his fists clenched.

Colin reached a calming hand toward him. "I'll look around—"

"We'll stay together," the shorter cop cut in. "The more we know about the person in question first, the less time we waste running around. Let's step inside."

Martin led them to the door. Colin glanced around as they did—the yard looked dead, with little more than brown grass on it.

"Not much to see," Martin said as they stepped in.

The house was two-thirds empty. Bare floorboards and walls met Colin's eye everywhere, with the rest covered by stacked boxes or a few last bits of furniture—battered old ones at that.

Martin waved around, and wiped his hands on his dirty t-shirt. He and his father might have been packing their lives away an hour ago. *And now his dad might be* gone. *A thing like this should never happen.*

"You getting away from something?" the taller cop said.

"We're getting away from *nothing,*" Joe Martin burst out. "No jobs, no friends left here…" His eyes went wide. "Don't you *dare* say Dad just gave up and ran off on me!"

"Why would we?" the other cop said. "Is there any reason to suspect that?"

"No!"

Colin fought down the urge to push in between them. Simple abandonment might be the best Martin could hope for; if this was Eric his father might be already dead. Just one unlucky man fed to the bastard's skein.

A flash of pale green caught his eye, on the counter with a few other scraps of mail. He stepped over and picked up the envelope.

Gently as he could, he asked Martin "You're selling your house? To Gardner Development?"

The two cops' eyes flickered at the name. Maybe…

"Not them," Martin said. "One of the big nationwide agencies took it. Dad just closed the deal this week."

"Oh." It shouldn't matter—Eric's schemes were his own, not some company conspiracy. Until they started defending him.

Martin added "Had to explain that to their man today, that it was too late for them."

The cop frowned. "So a Gardner agent was the last person your father talked to?" *Right, so these cops heard about the Gardners interfering at Eric's home.*

"One of the last," Martin said. "You think that's important?"

Was it? They'd come because Eric *could* make someone disappear this suddenly, but they had no idea if he'd pick this man, and less what Gardner as a corporation could have to do with it. But Colin watched the son's eyes brighten with the beginnings of hope.

"Probably not," the tall cop said. "Not their business, and it's a done deal anyway. What else can you tell us?"

Colin ground his teeth. These two cops had no respect for Joe Martin's fear, and even less for himself being with them… He followed their questioning for any other hints of what had happened, or any chance to step in and offer Martin something besides their rough help.

Then he sighed and stepped backward, out by the front door where the boxes were piled highest. The Gardners' attention had to mean *something.*

He sent a quick call out. Bea said Eric's old boss had been out of touch, but it was better than trying to spot which of Martin's memories could still lead anywhere.

Then Dennis Fields picked up. "Colin? Did they catch him?"

The eager hope in that voice had to be sincere—even after seeing Fields shuffling in the background as the Gardners defended Eric. "No, sorry. But there's something else I wanted to ask you about."

"If it helps, sure."

"Joe Martin. Have you heard anything about him?"

"Doesn't ring a bell. What's his connection with us?"

"I'm not sure. But he went missing, after he turned down a deal with Gardner."

"And you assume that ties us in to it?" Fields gave a heavy sigh. "I'm sorry you could think that. Eric Rowe is *not* this company... but I suppose you heard that company lawyers are claiming he's being railroaded?"

"I heard." Colin kept a grin off his face.

"I don't know what to say. They must think something about the evidence is off."

Zara and Terri saw *him, and so did I.* "Would they? More likely... Eric's threatening someone up there." That made more sense; Eric had already tried it on Fields.

"He can be intimidating, yes. I keep telling my superiors he's going to drag us all down. That's not what team loyalty is for."

"Careful—"

Colin froze. One of the cops, the taller one—the harsher one—was standing at the doorway watching him.

"I understand," he told Fields. "But, look after yourself, alright? Eric's a killer, and it looks like the company has a blind spot for him, or worse. Keep your head down."

"Believe me, I know. Thanks."

When they hung up, the cop stepped closer, eyes probing. "So what was that?"

Something that's closer to Eric than you bullying Martin. "A contact of mine at Gardner," he said, and he caught a hint of smugness in his tone.

Those eyes only squinted tighter. "So you talked to him first, and now he's all set to tip the rest of them off."

Just like that, because it was Colin's idea? "Fields isn't like that. Detective Bea Simms trusted him—he's part of how we found my sister—"

"Look, just *try* staying with us," the cop said. "And staying quiet."

They moved back inside—only to find Martin and the other cop walking out to meet them.

"I've got what we need," the officer said. "Time for a look around the place."

They stepped out to the yard.

The cracked paved walkway led from the door out to the street, where the older Martin had been heading for his car. Dirt and grass lay around it.

Colin looked around at the little neighboring houses, trying to count lights on, cars in place, or just the number of toys, people, and undamaged walls in view that said there might be enough people here to notice the few moments Eric might need to strike.

Would he have stood in wait behind the car? Dashed out from the side of the house? Colin turned toward that.

The two cops closed in around him. "Alright, Martin's back inside. You see something now, you tell us."

"I wish I could, believe me. I don't know much about footprints, and it looks like the son's tromped all over this by now..."

"Amateurs do that."

Meaning me too. Colin kept his eyes on the ground, easier than smoothing the resentment off his face.

The other cop, the shorter one, said "So was it Rowe or not?"

"Hard to say. I mean, he could have just picked the name out of some Gardner records before he left. But Eric blames the people who *stayed* with our town." Why couldn't this have been simpler, a nice straight line to their enemy? "I could see him scaring people away too, but not..."

"Not a guy who's already leaving. And this could still be some random mugger. So we've got nothing."

"Do we?" his taller partner said. "Da Costa, you're supposed to be the expert on Rowe and what he does. You've been saying he could pop up anywhere—but you think anyone could grab Martin that fast? My money's on the man running off with some skank."

Enough. That was one sneer too many, and now they were sneering at Eric too...

Colin stepped around the house's corner.

When he didn't hear the cops following, he added "So Eric couldn't pull this off? You never know." With a wrench of will he brought the skein surging out around him.

"Yeah?" came the cop's voice. "And you think you've seen it all?"

Colin faded from sight, and stepped around the corner.

If they see my outline, hear my feet, I'll show them the truth and to hell with Hoyle's schedule...

The two cops only stood there, glancing blindly at each other. One hooked a mocking thumb toward the corner where he was supposed to be, looking right past him.

Colin slipped around behind them. He glanced around, and took in one slow breath as he sucked the skein back out of sight, behind his cuffs and his collar.

—Eric might be even faster, grabbing Martin and covering him with skein to hide them both. He *could* have done this.

"I've seen a bit," he said.

Somehow he kept his smile in check when they whirled around.

* * *

The uncertainty on the officers' faces wasn't trust, but it was better than the contempt they'd showed him before. At least now they might listen... but Colin was still left looking at the Martins' home and the streets around it, and wondering if he'd know a real clue if he saw it.

The most he found was when they climbed into the squad car and drove around. He could see both men eyeing the neighborhood for places a man might have been mugged, or even tumbled out of sight after an accident. Then Colin looked away down the hill, and recognized the blockier buildings there in the twilight.

Cherry Street, where the first of the two Beast Killings had been.

That was more than thirty years ago, and plenty of sites are within blocks of the Martins'. What would I tell the cops, that they should search the house or the whole neighborhood for some connection?

Instead he stared at the big outlines that had grown up over the years there, and wished he knew if they were part of the puzzle at all.

Or if Eric had done this, or what he'd want with Joe Martin. Why?

When the night deepened around them, they headed back to Terri's hospital—that extra attention had the cops grumbling too.

There were more police on the floor now. They led Colin to the back of the wing, past fewer hospital staff and probably more empty rooms, to a different and more secluded room.

Here Terri's bed and monitors were crowded in with two other cots, both stacked with a change of clothes. *Awkward, but if that's what it takes for them to keep us under guard...* The room wasn't much smaller than Terri's last room, and at least it had no window.

"How are the Martins?" Zara asked.

"We couldn't do a damn thing." He sat down on one cot, but his legs wanted to bounce him up again, or even try pacing around in the few feet he could move. "It's all weird. You know the Martins were leaving town too? They'd already sold their house, and not to Gardner either."

"But you think Eric took him?"

"If he's the only one who could," Terri declared, "that makes it him."

"If, yes, but we don't know that for sure either." He shifted his weight on the cot. "Just one other thing: their house is a few blocks from the Beast Killings, but then anywhere could be near there."

Zara frowned. "Maybe. Or you could be right about their timing and the Vargas records…"

She stopped, shook her head.

"But I think that's enough for one night, don't you? We ought to be grateful we're together again. So let's put some buffer between today's nightmares and our sleep, shall we?"

"I'd like to try that," Terri added.

"Of course, sorry." *I just can't cool down, can I? And Terri's lived with this horror for years.* Colin got to his feet with a sigh. "Be right back."

He walked out and trudged toward the nearest bathroom. Two or three cops watched him as he went by, and he wondered if these conditions were so different from the life in the barracks that he might have had.

But just thinking about the Army, that meant his father's death in action… and it looked like Joe Martin had just lost his father too…

The bathroom was empty, and he slumped against the wall.

That whole time at the Martins, he'd been useless. *No, ever since Eric first came looking for skein, I've just been watching friends die or turn enemy. Bea's still facing jail.*

He leaned against the sink to look in the mirror.

Those scars *were his face,* now. His jaw, his cheek, too much of them were swallowed up by those fine lines. Not quite ordinary scars, not burns, but so many tiny gashes where the skein had taken a piece of him.

My face. That's me, I'm the guy with the scars *now, that's what everyone will see. Always.*

Nothing was the same anymore.

He sagged against the sink as that seeped through him.

Fighting meant scars, right? He should be ready for that…

Instead he clenched his eyes shut, around the deep, bitter wish inside him: that he'd let Eric go from the start, that all this had passed them by.

Or that he *could* be someone who let it pass.

* * *

Sleep came hard.

Waking was strange, lying there listening to his mother and sister breathe like he'd been dragged back to boyhood. The monitors on Terri hummed, softly, but in these quarters they felt like they were right at his ear. And strangers marched on by outside, each one fighting their own unconnected battles.

When his phone told him some of the morning had crept up, he lay there and began searching by the screen's light. There had to be a way to know if Martin was one more victim of this.

The Beast Killings—a woman killed on upper Cherry Street and later her boyfriend killed a few blocks from there. He tried not to think of Joe Martin Senior somehow being torn up the same way. And he still saw no real tie from those deaths to Matt Vargas, or Eric's moves, or the Gardners, except the worst case of what that kind of damage and a never-caught killer could mean...

Light flooded the room. He blinked and stared around—he hadn't even heard Zara wake up.

She glanced at Terri, still asleep. "I thought she had enough sleep... but, shhh." She crept over beside him, with the brisk eagerness she would have had before their world cracked open. "What do you have?"

"Some Vargas notes from the time of the Beast Killings, but there's still no connection—"

He stopped, scrolled back to the image of the last note. Those words Vargas had scribbled on the side didn't say *Rayo Hill,* they were *Rayo Spark.*

"Rayo—of course lightning has its sparks," Zara said. "Is that someone's idea of a 'clever' project name, and they forget it was lightning that wiped out the last mining camp? Or is it another Vargas clue?"

They found nothing more, even with Zara searching beside him. She flipped back and forth between those records and news about the sympathy that the younger Martin was drawing from the community, while Colin could only sit there and *not* have an answer for what had happened to his father. The sounds of the hospital outside thickened and gathered force.

Terri was awake by the time one cop opened the door to check on them. Another man Colin hadn't seen before, with a fixed, profession-al smile plastered on his pale face.

"Any news about Joe Martin yet?" Colin asked.

"Still looking. And yes, for Eric Rowe too."

Colin fought to keep the frustration off his face. The room felt so small, and Eric had to be somewhere...

And all we do is wait for him to let the cops spot him? Wonder helplessly if he took Martin, or what he might tear into next?

"There's a sort of rally gathering at the Martins'." Zara looked up from her screen. "He hates to sit alone in that house, so people all over the Hillside are coming to help him finish packing. Even on his way out, he's a neighbor."

Terri said "I've missed all that." Colin had to look away—for three years she'd missed so much more than that.

But, the morning was far enough along that he could finally call Bea. And after so much else today had held him up, she answered at once: "What's wrong?"

"Nothing. Or nothing urgent," he added. *Of course, that's where we all are these days, checking if something's exploded.* "How about on your end?"

"Waiting, and more waiting. That's what 'a hearing' means."

"Hoyle said he'd try to help you there. Say, have you heard any-thing more about the search? Any signs of Eric?"

"I don't know," she said. "I've got a real chance to beat this thing now, so I don't want to make waves until it's settled."

"Got it." He felt the frown twisting at his face, and tried to keep his voice even. "We could have used you yesterday."

"Eric's attack."

"Right—" Could they have stopped him cold if Bea had been waiting? For a moment Colin let himself wish it had gone that way, but then honesty made him add "Or, I was thinking of when we went to Joe Martin's. None of the cops listened to me—but that's okay, I had nothing to add anyway."

"Something always turns up—"

The door opened.

Lieutenant Hoyle stepped in, moving boldly into the tight space as if they were the ones crowding him. "Good morning, to you all."

"Hoyle's here," Colin said.

"Okay. But, watch yourself."

What? About Hoyle, she means? But Bea had already hung up.

The lieutenant was saying "I hope you're settling into the new room. I thought we'd see about breakfast, and then we can go through all your stories from the top."

Colin nodded. All this attention from Hoyle should be a good thing. Or else he guessed how much they were still holding back.

Zara said "The community's gathering at the Martins'."

Hoyle folded his hands behind him, studying her. "I wish we could do more to bring Mr. Martin home. But... do you have any firm reason to tie this to Rowe?" And he turned to Colin.

"No..." Colin squirmed under that gaze. Of *course* it came down to him, nobody else could say that Eric's obsessions were more likely to put him at the Martins' than some thug with a gun—

"There *is* a reason."

Zara's voice cut through the room.

She held up her phone. "One of their neighbors says he saw a ghost outside the house yesterday. A dim, transparent figure—he thinks it was simply an omen about Martin."

"A rumor." Hoyle glared back at her.

"You wanted to know if this could be Eric. I'm telling you, you can listen to these people."

Hoyle sighed. "We'll have someone interviewing them, yes. But we're stretched thin. And you ought to know eyewitness accounts are never as simple as they seem."

Terri said "Your plan was to search the city until you found him? Someone found him." Her clipped whisper came from behind Hoyle's back; they had him surrounded.

"I said I'd look into it. The priority now is to tell me about Rowe, so we can follow up on *all* the attacks as well as the Gardner connection—"

Colin snapped "And ignore the newest clue you've got? Give Eric more time to go after someone else, or someone right there?"

Zara said "Colin and I are going to that rally."

Hoyle twisted toward her.

"We're going," she said. "We can give Joe Martin our support, and we can also ask the people about that 'ghost' as well as any other reasons Eric might have picked out his father—"

"You're too valuable to this investigation," Hoyle said. "None of us know what goes on in Rowe's head. And you're *safe* here, or as safe as you can be. You know how hard it would be to protect you both, in a crowd?"

Colin stared at his mother. "Hold on, you can't be using yourself as *bait!* You can't do that!" He wanted to shake her, or hug her—

"Actually it's not," Zara said. "It's because you believed this was Eric's doing, and now we have even more reason to trust that. That means Eric wants something—"

"What?" Hoyle said. "What could you learn there, that's worth my letting you out there?"

Zara smiled. "We don't know yet. We might find something about why Eric chose him. Or that Eric will be going after more of the people there. That's what we need to explore."

Colin added "We could go without you. I can look after Zara."

And you can't stop me—but he knew better than to say that. Instead he said "But I think you want to be there too."

CHAPTER SIX

RALLY CRY

Young people, but also older ones, even a few children... there had to be two dozen of them milling around in front of the Martins' house, and more trickling in. The summer sun pushed most of them into the shadow of the orange moving van, or the house, or the food cart and canopy that had set up by the sidewalk.

If there had been any momentum toward emptying out that house, the work had fallen away into chatter. But the murmurs felt oddly subdued for this large a gathering, spiked by moments of anger.

And Eric could grab any one of these people to grow his skein.

Zara waded into those currents—

"Good to see you—"

"Where do we start?"

"Looks delicious—"

—as if she hadn't been in seclusion for one minute. The great constant in Colin's life, watching her in her element.

Seeing her among them now, he realized that her simple, safe-room clothes fit the tone of a moving party as if she'd planned it, and her bright necklace and smile made her stand out. He moved along behind her, trying to watch the still spaces where Eric could hide instead of all the faces turning toward his scars.

One young woman called out "Why the cop cars? Why're they watching *us* instead of looking for Martin?"

Colin swallowed. Every officer out here—or back with Terri—*was* one more pulled away from hunting Eric himself. But Zara fielded every question and comment that came her way.

The younger Martin stood by his front door, eying a knot of people around a small table in the yard. Zara went straight up to him.

"I hope you're holding up."

"Ms. da Costa?" The young man flushed, looked shyly away from her smile. Colin had seen that reaction around her too.

"It's Zara, always," she said. "How is the loading coming along?"

"Okay—" He stopped and stared at the police moving to the crowd's edges. "Why are they here? Is Dad... really gone..."

A whisper rippled around them, pushing people's voices to a nervous, waiting hush.

"No, it's not that."

Zara took a step away from him and turned to face the crowd. Colin edged back to watch the spaces around her.

"You see the police out here?" she called out.

Someone muttered "Yeah. They only show up *now?*"

Her voice swelled. "The police were investigating here yesterday, and they're committed to finding our answers. You'll see them around us while we're here—so please, if any of you have seen anything or have any ideas that might help, I hope you'll take this chance to share them."

"Too late," snapped a voice from over at the table, an older man—*what was his name again?* "The cops can't save Marty. They couldn't save *four* of their own—"

A woman's voice cut in "It's a spree killer. They flare up and burn out, and then almost all of us go back to our lives. And the police did bring Terri back safe."

Jessie. Colin watched her at the table, her red hair mostly gone gray. One of Zara's oldest friends, but she'd said she was moving away too?

"Safe?" the man said. "You mean besides *that?*"

And he pointed straight at Colin, at the marks on his face.

"It was worth it—" Colin began, but the words came a moment late to head off the murmur of voices that rose. One couple eyed him and edged away toward their table.

Zara moved toward them. "What are you working on there?" and she motioned to a clipboard they'd set out.

The man glared at her. "Names. Of anyone who can be ready to help when the next people want out of this town!"

Zara froze. She *froze,* looking at that table and its list, its bleeding wound to the community's strength...

"That's a good thought," and she flowed toward them. "Not many neighborhoods would be so generous in helping someone leave them." A couple of faces looked away in embarrassment.

Colin grinned. He drifted back a step, and concentrated on searching the corners of the yard, the gaps in the crowd—anywhere a hidden Eric could be watching without someone bumping into him.

He could slide through the crowd and just stab her, if he wanted...

Colin shoved that image away and looked around.

A pair of sunglasses glinted on the dry grass. An idea sparked, and he picked them up.

"Did anyone lose these—" he began, when a motion caught his eye.

A car, one of the pale green Gardner Development cars, settled to a stop by the street. Two men and a woman stepped out, suit jackets over their arms. Dennis Fields was the one in the lead.

A voice from the side of the crowd growled "What're the vultures doing here?"

"We brought some extra hands." Fields hesitated only a moment in the face of their hostility. "The work here could always use more, couldn't it?"

"Can't wait two minutes to snatch up the house?" someone jeered.

Martin called out "Hold on—I already sold the house, and *not* to Gardner. And the folks that bought it are nowhere in sight."

Zara added "Much appreciated, Mr. Fields. Now, is anyone in charge of checking how well the van has been loaded so far?"

On a simpler day Colin would have filled any hesitation by stepping forward himself. Instead he watched the Gardner team move at the edge of the crowd, still less than welcome. Fields's generosity seemed to fit the good nature he'd shown, but his company was still finding a reason to *defend Eric.*

The Gardners edged along the crowd, closer to the table and its list of people who were *so* interested in leaving the Hillside. That was two threats to the community as they knew it, too close together...

Or any of these people could be dragged away today, if Eric wants them. Colin gripped the sunglasses, hoping his idea could work—

One of the uniformed cops stepped over to him. "Give your mom some space. I'll watch her while..." and he nodded to the side. Hoyle was striding toward him.

Colin let the lieutenant lead him through the crowd out to the sidewalk, by one of the police cars. Hoyle gave a slow, expressive glance back around the people, and the several cars' worth of cops that stood around them.

"We don't have the men for this, but I went along with it." Hoyle paused, and Colin felt himself flinch under that gaze. "You're so certain that random rumors are going to give us a break? From where I sit, it looks more like getting my officers blamed that Martin isn't already back."

"Just give Zara time." Colin looked back to the crowd—Zara was in the thick of it, the safest place. He saw no shadows lurking around its fringes so far. "Anyway, your just being here might head off another attack."

"We may never know," Hoyle said. "But you're always careful to remind us our manpower can still make a difference, against someone who can... do what I saw," he added softly.

Colin glanced around the people again. "Harden the target, right?"

Hoyle stepped in front of him, blocking his view. "Right. But, why would Martin be a target? Why think Rowe would go after anyone except you three?"

Colin sidestepped to keep them in view. "But Eric *was* spotted here, that 'ghost' had to be him."

"Had to be? You think that fits because... he hates the town, right?"

"Right. He blames all of us for Terri—"

"So he grabs Joe Martin, a man about to *leave* Rayo Hill?" Hoyle stepped into Colin's sight again, and he shook his head. "The Martins ought to be the safest ones around."

"I know, I know. Unless Eric was... he could..." Colin's mouth felt stiff, clumsy.

"Humiliate Zara? I can't see it. What would he be after?"

"That's what we're *trying* to figure out," Colin managed. "Something about Martin, maybe."

Maybe that he's a human being Eric can feed to his skein. It was the worst, most explosive secret they had, but without it Hoyle couldn't see how nobody was safe...

Then Hoyle turned away to watch the crowd again. "We'll find something. We've even got some Gardners here again—they have to be in it somehow."

"Somehow, maybe some of them. Want me to introduce you to Dennis Fields over there? He helped us find Terri, and he's seen Eric coming unglued—"

"I think I can handle this."

Hoyle marched off toward his suspect.

Colin looked back to Zara. She stood out by the van now, watching three men sifting and repacking its contents. Her back was exposed to a whole swathe of open space where an invisible Eric could...

Or Eric could wait and pick off anyone, anyone, just to build his own power. Or *anyone* could start building up that same unstoppable power, with a scrap of skein and enough ruthlessness—and Hoyle needed to *not* know that?

Because Bea warned about him. Colin pulled out his phone and punched up a call to her, but he only reached her messages.

He started toward Zara again, as he said "Call me back. It's about someone you suspect, that wants to know more—"

"What is it?" Bea's voice came on.

Colin stopped, pulled back from the people ahead. "Sorry. You busy?"

"No. Not if it's urgent."

But only then? He looked at the pavement. "Not that. Just... what makes you so sure about Hoyle?"

"One of his officers, once. A rookie who came under some heat for screwing up, and when the media got hold of it Hoyle just cut him loose. A good kid, but he wound up forced to resign."

"That's... not so bad. I mean, of course you need a leader you can trust, but it looks like the other cops under Hoyle do trust him." What was Bea getting at?

"You haven't seen the details. And do you really want a cop who's thrown a man to the wolves once? On a case this radioactive?"

"I *want* to catch Eric! And he's helping me"

"You want..." Bea broke off, then began again: "Look, give me a few minutes and I'll find you the records about the case. You'll see. But this time, can you believe I know what I'm talking about?"

"I'm trying to."

They hung up, and he moved back toward Zara. The people had finished repacking what had been loaded so far, and they were drifting around her and the van, the yard, and the food cart, all with the uneasy movement of people not quite pushing themselves to start the next work.

Let's see if these sunglasses help.

He palmed a tiny dollop of skein, and smeared it over the inside of the lenses, silvery green spread thin against smoky green. He slipped the glasses on and felt the skein pinch against his nose, ready for his command.

The sunlit street looked doubly hazy through the two layers. He stared at one open corner of the yard, searching the skein for any invisible shapes there... but no Eric appeared behind the crowd, or up on the rooftop, or anywhere.

Colin drove his thoughts at the skein every way he knew—anything to feel how it bent light to hide him, or to somehow *unbend* what he saw, or pierce through it. Bea could do this.

Nothing. Assuming Eric was watching at all.

But at least the shades could hide the skein over his eyes and let him keep trying...

Except they also blurred all of his sight. He pulled the glasses off for now and moved to Zara's side.

The tall young man she stood next to was looking toward Joe Martin. "You better get this moving, and don't look back. The whole Hillside is cursed—the quake, the House, now Eric turned killer, how many signs do you need?"

"Give it a rest—ghosts, now?" grumbled the man next to him.

Ghosts? Colin looked at the first man again. If this was the one who'd glimpsed Eric and called him a spirit, Colin had expected someone more eccentric, not this clean-cut young giant.

"Cursed," the man said again. "Not that anyone wants to hear it."

"But you've given your warning," Zara told him. "Here, are you as thirsty as I am..." She eased him away toward the food cart. "You saw what you saw."

"What I saw was a ghost! An hour before Martin's dad was gone—right over there." He waved at the corner of the house. "Looked like a man there, and then he walked away like one, but he was all misty so I could just make him out. An hour later, *bam!* missing person. And they say it's no curse."

A sound ruffled through the people, an uneasy tone. One woman pulled her child closer.

Colin slipped the glasses on again, trading sun-clear sight for another chance to wrench that hazy view into something more. Still no sign of any enemy.

He pulled them off, and saw all the more clearly how many heads were glancing over toward the table and the list of move-enablers waiting on it. "So it's been a rough month," someone said.

"Or it's all a scam by the Gardner folks," and a gray-haired man waved at Fields and his team, white shirts by the food cart.

Then Zara was at that man's side. "We have a killer, not a conspiracy. A crisis like this comes and goes—and it *will pass,* soon," and her voice rose just enough before she went on, "but it always comes back to our own choices. How we want to live, and what we fight for. Our ancestors knew that when the first mines played out, and we still do."

Colin tried the glasses again. Nothing took shape.

"Of course it's no scam."

That was Jessie's rough laugh, and Zara smiled to her friend.

Then the old woman added "It's been going on for thirty years. Just look at the economic reports—Rayo Hill has been slipping *downhill* that long." She raised her hand and traced a shallow sloping line in the air. "Take two-year or three-year increments to look past the blips, and the employment and average income drops every time. A lot of us that stayed do alright, but you're getting fewer. It's all on government records, if any of you would just *look.* "

Zara didn't move. Colin saw her standing frozen, no answer, not even a flicker of reaction on her face. To hear that from a friend...

The people's voices lay in a hush, a pocket of quiet and cold uncertainty under the morning sun.

One man's voice rasped "So the joke's on you Gardners? You keep buying us up and throwing your money away?"

"That is not true." Fields turned away from his team around the food cart and walked toward the larger group. "Look, I think I see some of you here who bought or rented Gardner properties..."

"Sell-outs," came a voice from back in the crowd.

"Our mission is *community*," Fields said. "Here—if any of you feel you've been overcharged or cheated, or you're unhappy in any way, I hope you'll tell me why."

A different hush fell over the people, waiting and glancing around for the first one to raise their voice. Nobody did.

Colin used that silence to slip the sunglasses again. No good.

"We appreciate that," Zara said to Fields. "Of course it's not a thing anyone can just hand out. A community is what the people have grown between them, not who's living near who."

Jessie added "It was never about nearness anyway. How many reports did we fight over online before I dragged myself out to see you?"

She grinned at her, and Zara returned it. Colin felt a knot loosen at the back of his head; his mother couldn't lose friends that easily.

"There you go," Fields nodded. "Opportunity—that's the best thing any of us can give to a place."

Jessie said "And Gardner has been investing in this town for years, right? You've seen the values go up, and down."

"What was that chart you pulled together once, Jess?" Zara said. "That the Gardners didn't prey on us when we're vulnerable—the pattern is that they lose interest whenever the Hillside is in the most trouble?"

Dennis Fields burst out coughing. Then he cleared his throat and said "I'd like to see that one."

Somewhere deep in the crowd, a young voice said "So it's just us who live here that care for real. And we all knew that."

No single sound followed that, but the murmurs and rustles of the crowd rose a fraction, as if their voices were reaching to draw those words in. And most of the people had drifted toward where Zara, Jessie, and Fields spoke, leaving the table of defectors and enablers alone.

Into that hush, an older man said "Now, we going to pack the rest of this up?"

"What's the rush? I want a snack," someone said.

Smiles spread around the crowd. Some of the nervousness smoothed away, and their voices sank lower, thoughtful.

Colin looked back to Zara and saw her already slipping away, toward where Joe Martin stood at the house's doorway. He moved to join her, as she asked Martin:

"I was wondering. From what I've heard, this whole gathering wasn't really your idea, was it?"

Martin looked away. His voice was so low Colin could just catch it: "No. It just... happened."

"These things can," she said. "Did anyone ask you if you still wanted to leave, before you know about your father? You know it's okay to wait here for him, and hope you can leave together. Some things a family shouldn't miss."

"I know..."

Then he turned back, and tears streamed from his eyes.

"But nothing's changed! Dad is *gone,* I know he is, and I can't stay here and face this alone. Maybe, maybe I'll get to come running back if he's found, but *this place..."*

He wiped his eyes. Zara gave him a gentle nod, and he walked out to start the crowd loading his remaining things.

When he walked away, Zara's own eyes closed, and Colin saw the corners of them trembling. Her breath hitched.

Colin wanted to reach for her, but this was the same brittle edge-of-collapse his mother had stood at yesterday. If he spoke to her, touched her, here in public, would she crumble?

Then she opened her eyes and sighed, and walked out to the crowd herself.

He scrambled to stay behind her, and he looked around at the tone of the people now—sorting themselves and lining up to start clearing Joe Martin Jr. out. All the people they *weren't* losing, and the hesitant, reluctant way they went about sending one of their own away without his father.

When any of them could be next to go missing.

Hoyle stood at the back of the crowd, watching his officers stand watch against a threat he still wouldn't explain to them.

Colin glanced at his phone. Still no "details" from Bea about Hoyle...

No.

He marched toward the lieutenant, too fast to let himself back down. When he reached Hoyle, he gave him an urgent wave off to the side and away from his officers, and Hoyle followed him without a word.

The voices of the people rustled behind them. *I should be embarrassed to come clean after so long, but I can't slow down.*

"The skein that gives us power," he whispered, "someone *made* it by dissolving human flesh."

"What the hell? And you were—"

"Yes, I held out on you! But that is how the stuff's made." He rushed on "And Eric's done it. I keep thinking, all he needs to make more is people. Anyone. We have to figure out why he picked Joe Martin, or find some way to get ahead of him, or... or..."

"Or *anyone* could disappear." Hoyle glanced up at the sky, silent for a moment. "Maybe there is no likely target. And all we can do right now is be ready. You go watch your mother."

Colin's knees shook as he headed back, feeling how much worse that could have gone. *Sorry, Bea—I had to. And I didn't mention how we know the spell too.*

The crowd was in full swing now, hauling boxes and armfuls of possessions out to the van. Colin moved toward Zara, glad that keeping her safe gave him an excuse to not help hustle Martin away.

Jessie sat on the grass a dozen paces away from her, beside where a couple of other older neighbors stood. Colin kept his eyes on Zara and backed around toward her friend.

He sank down beside her. "By the way, thanks for bringing up those Gardner figures for Zara."

"Thank me? Numbers are just my hobby. I didn't remember the correlation she used at all, until she pulled it out." Jessie gave a crooked smile, and he wondered if she hadn't known just what Zara would do with that reference.

"Well…" *Please don't move away, Zara needs her friends now—* he swallowed that thought and said "You mentioned a spree killer, didn't you? You mean because we're just a few blocks from the Beast Killings?"

"Oh, those." She sighed. "I guess I know a bit of history. It's not hard—your mother only likes to stick to the town's nicer stories."

"I noticed that." He tried not to chuckle.

" 'Beast Killings.' That's just a trashy name for two people being killed—they thought it was the woman's boyfriend, until he was torn up too. But why put a label like that on two deaths?" She puffed out a breath. "And they were more than forty years ago—what's it matter if they were near here? Even the sites are buried under some warehouses."

"I thought so, thanks. Like you said, shocks come and go." *And Eric* will *be history too.* Colin pulled his feet in to stand.

As he did, Jessie said "Careful with Zara. She looks fragile today."

"You *are* her friend." The words were out in an instant—Jessie had *seen* all that in her, right through the crowd? "And you're really moving away on her?"

The old woman looked at him, and her face creased in a frown. Then she said "The sale's not final yet."

Colin felt a slow smile broadening across his lips.

His phone chimed.

Jessie laughed. "I'll see you around, maybe," and she stood up and walked away.

Colin grinned and stepped back from the couple Jessie had sat with, as he pulled out the cell.

Bea. Calling back *now*.

His throat tightened. She'd promised him real reasons for keeping their distance from Hoyle, but... He glared at the screen, then looked up around the neighbors, bustling around with only a hint of the danger they were in.

I had to tell him. Please don't make that a mistake now.

"Hi," he said.

"Hi..." Bea's voice hesitated. "I, well I found the history about Hoyle's case."

"I already told him. About... feeding." He looked at Zara, the crowd, Jessie strolling toward the sidewalk.

"You *told* him—"

Bea broke off. Then she said softly:

"It turns out, the truth isn't so bad. That officer Hoyle forced out, he *was* guilty of misconduct, and it was weighing on him. Yes the media attacked him, but he wanted to resign anyway. And it looks like Hoyle did his best to let him go with dignity."

"I see..." The tension loosened, fell away. So Hoyle was innocent, even when Bea assumed he'd throw his people under the bus.

Like her, *only he hadn't. Was she really thinking about Hoyle and our secrets, or was she simply paranoid about her own hearing?*

She added "But, you told him. Again. First I asked you not to give him anything more, and you did. Now you're telling him about—appetites, all of it?"

"About *what* Eric needs." But not *how* he did it, she needed to hear that difference in his words. "Of course I did."

"After everything we've faced together." Bea's voice was measured. She could have been ticking off points on a shopping list. "I told you I had information you didn't. But you simply put your judgment ahead of mine."

Ahead of someone who's not here? Colin stole one more glance around the crowd, at Zara. "I was trying to protect people. So I made a choice."

"I guess you did. When we should have made it together."

"I was…" He cut that off, it would just be repeating himself. And what kept her away was a shooting hearing, that could still land her in jail. "Well, I hope we can get back on the same page soon."

"I hope so. I hope there's still time."

What did that mean? Colin felt for words as the silence stretched another second, another, an island of stillness in the busy sounds of the people at work.

Then she hung up.

He looked at the screen a moment, thought of tossing one follow-up text over to her. But he'd left Zara alone too long.

The lines of people were slowing now, carrying smaller boxes and possessions to the van—winding down with the last of the work. More and more of them milled around the tailgate with their loads, only waiting for a plan for how to tuck them inside.

He moved up beside Zara at their fringe, and said softly "Everything look okay?"

She smiled, her eyes never leaving the people. "I think hope is still alive for most of them. Even losing the Martins."

"Yes." He leaned closer. "And, Jessie may want to talk to you. She said, she *told me,* she might even stay."

Zara's hand brushed his arm. "Thank you."

She strode off toward the sidewalk, glancing around the crowd as she went.

Colin fell back a step as he followed. He slid the sunglasses on again, and fought to make their skein *show* something… but still no shadowy figure took shape near his mother. Eric simply wasn't here—or Colin's whole idea of testing his vision at random moments was a waste of time. He had to make Bea walk him through this trick, if they ever got the chance.

"Are you gonna wear those things or not?" A little boy was looking up at him, half hidden behind a cardboard box in his arms.

Colin managed a grin. "Both. I heard switching it up keeps the eyes healthy." It might even be true.

Parts of the crowd had begun to peel off, a few walking toward their cars or the street. More gathered into smaller groups, most of them around Joe Martin at the van. It made it easier to look for Jessie.

Zara still moved back into the thick of the crowd. "Anyone? Have you seen Jessie Chapman—the red-haired woman going gray? With the attitude?" she added.

"Nope."

"No. Must have gone home."

"But," and she pointed up the street, "her car's still there... Oh *no.*"

Zara dashed a few steps one way, another, peering around the van. Colin ran with her. That *was* Jessie's tiny black car up the block, and he'd seen her walking toward it, before any others headed out.

He caught at Zara and steered her toward the nearest cop—*six men plus Hoyle, and they saw nothing?* Zara fumbled at her phone. "She's not answering—"

"Stay with the police!"

He bounded away for the sidewalk. Skein gathered against his legs, bracing his steps and flinging him along faster. He heard one *What are you* from the cop behind him, and charged on. He *had* to be wrong.

The sidewalk and the few people on it flew by him, toward Jessie's car—

He stumbled—the skein over one leg not driving him to match the other—and pulled himself up and raced on. Jessie's car stood only steps away. If she'd made it that far.

The street around them was all blocks of houses... all emptied out by the morning work hours, the gathering at the Martins', and the usual Rayo Hill share of abandoned homes. All the places that could have seen Eric strike, if he were a simple kidnapper.

But once he yanked her away, just a few steps off the sidewalk would bring them in among those corners and walls and bushes...

Colin lunged in past the first house to be missing a fence. Brush crackled against jeans and skein. *All those times screwing around with the sunglasses and I still missed him?* He halted behind the house. The ground was caked hard in the summer sun—but there had to be some tracks.

He swung back behind the house, in case they'd pulled off the sidewalk sooner. He stumbled again, forced the skein to keep him moving. His mouth opened—no, he couldn't call out and warn Eric. He leaped one fence, dashed on past brush, all so damn *deserted* and so undisturbed.

There. He slammed to a stop, looked back.

A single print lay gouged in the hard ground, like the marks under his own powered-up steps. Leading away from the street.

Only that one track—like Eric could *really* disappear now?

But another mark lay some twenty feet off... twenty-foot strides? This track was shallower, harder to see. The next was lighter still and twisting off to the side...

The trail was already smoothing away, and Eric could be blocks ahead by now. Colin snarled and headed back toward the police.

How do I tell my mother I lost them?

CHAPTER SEVEN

NEAR AND FAR

Worried, uncertain voices were just beginning to prickle out of the gathering as Colin jogged back. He saw one couple start moving toward the sidewalk, and a cop shoo them back into the crowd again—and the voices spiked. Once he heard the name *Jessie* among them.

Two officers saw Colin approaching and moved to meet him. He angled toward Hoyle instead and they headed to him together. At least Zara was there beside the lieutenant, safe.

One of the biggest men on the lawn advanced on Hoyle, several friends in his wake. "So you don't know if she's missing?"

"Sure she is, same as Martin." That was the tall man who'd seen a 'ghost,' and his voice cracked. "She's just gone! We're all cursed—"

"Please—" Hoyle drew back a step and called out to the crowd. "Please! All of you, we're right here, and we'll deal with this. The more that you simply *keep still,* the sooner we can see what's going on." His voice pushed against the murmurs and actually tamped them down.

Zara moved to Colin's side. She didn't speak—the question was all over her face.

"It was him," he said. It had to be, from the stride of the tracks. That had to be enough to convince Hoyle. With Eric striking right here, out of nowhere with his speed and everything else... this time Hoyle would have to warn his people what they were hunting...

The lieutenant's balding face leaned in close. He hissed "Just tell me one thing. Did he dump her off in a ditch, or is there somewhere he's keeping her alive?"

At that blunt question, Zara started back with a grimace of pain.

Colin snapped "He never dumped Martin, did he? Think!" The sharp answer popped out by reflex, but then he felt the reason fall into place behind it: "I told you, how he needs people for…"

He stopped and drew his tone down, in away from the frightened faces around them.

"Well, it takes time," he finished.

"It does," Zara added. And she held up her hand, to show the raw scar along its back where Eric had dissolved some of *her* flesh.

But would he need Jessie alive? Colin couldn't say that.

Hoyle gave that mark a long, measuring look. Then he waved his officers over to him.

"Check doors and windows, all down the block! Anything that's broken, call it in and wait for backup and assault gear. And—"

He broke off, and heaved a slow sigh. Colin opened his mouth to demand a place in that search, but Hoyle turned and called out to the crowd:

"People! There is a chance, a *slight* chance, that the attacker may be hiding in some nearby home. If you live within a block of here, for your own safety, please stay here until we have a chance to clear your homes—"

Shouts exploded. Men and women yelled, half a dozen people swarmed toward Hoyle, to be blocked by his cops. A few figures bolted for their cars.

Zara moved to meet the crowd, raising her arms. "Please, please, *let them do their job!* Jessie needs your help. She needs you to *listen.* Here, Kitty, let me take…"

She slid in among the people and went to work.

Hoyle drew back a few steps, and waved two of his cops up the block. "Doors and windows, now. *Not you—*"

He grabbed Colin's arm.

Colin turned ready to wrench it free, but the lieutenant was already snapping commands on his radio, a flurry of police code with the words *mobilize* and *vehicle patrols.*

Colin settled back and did his best to follow it. Hoyle released his arm and began directing cops up and down the block, alternating between gestures and different channels on his radio. Colin listened, trying to build a picture of the search and where he should demand he join it.

His gaze swung up and down the block, he dashed one step to watch another police car pull up to join them. The big question seemed to be, would Eric hole up somewhere close, or risk taking his prisoner clear out of the neighborhood? Near or far, near or far?

The phone's chime made him jump.

Fragmented guesses rattled in his head, as he clawed out the cell. Some man's name he didn't know—*is this one of Eric's games—*

"Colin?"

The faint, controlled voice was *Terri.* Noise from the crowd tore at that sound and tried to trample it, and Colin dove a few steps to the edge of the yard to clear his hearing. "Terri? What's wrong?"

"Not that. I'm on a cop's phone. They thought I could help." Every syllable had the sharp enunciation Terri used to make her thoughts clear. "Tell me."

"Jessie. You remember, Zara's friend."

" 'Course."

Right, Terri's only been away three years, she still knows her—one friend Zara can't lose— He pushed the wave of guilt down. "Eric grabbed her."

"For *me.* " A sob broke through her voice.

To heal her, by making skein from innocent people. And Eric's whole spiral only began when Terri disturbed some skein and collapsed the church on her—

"This is on Eric, all of it." He flooded his words with all the certainty he could give them. "It is *not* your fault he's gone crazy trying to 'help' you. When someone can talk like a real person one minute and then spit curses at everyone around him…

"Forget that. Try this, Terri: don't think about who he's doing it for, how about who he took? Martin, now Jessie—why would he want them, where would he take them?"

"What do you *think's* been going through my head? All day?" Terri shouldn't even have enough breath to snap at him, but she did. "He wants… to help me. Prove the town's doomed."

Like Eric already told them. Colin gritted his teeth, wanted to apologize and let Terri rest, but the cold back of his mind whispered something else: *If it was me, I'd need a purpose.*

"I know," he said. "But why take Joe Martin and Jessie? That's two people that were already leaving the Hillside."

"Don't know! I—oh." Terri gasped.

"What? What is it?"

"The town. He's proving people are leaving. But if he took someone who's staying, the rest could be—" She halted, wheezed for breath. "They'd be leaving because of him."

Colin looked around at the churning crowd, at Zara darting around it trying to keep them calm, at Martin Junior huddled against the van. This was Eric *not* forcing them out of town?

But for Eric, that probably counted as fair. If he didn't punish them for staying, he could call their being so rattled as proof…

Lieutenant Hoyle stepped into Colin's view, too close. "What have you got there?"

"Terri. She's got an idea about Eric."

"Well? Not getting any younger here."

"It's not about where he took them. More that… we thought wrong, that Eric wouldn't want Martin because he was already moving out."

Colin waved to Martin's van, and fumbled for words to make it clear:

"Yes, for one thing, he took them to use their bodies. Thinks he can help Terri, and build up his own strength. But the other thing is, you heard Eric in the hospital—he's out to prove Rayo Hill was never worth Terri getting hurt at all. So he's grabbing people who are already leaving. That way he can scare us all and show what we're made of, without us saying he's scaring us *away*. Guess that's enough for him," he added. *Please, let that make enough sense.*

"Maniac." Hoyle spat the word. "And it's him who's got all this power."

"That's Eric alright. And every minute he has the stuff working on someone?" Colin pointed at his own damaged face. "That means more power for him."

And I'm still standing *here. Where do I go?*

"So where is he?" Hoyle said. "When does the... is there still a chance he'd duck in an empty house here and take what he can get? Or would he have to be long gone?"

Colin swallowed. Those were good questions, but Hoyle sure adapted fast to the idea of how nasty the skein could get.

Hoyle added "Come on, think! God, I already told all these people they could have a kidnapper in one of their homes, we have to know if that's—hell, what now?"

He raced away, toward a trio of people converging around Dennis Fields and his team. Colin charged after him. The Gardners had been cut off just short of reaching their car.

One of the three in their way waved a phone at Fields's face, but Hoyle snapped "Alright, back off!" Other cops closed in around them.

"Their man Eric did this," the man with the phone said. "And now all of them come around here—"

Fields said "He's not ours—"

"You're putting out lawyers for him. While he's kidnapping..." His voice gave way to a growl.

Colin stepped around Hoyle, aiming between the two.

"That is enough," Hoyle said. "I'll do the interrogating here."

The man opened his mouth, but Hoyle locked his gaze on him and he flinched. The officers moved in and herded him and his friends away.

Hoyle closed in on the Gardners. "Alright, this time let's have the real story. Why did you come out here, when Rowe was the reason Martin was missing at all?"

A woman behind Fields said "That's not certain, that Eric—"

"Do *not* start with me," Hoyle cut in. "What are you doing here?"

Fields said "I keep saying it: to try to rebuild our reputation. And just give these people some help. I didn't expect to catch the blame for everything Eric Rowe has done."

And Fields *wouldn't* be part of that. Colin opened his mouth to say it, but Hoyle pushed right on:

"So you haven't had contact with him?"

"No."

"You're not sheltering or supporting him. Even though we've had a manhunt out for two days now, and he's still at large?" He swept a glare over the whole team.

"No, we're *not.*"

"And I should believe that? Rowe used one of your properties for years to hide his first victim, and you 'never guessed.' "

"No!" Fields stumbled back a step.

Colin moved between them. "He didn't! Fields was the one who helped us *find* Terri. He's seen what a menace Eric is—"

"I think I said, this is my interrogation." Hoyle stepped around him and cast another slow, sharp gaze around the Gardner team.

One of them, the woman, took that moment to straighten her blonde hair and screen out his gaze.

"This is a cop-killer we're hunting," Hoyle told them softly. "If we find any connection between his trail and you, nobody's getting away clean. You have to know that. And yet you're already sending lawyers to block us in court."

"No..." Fields tried again.

A new voice added "He's giving you a chance."

And Bea, *Bea,* walked up to take a place beside Hoyle. Colin wanted to stare, just be grateful for her presence here when they needed her most. He forced his gaze back to the Gardner team.

The woman there was edging back a step, away from Bea.

Hoyle focused on her retreat. "Is there a problem?"

She stopped, then drew herself up to meet Hoyle's gaze. "Alright. Yes there's a problem, that's the woman who *shot—*"

"Careful." Hoyle's voice stayed low, but it cut the woman off neatly. For a moment the group was quiet, and the nervous, volatile mutters of the crowd spilled into the stillness.

She began again, softer now. "But she did shoot a helpless prisoner, a man we've worked with for years. And you wonder why we think this could be a witch hunt?"

"Helpless? The man is still out there, and he added to his body count on the same night." Hoyle studied her for another, long moment. "You claim to know a lot about Detective Simms, and less about the man you're sticking up for. Someone that well-informed makes me curious—and someone *selectively* well-informed makes me uneasy. But you ought to be concerned yourself, if someone showed you just that side of the picture."

He eyed her again, then Fields and the other man.

"You go tell your lawyers we'll be looking into this," he sighed. "When I don't have an abduction to track down."

He waved them away.

Colin watched them slink away toward their car. For a moment, before his gaze swung back to Bea.

"You're back? They cleared you?"

She said "The hearing is... calming down. Looks like I have friends over there."

She looked at Hoyle—not a smile, an odd, measuring look.

Then she added "I haven't been cleared, but they won't scream if I pitch in some support here."

Colin waited for the next words, for her to ask for the situation and what her place in it would be. Instead she stopped there, like all that could be taken as part of what she'd said. That was pure Bea.

A voice rose behind them, from the people in the yard:

"And when *are* you searching my house?" One stocky man shook his finger at one of the cops. "You told us the kidnapper was hiding around here!"

"They said he might be." Zara moved up beside the man, drawing his gaze away from the cop. "And they have only so many officers to search these houses and their other leads. You don't want to be the one slowing them down, do you?"

"I 'want' to go home! You think I can stand out here all day?"

"Would it be worth it, if it saved Jessie's life? You know the police are using every resource they have for this search. And they're trusting us not to try and put ourselves first right now. They do have to search here, but they also have to look for whether he's already taking her farther away…"

Her voice softened, and the big man steadied, beginning to listen. Zara had this under control.

Colin looked around the blocks again. Like Zara said, Eric could be hiding close by, in one of the simple Hillside houses on this block or the next. Or he could be heading further away, like the few cars that rolled along the block, if he risked being seen at the wheel. Block after block of often-empty houses one way, while down the other way were the rougher silhouettes of industrial buildings.

Hoyle was fixed on his radio, issuing more commands to his troops. He'd barely looked at Bea.

Colin caught at her arm and drew her aside a step. "You're really back?"

"Like I said, some of the pressure's off me. If you mean do I get my badge back, we'll see." The edge of her mouth moved in a smile.

That was all. No reassurance, and no going after Hoyle *demanding* to pull her weight now that there was a life on the line?

"We'll *see?* After you *trap* yourself by shooting—"

He cut that off and tried starting again, quieter.

"You risked your career trying to stop him, and now you're just waiting for them to—"

"It's the only option I have," she said.

And that was the end of it? *You'd* better *come out of this okay. I need...* He shook himself and tried to focus. *I need you and me to get back on the hunt, I need us to run Eric down with no more mistakes, I need...*

Finally he said "I need to be able to see if he's around. I've been trying to watch all morning," and he pulled out the sunglasses.

She looked at the skein-coated lenses, and smiled. Had his trick actually impressed her?

That moment of confidence sobered, as he stepped closer to whisper "It never worked. I was hoping there was just no Eric around here to see, but he got Jessie anyway. So I was wrong *and* blind, and I need your help."

"And you think I can just explain it?" She sighed.

Her breath brushed his face. They were only standing near to whisper, but—

Then, then, she said "I can't do that."

She blinked, swallowed.

"It's true, I told you once, how making a thing invisible felt like bending the skein? But for this, how to see through that technique... I don't think there *are* words for how I do that. And it doesn't make the glow much more visible anyway."

She pulled away a pace.

Voices chattered around them, frightened, helpless.

"You heard about the Beast Killings?" a woman said. "Three dead, just down the block."

No, it was two *dead. Jessie could have told them that.*

Jessie. And we're still only standing here.

Hoyle was still only a few steps away, still on his radio.

"Where's the best bet to search?" Colin said. "I'm going out with them, now."

Hoyle's eyes narrowed. "You're staying put. You go where I tell you to."

"Let me help! We're still the only ones who know what we're—"

"Quiet!" Under his breath he added "I have a plan, to explain this without launching a panic."

Sure, Hoyle and his "plan," if he ever had one.

Colin felt Bea beside him, watching, still just letting Hoyle sideline them.

Her head turned. Colin followed her gaze, up the street where a cop was stepping out of his car, and letting out a dog.

A lean brown and black shape, with cheeks that sagged past its muzzle—was that an actual bloodhound? Two other officers joined the dog and its partner and led them up the sidewalk, toward where Jessie had been grabbed.

Colin scrambled after them, Bea right behind him. To their rear he saw Hoyle had chased a few steps after them, then halted with a scowl on his face. But they'd sat out too much of this already.

"A dog," Colin grinned. "Quickest way to check if they're still in a nearby house."

Bea nodded. "At worst, we free up some manpower for the rest of the search. At best, be ready."

Ahead, the officers neared the open yard where Eric's footprints waited. The dog's handler, an older cop, led it carefully off the sidewalk.

The dog edged forward, turning one way and another, exploring the scents. Its nose dipped toward the ground.

The dog stopped cold.

With a single whine it dropped to the ground and cowered.

The handler coaxed it back to its feet and nudged it forward, leaning in close to reassure it, but the dog only pulled away. He tried leading it around from the side, and it flattened to the ground again.

"I don't know what she smells," the cop said. "Is there a goddamn *bear* around here?"

"Don't let them hear that," one of the others said.

They turned back toward the sidewalk, eyes on the crowd where Hoyle was, and Colin and Bea started back ahead of them.

Colin's fists clenched. They'd been so close to narrowing the search, but the dog was beaten by just the *smell* of Eric's skein?

He glared around: more Hillside houses to the left and right, the industrial silhouettes off in the distance, nearby a sidewalk still helplessly lined with cars...

Behind them, the dog whined again.

My skein. It smells it on me too.

He glanced back and saw the handler just starting to look down at his partner. Colin quickened his step, wondering how many seconds they had before the dog panicked on top of every other disaster—

Hoyle stood at the edge of the crowd, advancing right on them—

"Just *go,*" Bea whispered. "I'll call you soon."

She gave him a push forward, and strode past him to intercept Hoyle. "The trail's no good," she began and drew her boss into a close whisper. Distracting him.

Colin followed her shove toward the thick of the people, out of Hoyle's sight. How, how could she read him that well... but he still had no idea where to look... but he had to do *something*...

He slid through the ranks of the crowd. Zara stood near the center, between two women and probably calming down an argument. In the whole nervous, rumbling throng, she might be the safest one there.

Then, out the back of the crowd. Around the side of the Martins' house. One more look around for anyone who could see him. Right at the same place as he'd done yesterday, as if that stunt had been pre-paring for this.

Still walking, he called the skein out from under his clothes.

It slid out—and *lurched* once to freeze up along his sleeves, before it flowed into place around him. Another thought twisted him from sight.

Then the skein drove his legs to fling him faster, faster, over the ground and toward the far sidewalk. Thoughts rustled in his head about the risks he was running, but he darted past two police and saw them barely glance toward his glimmer of light. And another idea set-tled into shape:

None of the police would spot Eric either, with not Hoyle keeping them blind to what he could do. And they were still splitting their search in case he went to ground nearby—but Eric wouldn't bother, he could simply wrap Jessie up in skein and slip right past them all.

Colin dashed past another officer reporting on her radio, and a nervous woman eyeing her from a distance back. Houses and low walls and brush flew by. If Eric was still anywhere nearby, he'd never spot him down in the thick of these obstacles.

Two blocks ahead, the warehouses and factories rose from the street.

Now and then a car rolled past him. *Or Eric could have just driven out, risking his face being seen, so he's miles away now...* Colin pushed that from his head; *this* was the only scenario where he could make a difference.

The warehouse loomed pale in the sun. Cherry Street was one of the few blocks where industry had tried moving up into the Hillside itself, and some of its buildings were the tallest spots in the area. He charged for the wall and threw himself upward.

The skein around his legs spasmed, failed—he stumbled and fell against the wall.

What is wrong *with this thing? And why* now?

He locked the invisibility tight around him before the two workers came into view, searching for the noise. No time to hesitate. He slipped around the corner to the back wall, clenched his strength and his will, and leaped.

He landed against the wall just ten feet below the roof, claws sinking into the surface to catch him. Scaling the rest was simple.

A breeze blew along the roof, a cooling, freeing touch that helped Colin step away from the fears and look around below. Streets, houses and yards, broad blocky shapes and loading areas, all spread out below. Jessie could be somewhere in there, with the bastard that took her.

Only if I'm lucky—

No. They'd tried everything else, until all that was left was piercing Eric's invisibility. *It will work, because it has to.*

He stared down at the streets. Through the gauzy blur of his mask, he saw house after house, some already long empty, while tiny shapes buzzed around the car-clogged space that would be the Martins'. Black and white police cars moved about on their own patrols.

Or there was just nothing more to see here—

His will pushed at the skein across his eyes. Strain... twist... relax into it... reach out... pull, hammer at it... Every technique he'd learned, his will tried and twisted and twined together. Heart pounded, head turned to sweep the streets—Eric could be long gone—no, no room for that, *stare*—

Eyes blurred. Vision went gray—*no, do it*—

A shape bloomed below him. An outline, a soft gray halo that limned an empty shape, creeping between one broad building and the next.

Eric.

Alone. His breath caught—Eric was done with Jessie?

No hesitating, I can finally do something...

The figure that was Eric moved slowly from one mini-factory to the next. The "halo" was still a dim thing, too easy to miss at a distance if Eric's outline wasn't swollen with all the extra skein he wore.

Eric stopped in his tracks, moved back toward the plant he'd just left. He could be keeping out of sight of the few people down there, or even keeping watch around an area where he'd stashed Jessie. While the skein burned its way into her.

And Colin was still standing straight up on a rooftop, trusting to the same camouflage he'd just beaten. He crouched down on the hot asphalt roof.

The Eric-aura flickered from sight—Colin's twist of perception had slipped. He beat down the swell of hot fear to fumble for vision again. *There, wider...* Eric took shape again.

Colin drew out his phone. The cell slid out from under his skein, *appearing* in the air beside him, in his own halo-limned hand.

Bea answered at once. "Anything?"

"I *found him.*" The whisper thrilled in his throat like a shout of joy. "No sign of Jessie yet."

"Impressive. In one of the houses?"

"The Cherry Street storehouses." Eric was still edging along below. "I went looking for a vantage point, but he's right here."

"Of course you got him. Let me—"

The line went quiet. He kept his eyes on Eric, still making his way slowly through the block below. That had to mean something, that he hadn't simply finished with Jessie and raced away.

"You found him?" If Hoyle's voice could have reached through the phone and shaken him, it would. "How?"

"Lucky guess, and finally learning to see invisibility. Listen..."

"Where *is* he?"

"I found him, so you listen to me!" The words were out before he could think, but they felt so good. "I'm watching him right now. If we keep an eye on him, he might lead us to Jessie."

"Surveil *him,* when we've got just one chance to bring him down? No, we're surrounding him and bringing all the heavy-caliber force we've got."

"I know, of course you are! But Eric's not going anywhere." The shape was still stalking between the buildings, hiding or searching. "I just mean, try closing the net slowly, I'll guide you in. We could have a chance to trap him. And find his prisoner, if we do it this way."

"So we've got time? Alright. Now where is he?"

"In front of... It says Lipnik Machinery. Here." He swung the phone out and sent them a quick picture of the building's empty-looking face, then some shots up and down the street to orient them.

"Got it. If your mother can keep these people off my back."

Colin crouched lower. The roof already felt hotter than it had when he'd climbed it. Jessie could really be alive... they'd finally gotten the jump on Eric.

Out at the end of the next block, a black and white car pulled up and settled on the street. The police were moving into place. And Hoyle could be right, big enough guns—and *enough* of them—were the best chance to break through Eric's skein, as long as someone showed them where to shoot.

Eric stepped around the building's corner, out of view. *Doesn't mean he spotted me, it looks like one more part of his sneaking around.*

"Careful! He just went behind Lipnik—here." He sent them another shot. "I can't see him now, and I don't know what he can see."

"Got it." That was Bea again.

Colin stared down at the machine plant. It looked still, not shuttered but maybe shutting down, one more slow loss in the years after the earthquake.

Eric wouldn't just step back into view, would he? One observation point couldn't track him forever.

Colin moved out to the warehouse's far corner, still not far enough to bring Eric back into view. He dropped from the roof.

He hit the street—and the skein's strength failed again. Instead of his legs catching him, he crashed down and toppled across the concrete, saved by its shock-absorbing protection—*the only reason I'm alive.*

"Huh? You hear that?" someone said.

He tightened the invisibility again and headed down the street on wobbly knees. What was *happening* with the skein? Starting and stopping like that, that wasn't like the stuff. And he'd known that and jumped off a roof—smart.

And now he was running toward the killer who had more power than him.

What few people were on the sidewalk, he wove around. The corner of the Lipnik building waited ahead. Just one glimpse of Eric, *please don't let him be already gone...*

Up the street, the police car moved closer. They could all be closing in, too late.

Eric stood at the rear of the building. Walking back toward him.

No, wait, he wasn't glancing around yet—Colin sidestepped to the wall, the same smooth motion he used to keep his shimmer from catching someone's eye. The Eric-halo never turned toward him, and he ducked back away behind the corner.

Eric stepped onto the sidewalk, and glanced around.

The halo flickered from sight, *gone.* No—Colin locked his eyes on the faint shimmer Eric still left in view. He clenched a fist, and even that felt weak. If Eric took one step back toward him he'd... *I don't know what I'd do.*

Eric looked away, on up the street. At the police car.

Then he strode away across the street. Colin stared after him, fighting to master the skein over his eyes—Eric's shimmer dwindled in the distance, but finally the halo sprang out around him again.

Eric reached the warehouse. He leaped for the roof, and sailed up to it with one clean jump. Colin watched the hulking shape move away down the roof. His control looked effortless.

Colin pulled out his phone. "He's up on that roof now, see there? I'll keep an eye on him."

He slipped back across, to the side of the warehouse wall. With Eric up there somewhere, right below him would be the best shelter from his sight. He crept along the wall.

He reached its far corner and peeped out beyond it. No hidden shapes on the pavement there.

Up above... Eric stood on the edge of the roof, looking out around.

Colin pulled out his phone again.

The distraction must have been too much—the light-twist around him flickered and faded like shade parting from above him, and his body flashed into sight.

As Eric stepped down to the ground.

CHAPTER EIGHT

HOLLOW

Colin jerked back around the warehouse corner. *Not enough, Eric's too close and the skein isn't hiding me*—he had one instant to stare around for cover, at nothing but open yard and the wall beside him.

And one doorway in that. He dove through that, two quick steps, silent, *safe* into the building's stillness.

His knees were trembling. That was a wave of sheer, primal relief—his teeth clenched against that, as he edged toward the nearest crates for what concealment the space had.

Eric stepped into view. The broad, skein-swollen outline stepped in front of the doorway.

In the moment before that head turned toward him, Colin slid behind the crates. The warehouse floor was wide open, dotted by only a few boxes and objects like the last bones of some huge skeleton, and the fluorescent lights drove any shadows away. But Eric hadn't looked toward him, and he wouldn't come searching for something right in *here*—nobody's luck was that bad.

Eric moved away.

Colin let out a sigh, that filled his nose with the room's smells of staleness and oil. His will pulled and turned at his skein for that one *twist*... and the cooling feel of invisibility slid over him again.

Eric paced back into the doorway, but the camouflage held.

What's wrong with me? I've never had the kind of power Eric does, but I was always ready to face him before. Now I've got enough skein to have some chance, and as soon as it starts failing me, my only instinct is to disappear?

He held his breathing even, crouching behind the crate and tucking his phone away. At least Bea had some idea where Eric was now—*and what's that, me waiting to be rescued?* The police were never equal to Eric's power either, and it had always been Colin and Bea trying to drive him off. Or trail him to Jessie.

Invisibility flickered against him, like a lightbulb struggling to stay dim.

Eric walked inside.

Colin had one glimpse of him stepping through the doorway and peering around, before he moved toward the far side of the floor and out of view. His soft-echoing steps on the concrete moved slowly, me-thodically—not a man sensing danger at all. More like, searching for something.

Colin peeped around. Eric was eyeing, not the limited crates or the shadows, but the signs along the walls. Those looked like a typical smattering of instructions, colorful icons, and other simple guides for whatever daily work they did here. Colin crept over a few feet from his low crates to behind some kind of long metal rack, for a clearer view.

Eric studied one large sign, then turned away, then to view it again. Colin held still and felt his invisibility steady.

Eric's outline started around the room. His head turned right past Colin, toward the corner beyond his hiding place. With the same slow tread, he started toward that.

And toward me. Or, if he didn't see me but I pull back now, the shimmer's motion itself could still give me away...

No. Colin locked the nerves down, held his body still against the cold metal and his will tight through the skein.

Eric turned away toward the corner. Breath still held, Colin took the moment to edge further back behind the screen, out of sight.

One footstep broke Eric's rhythm, one shifting sound in the echoes.

Colin flung himself clear as the juggernaut slammed into the rack.

The crash of metal hit like a blow itself, but Colin rolled to his feet before Eric spun around toward him.

Eric halted. The green-covered head—all stealth gone—twisted left and right. Like he'd lost sight of his target.

Footsteps sounded outside.

Oh God no...

Eric winked from sight before a man, a single older man in a blue watchman's uniform, strode inside. "What in hell—"

Silence fell. Colin felt his invisibility hold firm and cool around himself. Eric stood frozen, an unseen outline of menace. The watchman gazed around at the open floor.

Finally he stepped toward the fallen, dented rack, and bent to try lifting it up. He gave one pull, then let go. "Hell no. That's no one-man job."

As he turned away, Eric stalked toward his back. With one rising hand forming claws.

Colin charged. With all the strength his skein had, he flung himself at Eric—

For one instant Eric turned *away* from his target and toward the doorway, then the next he began to whirl back toward Colin's footsteps—

Colin's fist slammed home into his stomach. Straight to the lower center of the body, the force lifted Eric up and pitched him away, clear of his intended victim and crashing against the wall. He tumbled into sight as he fell.

"Whaaaa—"

That was the watchman, he had to be staring at the green-sheathed figures that had burst into sight. Colin gasped one breath to say, *"Run."*

Footsteps scampered away.

Colin kept his eyes on Eric. The huge shape was already rising to his feet, as smoothly as if the punch were nothing.

"So you can see me." Eric hissed the words as he stepped forward. "You think you're catching up with me? You know I've always been the one ahead, always."

Colin braced for the attack. He could still deflect his fastest strike, if the timing was perfect.

But Eric's gaze, his stance, were angled just past him. They swiveled back and forth... *and he's bragging about invisibility, when he couldn't see me before, it's a* bluff.

And Colin's stealth flickered away. The distraction worked.

Eric hurtled in.

Instinct turned the first punch away, the second flicked in and clipped him—

Flying, frozen in time and then crashing back against what had to be the wall. He tried to stand, to see, to just breathe, *Eric's too strong, he's got to be charging in...*

Colin wheezed *"Gratshay"* and flailed out blindly. His vision cleared to see Eric darting back from his touch, and he broke off the spell there. Was he already that desperate, using a weapon that would tear himself up too?

His enemy gathered for the next lunge, a slow, deliberate motion of Eric *letting* him know he'd be unstoppable.

Don't let him move, try anything! Colin flung out words: "Is Jessie alive? Why, why her?"

Eric paused. He stood still for a breath, two, and then he yielded to the question in the air: "To feed her to the skein. For Terri, of course," he added. The last came just a fraction too fast.

"Terri doesn't want it! You heard her! What are you going to do, keep killing people and think she'll be so *impressed*—"

Eric struck. Cruder, more telegraphed—Colin twisted and tossed him away with his own momentum, but Eric slid off the ground and began clambering to his feet, still unhurt.

Colin rushed at him, but his skein's strength faltered again. His stride floundered, he toppled forward into Eric's wide, wild swing. The blow slammed into his block and sent him spinning back. He caught his balance, staggered up.

"In here, c'mon!"

Sharp, angry voices sounded right outside.

Eric *snapped* out of sight. Colin wrenched at his own stubborn skein and pulled his invisibility up, and then the halo sight to track Eric's moves. As the people rushed inside.

Three men behind the watchmen, a mix of young and middle-aged, one gripping a crowbar and another with a gun. All staring at the damage and the empty warehouse floor.

Eric edged past them all and slipped outside.

Colin crept out slowly, giving the workers a wide berth but holding his real focus on the skein. Outside were more people, two uniformed cops shouting warnings and leveling pistols—no match for Eric either.

But Eric... Colin caught one glimpse of a haloed figure ducking away on the rooftop, doubly hidden up there.

The shape leaped, across from that roof to the next. Colin moved into the street after him, into the thinner and more scattered sounds.

He said Jessie was alive! No, he said he fed her to the skein—does that mean alive or not? Colin reached for his phone, but pulled his hand back. Better to stay focused, keep Eric in sight. He was the only one who could lead them to Jessie now.

The next roof stretched past where a police car sat parked, and two cops stood on the sidewalk. Speaking on their radios, with gleaming black SWAT rifles in their hands—two of Hoyle's team. With the weapons that just might blast through Eric's armor.

The unseen cop-killer thudded down beside them.

Colin yelled "Look out!"

The cops whirled, looking around at all sides. But Eric ran *past* them, up the street and behind a corner.

Colin could just make out a "did you see—" and "said he was fast!" from the police.

Eric's face peered back around that corner. His real face and shoulder, *bare* of skein. Recognizable.

"Hold it, Rowe!"

The cops rushed after him, rifles ready. Eric darted back beyond the corner and they closed in.

Colin charged after them. His invisibility flickered, but it still held. Up and down the street, what people were out stared at the officers out in force.

Colin turned the corner. The police were still advancing along the wall, but he saw Eric invisible again, falling back toward its far end.

Luring them into a trap... no, Eric didn't *need* traps. Out in the open he had enough ways to just bypass anyone who had no skein. He had let those warehouse workers go, too—and he'd targeted the watchman only while it could have stopped him bringing help, when it would still have let Eric finish with Colin in private.

The police closed in on the far corner, one in the lead. The other hung back to cover him, and glancing around the area. He glanced back and whirled—

Colin clamped down on invisibility as the rifle swung toward him—

The officer froze, frowning at "thin air."

Down by the corner burst out *"Hands!* You stop and show me your—" from the other cop. Eric was ducking out of sight at that end.

The two officers charged after him. Colin let himself stop and breathe, trying not to think what one panicky shot with that big rifle might have done to him.

The cops' voices were still chasing, searching. A soft thump sounded on the roof. Colin craned his neck up and waited, but Eric had to be heading the other way along it. He'd drawn the cops down here... and now he was backtracking along the street?

Colin eyed the corner, thought of leading the officers toward Eric. No, that could lose him time or worse, if Eric was slipping away. Even using his own skein made him a target if he kept fading in and out of sight...

He glanced around the street. What few people were out each seemed to be looking in some direction away from him. Now or never.

Colin pulled his skein in under his clothes, jammed on his sunglasses, and stepped back onto the street.

A figure of unseen light was already half a block up the street, and moving fast.

Colin charged after him. One broad mini-factory or office after another lined the streets, half of them surrounded by chain fences—bare of cover. Without invisibility he had to hang back to a distance where Eric was barely a glimmer. Only Eric's halo and his bold jog up the street let Colin tell him from the few people around him.

Just keeping up took all of Colin's attention, when he tried not to rely on his skein's speed either. It was only when Eric slowed at a corner to let cars pass, that he stopped and pulled out his phone.

Bea's first words were "Where are you?" Eager to know.

That need let him calm his thoughts. "Following him." He gave her a long view of the street through his lens. "You know this spot? Eric's heading for something and I hope it's Jessie."

"Copy that. Keep us updated."

He rushed on. Eric was eating up the distance, but once again he had a blind spot for anything behind him. *You'd think that growing up as the most bullied kid around, he'd have a hair-trigger sense for enemies.* Or maybe now that he was so powerful he refused to trust those instincts.

Eric halted in the street.

Colin couldn't risk stopping—he could only slow from a run to a jog, two-thirds of a block away and hoping that slower change would keep Eric's eye off him.

Eric raced across the pavement, up a side street.

Slower now, Colin closed the gap to that corner and leaned around it. Four doors down, he saw Eric's unseen form cutting a wake through a mound of old papers. A sign hung on the wall:

Its largest letters said *From Rayo Spark and*—some computer logo. Eric stared at the sign, for two breaths, four...

He slammed his fist into the wall, sinking a deep dent in the surface.

The next moment, a door swung open. Two steps from where he stood. A woman stepped out, dark hair swirling as she stared at the crack, the indentation in the papers under those unseen feet.

Eric spun around and raised a claw—

And twisted himself away. He turned, leaped upward, and a familiar *thump* came from the roof.

Eric had been one instant from killing her, just for another flash of his temper. But this time he'd reined himself in.

Colin lay against the wall's warmth for one more moment before he stepped out and looked around for his enemy. Back on the street, heading up the same way again.

As he started after him, a sound crackled over the streets. A loudspeaker, blocks away, pouring out music into the morning air— something about a "Rising." They'd played that tune after the quake too.

Eric raced on, and Colin tried to balance the distance. Falling back was easy, all too easy, but just keeping him in sight made his breath come harder with each step.

And still no police in sight, not even the ones Eric had evaded a few blocks back. *Am I really trying to follow him alone?* But Eric could dodge anyone who couldn't see him, or cut them down... *Doesn't mean I can do better.*

The far-off music jerked to a stop. Instead a man's voice shouted what could be the words "how long" and "killer," and "earthquake" too. Did that make those voices the crowd at the Martins', still not so far away?

Eric turned off the street and toward a building.

The place was a true abandoned plant: empty parking lot with earthquake cracks still running through the asphalt, long blocky building with lightless windows of dark glass. Its door should be locked, but Eric swung it open and stepped inside.

A new voice sounded on the distant speaker. "Some of us leave. Some of..." Zara's voice.

Colin brought up his phone.

"He's gone into this empty spot. Looks like he's been here before. Get the police here—I'll take a look."

Bea said "Just remember, you don't have to do all of it alone."

"Thanks." Was that Bea's understated way of saying *Don't get stupid?* The trouble was, nothing he or the police did was bringing Eric down.

He edged into around a corner and watched the street until the few people in sight looked away. Then he drew out his skein and settled it around him. If he just got inside there'd be nobody to startle if he flickered back into sight, and he didn't mean to let Eric spot him at all.

This time he faded cleanly away. He crossed to the door and swung it open.

Whatever the place had been used for, it was a hollow shell now. The front room and the corridor beyond it stretched wide, like empty hands spread to show they'd once been filled with... something. The paint looked deep gray in the limited light, and the smell of dust hung in the air.

The loudspeaker outside faded when he shut the door behind him. Its last clear sound was the man's voice cutting off Zara's again.

A different voice murmured up ahead in the corridor. This sound was muffled too, but closer, and more vicious. Colin crept forward.

The first door there hung open a crack. He leaned toward it.

The *smell* hit him—not dust or stale things this time. Blood.

A dead man lay just inside the room. A blind, staring face, an older version of Joe Martin Junior.

The missing father had never had a chance.

Eric whispered "Now tell me! Why did Rayo Spark build here?"

"You *bas—*" That weaker voice cut off.

Because Eric's hand closed over Jessie's mouth.

She lay tied up against the wall. The room's covered windows let only tiny cracks of light inside, but the position she lay in beside her captor could only mean she was bound. A lump of skein glinted on the floor beside her... and a broad patch of flesh down her arm looked eaten into already. A blindfold covered her eyes.

Eric, still coated in his green, said "Again. Why did they set up here? Was it the Beast Killings?" He drew his hand away.

"What's Rayo Spark—*help!!*" she screamed, for one moment before Eric silenced her again.

Rayo Spark again. The one note Vargas had made, about the time of the Killings.

In the sudden stillness, one sliver of the voice outside filtered through. Something about *room.*

"Hear that?" Eric said. "They're out there shouting how this whole place is *doomed.* You saw it too, didn't you?"

Think, think! I can't take him, not the way my skein is.

"Saw what? I don't know what you want!" Jessie cried.

"Are you sure? Not about the Killings?"

I could drop my skein and use the spell... but then I'd be too slow to touch him, easy meat... That was fear curling in his gut.

"Just... a girlfriend and boyfriend that some freak fixated on, that must have been it. Nobody knows who."

"No?" Eric said. "Was it 'some freak,' or did he kill her?"

"I don't know! But please!" she said. "Just let me go!"

"Rayo Spark did start building here, so something brought them. *Was it him?"*

"I don't know, I don't know..."

"Maybe you don't. But I'm still giving you a chance."

He reached over for the skein he'd used on her.

Then he pulled out a gag, and leaned in to begin tying it in her mouth.

Colin held his breath. There it was—before Eric triggered that patch of skein to consume her again, he'd have to remove all of his own. For one moment he'd be vulnerable, one chance for someone fast enough... feet shifted on the floor, ready.

One twitch, one motion of awareness from that masked head—

The next moment Eric was a roar of rage and a wild lunge at him, and the doorway shattered to fragments as Colin found himself leaping back and clear of it.

He stood up tensing his skein for the fight—it was still sluggish, *weak.*

Eric paused in the doorway, and looked back toward Jessie.

No. Colin drew back a step, and called out "What's the problem? Now that you've got some strength, you only fight when you get to be the bully?"

Eric started toward him. No reaction showed through his skein mask, but his hulking, remorseless advance spoke louder than any reply.

Colin drew back, back, toward the front door.

Then he spun and dove out through it. That lunge bought him a moment to spin, ready as Eric charged in and swept a heavy fist around—Colin turned it aside and Eric halted for a breath. *Numb, my arm's not moving right.*

Blocks away in the open air, Zara's voice called "Thank you all for coming here..."

And those were police sirens. Colin edged back another step, fumbling for a way to stall. "Why Jessie? She doesn't even know what Rayo Spark is."

"And you do?" A hunger sharpened Eric's voice.

Colin twisted away and ran. At the edge of his sight he saw people, a woman up the street, a man in a car slowing to watch the two shapes in green…

The siren sounded closer.

Colin swerved to the side. Eric swept in—he dodged back and the all-out blow smashed down with a dull crunch of pavement.

No more playing, need some distance…

He leaped straight at Eric. Eric flinched back and yanked his guard up, pure human habit, but Colin drove his will into the skein and kicked himself on past him. Wrenched at the light along his skein. Twisted aside and lunged around a corner.

He rolled to a crouch just short of the wall. No good, Eric would only need an instant more to figure out where he'd gone and charge around after him, *can't run in time…*

Nothing. Against the scattered human voices and the approaching cars, he heard, saw, no trace of Eric. Not clearing the corner, not on the roof above, not behind him.

In the distance, Zara was calling out "Every one of us, we've struggled for so long…"

One watchful step at a time, he eased up and peeped around the corner. Two police cars *crept* up along the street—cops watching for traces and staying inside their protection for now. Colin looked up and down the street, but Eric was nowhere in sight.

Except he could drop onto the cops any time… no, Eric wouldn't care. Colin started back up the street to get back to Jessie.

How'd they move so far away, so fast? And the skein was still hiding him; what people he saw around looked right past him to eye the police cars.

Zara's distant voice was fainter now. "…will always remember…"

Colin moved toward Eric's hideaway, watching all around him for traces of an ambush. That mostly meant the roofs; he saw no invisible shapes and no *cover* down on the street, just a tiny concrete "park" with two peeling benches and a space that might have once been a fountain between them. Cracks and fractures from the quake still crossed the pavement.

Rayo Spark—but no, the plaque beside the bench said *Rayo Park,* along with the note *A reminder that good can grow over anything.*

Colin frowned. It couldn't be that simple, if Eric was searching for this *Rayo Spark* he'd never miss the chance that it was simply *Park.* But that *grow over* reference, it sounded like how this and the whole attempt at an industrial section rose over where the Beast Killings had been.

Over. One sliver of concrete had crumbled away between two quake fractures, showing dirt and some long-ago indentation—

"Look out!"

The voice, Bea's voice, flung him into a dive away as Eric leaped in and smashed a punch down into the concrete where he'd stood.

The ground, that shape under it, that can't be a footprint—

The instant passed, and Colin caught his balance and flung himself at Eric. One strike flowed into the next, every technique he knew to batter down a stronger opponent. One after another slipped through Eric's guard, but none of them forced him off balance.

Whatever that mark in the ground was, he had to force Eric away before he saw it, but his skein had no *strength.*

He fell back with slow and measured steps. Eric watched him—the bastard stood straight, unhurried, still unscratched.

Colin edged to the side. Toward the shattered pavement.

Eric charged.

The strike was slow, wide, meant to show an exhausted fighter *I want you to see it coming.* Colin watched it, and he caught at Eric's fist and twisted it down to tear across the ground to destroy the mark.

He wrenched Eric around and snaked in to grapple.

Something exploded into his side.

Can't be, he had no leverage, no fist is that strong... get away...

Feet stumbled for balance. Head rang. Eyes searched for the enemy. Jessie, he could still lead him away from Jessie. Wobbling legs forced him past a world of whirling color, walls and streets and cars all spinning...

The lights steadied. The low shape ahead was Eric's lair, he'd run *toward* Jessie after all.

He whirled. Eric swept in, and he had no strength to stop the blow.

It slammed into his stomach. The ground flew away, something shattered behind him—glass, a window—and he tumbled down into dimness. In wide, enclosed space. Eric's hideout.

Colin forced himself to his feet. The main light came from the smashed window behind him. That dimmed when Eric leaped through it.

Eric landed across the room, falling with the awkward abandon of a body that knew he couldn't be harmed. Colin hauled his head up to meet that masked glare.

"You," Eric said. "Always you, in my way."

He raised his fists.

Far out through the window, Zara's voice called "Whatever may come next—"

The sound was lost as Eric attacked.

He struck from all sides, jabbing and testing with none of the blind strength he'd used before. Colin blocked and backpedaled and shrugged off what he could. That *speed*, no way he'd match that now.

Then, from outside:

"The building's surrounded, Rowe." Lieutenant Hoyle, with the inhuman, tinny sound of a megaphone. "There's no escape."

Eric stared at Colin. "Why? Why didn't you let me go?"

You chased me in here! And— "Can't... can't let kill any... more." His lungs wouldn't break from their combat rhythm.

"I'm *trying* not to!" Eric burst out. "They don't listen, they never see how it's all crumbling away. There's nothing left here but saving Terri."

"She doesn't want your help! How many times—"

"It's the only way!" His voice shook with fervor. "Not Rayo Spark, not any of them! Why can't you *see* that everything here is over?"

Colin shook his head, drew in a breath.

Far outside, Zara's voice swelled: "Whatever comes, I know that each of us will remember how we came out here to share our support," and a wave of what had to be cheering.

Eric turned and faced the window.

Just outside, Hoyle called "We're coming in, Rowe."

Colin edged back. If this was the building's front room, a few steps back would let him block the way to Jessie...

Eric faded from sight.

Then the halo-shape spun toward the wall, and put his fist through one of the windows. Shaded glass burst and fell away. Eric crouched below it.

Hoyle said "I warn you, we will shoot. You're not getting away."

Eric spun to another window, and shattered that as well.

I see. He's splitting their attention, leaving too many open ways an invisible body could slip out.

Colin pulled out his phone.

Bea answered on the first ring.

"Eric's still in here," he reported. "Have them watch the windows on your left and right, and wait—"

Eric slammed into him. In one moment the shape blurred from over beneath a window to driving the world away in a shower of bright pain.

On the floor. *I'm lying on the smooth, smooth floor, and that mountain up there is Eric bringing his foot down on my head...*

The blow came down. Eric stomped down, and plastic shattered.

Eric had gone for the phone.

Colin wrenched himself to sit up, gasping for breath. Eric was already in motion.

A flicker of light, a single shimmer, dove out the first window. No gunshots sounded—Hoyle only continued his warnings as Eric slipped away.

CHAPTER NINE

RANK AND FILE

One thought pushed through Colin's mind as the trembling set in, as it sank into his muscles that Eric was *gone*—how the police still might not see that. He managed to slide the skein off his head just before they burst in.

So when he raised his hands and backed up to the wall, their first outburst of shouts and pointing weapons calmed, and swept past him to secure the building.

One officer paused and eyed him, rifle ready in his hands. "You had to wear the same freak outfit as the kidnapper?"

"Eyes on your work," Hoyle told that cop as he marched in.

Bea was at his heels. Colin turned to speak to them.

From the room inside, a weak voice called "Police? Did you get him?"

"Jessie's right in there!" Colin waved to the room—too wildly, too loudly, a part of him realized even as he went on "She needs help."

He stepped toward the room, and the cop moved to block him.

Hoyle said "That's enough," and the officer fell back.

Colin called to her "Eric's gone! You're safe now, they chased him off." The police were still spreading out around the plant, so he led the way to Jessie's room.

She still sat hunched against the wall, blindfolded head turning dazedly around. With the pale body of Joe Martin by the doorway.

Dead. The thought crashed into him now—the younger Martin, the one closing up that house, would never have his father back. Instead, tiny shapes buzzed over the body, and the smell...

The cops looked at the living victim and the dead one for a moment, glancing at each other and then turning to Bea. She was already moving toward Jessie, moving with an awkwardness he'd never seen in her. *Jessie wants another woman to reassure her now, and that's never Bea's strength.*

"Here, we're here, it's over." Speaking softly, she began freeing Jessie and looking at the skein damage to her arm, and she crouched to block her view of the corpse.

The other officers glanced at Martin, or pulled back and joined the clatter of steps and quick shouts as they cased the building.

Colin edged to the room's side, out of their way. But that brought him next to the splash of skein Eric had been using on his prisoner— one touch with his foot let Colin pull the stuff into his own skein, unnoticed.

And that's hiding crime scene evidence, even destroying it since I couldn't separate that one scrap out again if I tried. He hung his head.

Joe Martin had no skein injuries, at least not showing. Just a small pool of dried blood.

"You look like you'll be okay," Bea told Jessie. "Once they look you over. Where's the ambulance?"

A hand fastened on Colin's arm, and a cop pulled him out of the room.

"Alright, da Costa. Who *are* you? What the hell are you doing here?" The cop wiped a stream of sweat from his face, but his eyes never wavered.

Slowly, holding his voice to calmness, Colin said "I'm a friend of Jessie's. And the brother of Eric's first, real victim..."

The cop turned away toward one of his teammates, a smaller man watching the front windows. "We sure we even saw two men in here?"

"Hold up there. Da Costa was right there in the crowd until the woman was gone—"

"Was he?" The cop wiped at his sweat again and turned back to Colin. "You can be here and gone any time you want, you rubbed our noses in that. Just like the guy we're chasing can."

They can't *put this on me...* But, this was a chance to get the whole search up to speed at last. "I told you—" He stopped, steadied his voice. "Eric had my sister. He's hunted me before, I know about his tricks. Remember, I'm the one who led you down here."

The second cop laughed. "Yeah. And that fight? Over before I could see much, but *boom!"* He slapped a palm down toward the floor. *"Something* sure tore up the streets out there."

"Screw that!" The first cop stepped up to face Colin. "How'd you find him? We had to cordon whole blocks off, but you just led us to Rowe? I hear the last time you 'found' Eric Rowe, two cops *died."*

"Yeah..." Colin managed to keep his eyes level with his accuser. "Look, I've been working with all of you to track him."

" 'Working with'? More like you stomp into crime scenes and talk like you can give us orders. And they *let* you."

"No. Just..." His hands were rising up, inching out to plead with them. "Listen, I do understand how Eric keeps vanishing on you. Because I've got the same kind of tool, and I'm learning how it works. Or I thought I was, but today—"

"Our victim's trying to talk." Hoyle stepped into view, and looked straight toward Colin. "I need you to make sense of what she's saying."

The lieutenant spun away to where Bea was leading Jessie out, away from the room and the body. He didn't spare a glance to the scowls of the men behind him. *Sure, just when the cops say I'm getting special treatment you "need my help..."*

Jesse sat against the wall, as if nobody in the place could find a chair for her. Her voice stumbled through the words: "He said, he'd killed Joe Martin. He tortured me, with, some kind of chemical. But, nothing he said made sense."

"About what?" Hoyle crouched down beside her. He glanced back just long enough to wave the other cops away, and they glowered and moved off.

"The Beast Killings. He wanted to know… something, I guess."

"Something? What did he ask?"

"They happened forty years ago! Sure they're unsolved, but… I don't get it."

Colin leaned around Bea, where he'd found himself standing. "I heard Eric ask if it was the second victim, the boyfriend, who killed the first. You mentioned that yourself."

"You… heard that?" Jessie shook her head. "Yeah, it could be."

Hoyle nodded. "I know the case. Go on."

"The other thing was, 'Rayo Spark.' He was stuck on that too. Kept saying they built all these around—" she thumped a hand on the floor— "here. I think Rayo Spark was some kind of land deal back then, around the Killings' time. He said it came because of them…"

She stopped, coughed, and slumped back against the wall.

Colin whispered to Bea "The park, maybe. Something was—"

"Sh." And then, the softest breath: "Don't tell *him.* "

What, Hoyle? Are we back to this again? Colin glanced from her to the lieutenant. What was going on now?

Jessie said "He just kept ranting those. And how the town was dying, too. That's all I can remember. When he was with me, anyway— don't know where he went for most of the time. He just brought me here and…" She shuddered, hugged herself. "How could he get me here at all? The way he scooped me up… that's a crazy kind of strength."

Hoyle sighed. "We're still trying to work that out. But thank you. We'll talk more later—the medics should be here soon, so you can rest and think about anything else you can give us, anything. Simms can stay with you," he added, and he waved Bea toward her.

Then Hoyle stood up and strode over to several cops in the corridor, and Colin stayed behind him.

"Find anything?" Hoyle asked them.

"Nothing. Could be this is just the place he brought her and nothing else."

"Leave it for the lab, then. And keep watching the perimeter. Rowe's crazy enough to circle back."

"That's it?"

The words tore out of Colin and shoved him a step toward the lieutenant.

"You just tell them he's crazy and dangerous and leave it at that—
"

"Come with me. *Now.*"

Hoyle's demand cut him off. One twist of that balding head led Colin away through a door, and Hoyle slammed it behind them.

They stood in the room they'd taken Jessie from. With Martin still lying cold on the floor.

Hoyle snapped "I told you, the idea was not to panic them."

"Panic them?"

But Colin heard his voice going low, matching Hoyle's tone. Still, he saw a trembling in Hoyle's eyes, and his hands too before Hoyle shoved them in his pockets—

Colin motioned at Martin's body. *"That* is what Eric does. You just had those men chasing an enemy they can't see, and he got away—"

"I know."

"—because you didn't tell them what they were hunting. It's pure luck Eric didn't put any of them with him." He pointed at the body again.

"I know! But I've been *working* on this!"

Hoyle yanked out his phone and held it up. A list of names, contacts, ran down the screen.

"You think it's easy, telling the police commissioner there's a killer who can... Hell, just getting the right people in the room who can give me a real task force—and keeping out the morons that would shut it down? I'm working on all that, and you just want to yell it from the rooftops?"

"And how many people get killed while you jump through hoops, when we need to get in gear and *find* him?"

"Like you did?" Hoyle enunciated each word. "You tracked him all the way down here, and you still lost him."

"I—"

But the anger was already crumbling, as guilt settled over him. *It's not my fault, my skein isn't working, at least we saved Jessie...*

"You sure you have a plan?"

"Of course I do." Hoyle smiled thinly. "Until I pull this together, we keep searching for him. Plus, if Rowe is so interested in this Rayo Spark land thing, I need to see if the Gardner corporation was part of that. Since we keep seeing their fingers stuck in this case."

"Oh. Yeah, that does make sense..."

More words tickled in his head: the concrete park, the shape he'd glimpsed under it. How to use the spell, too. He could put everything out in the open.

Except Bea had said not to, even after all this. He still didn't know why.

Colin's jaw quivered. *I'm caught between two spooked control freaks. But Bea's the one I owe more to.*

He didn't answer, only followed Hoyle out to watch the police lock down the crime scene.

*　*　*

The back seat of the police car felt as soft as any high-priced couch, when Colin actually got a chance to lean his tired body back in it. To keep his eyes open he breathed deep in the stale smells.

Hoyle and his driver took them past building after building, so many with skeleton crews or even fewer people. Some of those people turned to watch their car, or the several other cars prowling around. The radio passed a few squawked directions between the searchers— Bea's voice was never among those.

Around corner after corner, up on the edge of each roof... Colin simply couldn't see any halo-shapes tailing them.

"I think he's long gone," he said at last.

"I know. Take the second left," Hoyle added to the officer at the wheel.

When they pulled over, it was beside the sharp, upper-middle type car Colin remembered Hoyle drove himself. The lieutenant stepped out to it with a glance back at him. "Come on."

"What's the plan now?"

"You'll see."

Did people really put questions off that way? But Colin was following Hoyle, at least until he could compare notes with Bea. He climbed in.

This time the drive was longer. The Cherry Street factories fell away as they moved downhill into the town's business section, and more and more buildings began to fill up, until two thirds seemed to be in full use.

Hoyle stopped at a hotel.

Colin stared up at the Bacara Hotel sign—was this really Hoyle's next step, or just getting rid of him? He followed him inside, feet scuffing weakly over the tiles.

A janitor paused his cart and gave Hoyle a sharp nod. What did that make him, a cop in disguise?

Then Hoyle knocked on a door, and Zara opened it.

"Good to see you back. Come on in—the lieutenant did say he'd find us a new safe house, and here we are."

"Here we are." Colin moved a few steps inside. An open suite, gleaming furniture and so many beige-padded chairs, safely sheltered and beckoning with comforts—

Terri lay propped up in one bed, in a nest of cushions. Samples of half the hospital's medical implements seemed to crowd onto her nightstand.

"That's really safe?" he said. "They let you out?"

"Sure," she breathed. "And, safer for the other patients."

Zara added "The nurses will be coming by regularly, and staying on call. It's all worth it to be sure."

Sure about what? This couldn't be the level of protection the hospital had, or the same treatment. It looked more like them shielding themselves from Eric by kicking Terri out.

Colin forced a smile onto his face. "You never told me this was happening."

"You had a busy morning. And thank you, for Jessie."

She drew him into a warm, fierce hug, and Colin leaned in and tried to keep his tired muscles from trembling until she moved away.

She added to Hoyle, "And, thank you for pulling this together. I honestly do feel safe here."

"We owed you." Hoyle's hands settled in his pockets. "I watched you hold that crowd together—you might have saved us a riot. We didn't know if it was safe for *anyone* to leave, until we found what Rowe was up to."

Eric... Awareness crashed back over Colin, and he pushed away from a chair he found himself leaning on. "It's not safe, nobody's safe. Maybe he'll grab someone like Jessie that he thinks has information he wants, or it could be anyone, anywhere, just to feed his skein. And you..."

You can't stick us here and leave me out of this.

He added "You said you'd be investigating the Gardners, right? I remember one thing about them."

Hoyle's eyebrows rose. "What's that?"

"The last time we saw Eric with Fields, and Fields talked about firing him? Eric said the Gardner *partners* might protect him. I don't think he meant because of his business sense, not after he'd started bullying his boss to get at Zara."

Hoyle's eyes closed, his head slumped forward. "And *now* you remember this. —No, it's fine, after the kind of days you've had it's enough that you remember it at all." He looked up, and a grin flashed. "What's next? You have records on all of Gardner Development's secrets?"

"Not like that. But, Zara is the community leader that keeps the Gardners from buying up all of the Hillside." It wasn't nearly that simple, but he had to push the doubt out of his voice now. "We try to know how far our neighbors can trust them. So if the only way left to catch Eric is to go through the Gardners, you need the best information you can get on them."

"And I suppose I've got that," Hoyle said. "The best that civilians have, at least. I'll be back soon to see if you found any leverage."

"Again, thank you," Zara said. But instead of showing him out, she sank into a chair.

Colin looked at her, as Hoyle walked away. Her eyes didn't show the same secret exhaustion they had at the rally, but still...

Then she swung her laptop open and the work began.

They started with a call to Dennis Fields—that Zara made, and Colin remembered Eric had shattered his own phone. Fields didn't answer, and they didn't risk leaving a message.

Without a phone or computer, Colin had to stick to thumbing through Zara's Vargas books for any reference they'd missed. Mainly he watched Zara search, for any mention of Gardner "loyalty" that might still explain their defending Eric, or any other strange dealings they might have.

Are they part of that Rayo Spark plan, that Eric and that note of Vargas's mentioned? Eric tied that to the Beast Killings too, and there was that shape under the park's concrete... So many pieces were missing, they might be no closer to catching Eric *at all.*

A knock sounded at the door.

"Ex...cuse me? It's Nurse Setter..."

The same nurse from the hospital—if a stranger's voice had been so afraid of its own sound, Colin would have wondered when Eric had threatened her too.

Zara said "Of course," and she opened the door the next moment.

The plump woman darted in with an anxious glance around, and shook off the coat that covered her blue uniform and the bag she hid under it. The smile and the well-meaning warnings were both gone from her.

Instead she went to Terri's side and began her tests and medications, too softly for him to hear. Colin sat still and buried his nose in the books. In bare minutes she was done and moving for the door.

"We do appreciate your help," Zara said. "Nobody would expect you to come near us again."

The nurse only looked at the door, frozen.

"I remember when Eric came after us, I thought this was the worst thing we'd ever have to face. And that meant there should be nothing that prepared us for it, and also that once we got through it we could handle anything."

Some choked sound came from Nurse Setter's throat. Colin heard a rumble of rage in his chest, and then she dashed away.

"Tense?" Terri was looking right at him.

"Nothing that actually *getting us* through this won't fix. Eric's still out there."

He began pacing, between the books and Zara, his feet scraping clumsily on the floor. Back and forth, back and forth.

Until *Bea* called from outside the suite. "Everyone alright?"

He spun to the door and swung it wide—and the smile on her face flickered away. *Too eager of me?* The doubts and suspicions thickened the air between them again.

He waved her in. "So... any news?"

"Nothing certain. Hoyle's keeping me busy finishing my hearing."

"Finishing?" Terri said. "You're a cop again?"

"I will be, if it continues the way it has."

"And you think that's from Hoyle helping you?" Colin said. "But you're still nervous about him. Why did you want to hide the—"

Before he could say *the park,* Bea cut in "He still keeps too many secrets, even when we're all hunting Eric and his weapon together. I'm simply not sure what his motives are."

Because he *hid* what the skein could do from his cops? *You do the same thing, Bea! You lied to Sergeant Jordan just to make him cover the stuff up—*

Colin drew a slow breath and pushed past that. "Listen, I need your help. The skein's been giving me trouble."

"Trouble? What kind?" Her eyes searched him, calm and measuring.

"I can see Eric hiding now. But all the rest it does, it's off and on. Sometimes I can't get at its strength, or I reappear. I've gone from fending Eric off to barely surviving today!"

He heard Zara gasp. He hadn't told them any of that, and now he wished he'd found less frightening words for it. But Bea was the only one who understood what he was losing.

She frowned. "It just... failed?"

"Yes. Off and on. Sometimes it..."

He held up his arm, and flexed his will. The skein "coat" he still wore slid its sleeve away under his shirt—then he brought it flowing back out an inch from the cuff again.

"Does that look right? I think it's still slow."

Bea watched it move. "It never did that to me, after I got the hang of it. You're carrying more of it at once than I did... you've used it more regularly... Are you eating?"

"Sure—not hungry at all now. Anyway, how could that explain all of this?"

"I don't *know.*" Bea turned away, staring at the curtained windows. "Surprise, I don't have all the answers. Maybe your connection to it's just changed. Or it could be the spell—for all we know, that makes the stuff *stay* hungry afterward, for nutrients if it can't get flesh… So you could start by eating more.

"But actually," she said, "I see two choices here. One, you keep practicing, and see if that helps." She motioned to the skein peeking out of his sleeve.

Zara added "Nurse Setter will be back tomorrow. We'll ask her to check your blood sugar—it might tell us something. Even about magic."

"It might," Colin nodded.

"And the other way," and Bea held out her open hand, "is that you simply give the skein to me, and let me take Eric on. But I *know* you'd never let that chance out of your own hands." Her arm dropped to her side.

"Hey—" He fumbled for words, some way to smooth over the pain of what she'd said. *And too much of that is* right.

"You know the worst part?" Bea squeezed her eyes closed. "You were using it better than I ever did, now that all this comes back to taking Eric in a fight. So don't you *dare* waste it. And watch your backs, all of you."

And she spun and walked out the door.

Colin couldn't move. Bea wasn't like that, she was calm, controlled…

"What was that about?" Zara said.

When Zara *can't read someone…* "Well, she said she's not safe from prison yet, for shooting at Eric." He tossed out the first thought to come to him. "Really, I wish I knew."

They turned back to the files.

Colin stared at the books, and watched Zara explore online. He put in a call for food, and shoveled his share down and barely tasted it— maybe he *should* be hungrier after this morning.

Mostly he concentrated on the skein. Bring it up his sleeve, and back out... fade his hand away and hold it... Again and again, trying for perfect control. It had to be perfect, it had to be.

"Here!"

Zara swung the screen around.

A long-ago news article captured online: *Land developed as part of the Rayo Spark plan... including Gardner Investments and...*

"See?" she said. "They could be a force in trying to industrialize Cherry Street. And that was soon after the Beast Killings, too." Her eyes clouded at that.

Just like Eric thought, maybe. Colin gripped her shoulders in a hug.

* * *

"So that's one more tie to the Gardners, if they were the ones rebuilding that neighborhood. Eric almost lashed out at a stranger in rage when he couldn't find answers." *Which might mean those prints under the park.* Colin tried to avoid Hoyle's eyes as he thought that.

"Rowe could have discovered something while he worked there." Hoyle nodded. "Plausible."

"So that's something. Then there are the records before that—one mention in Matt Vargas's notes that he was interested in the Gardners back then, and Rayo Spark. Just the fact that there's nothing more is weird."

"Hmm. I need to confront Josh Gardner about their supporting a cop-killer... if I hint Rowe might come after them next, and see what that shakes loose..." Hoyle stared at the ceiling.

"Then they might tell you something," Zara said. "Or you might persuade them to pull their lawyers back."

"They might." Hoyle looked down. "Want in on that?"

"What?" Colin heard Zara say it with him.

"Come with me. Rowe was keeping Terri prisoner on their land—let's see if some of that rage can rattle them."

Zara smiled. "Oh, I'm looking forward to it."

Hoyle raised a hand. "Sorry, I was thinking of Colin. I need someone who makes me look reasonable in comparison. That could be him, but not you."

"I suppose that's a compliment." She shook her head.

And there's another reason, that he's not saying. Hoyle wanted someone with him who could keep an eye out for trouble. Colin felt the skein ready around him—if he could still control it.

*   *   *

Hoyle marched straight into the building, walking like he never felt the corporate glares he pushed through. But then, he wasn't the one with the scarred face, the sweat-stained clothes, and the long morning still dragging at his feet.

Colin followed Hoyle into the pale green corridors, in among the cheerful, friendly voices that always felt so wrong to him. *Bea and I came here before, discreet as we could be, and the cops blamed her for bringing me along. Now it's Hoyle's own idea.*

But the sunglasses made it easier. They let him avoid their eyes, and hid the moments he glanced around for any signs of Eric.

When the elevator opened on the top floor, the trademark green trim was gone. These executive suites were a creamy white, and the air conditioner felt at least a notch colder on Colin's skin.

A woman in a tightly-buttoned suit led them toward the door at the far end. Hoyle never slowed.

The end door was five steps away when footsteps padded in the corridor behind them. Dennis Fields, out of breath.

He looked across at them, some uncertain expression twitching on his face. He could be about to shout to them, or run after them... but he fell back.

"Right in here." The assistant gripped the doorknob of the glass door.

Colin looked back at Fields, but the door was swinging open.

Hoyle muttered "Remember, *push him,*" and they walked in.

Josh Gardner sat there alone—Colin had to blink, he'd been sure there'd be a wall of lawyers forming here before their eyes. Instead there was one wrinkled man in his sixties behind his desk and smiling at them.

Something about him seemed small, as if the chair under him might be taller than it looked to help him fit the desk, as if people might glance past him in a crowd. And this was who they'd come to "rattle"?

Hoyle was already saying "Mr. Gardner. Thank you for seeing us."

"Of course. And this would be…"

Let it happen. Colin advanced on the desk and let the floodgates inside him crack open:

"Colin da Costa. And I want to know why your lawyers are sticking up for that bastard Eric!"

"That's a serious question." Gardner's smile narrowed, but his eyes never flinched away.

Hoyle said "Calm down, will you? There are laws about making accusations—"

"What are the laws about my sister being held prisoner, *on your property?*" He looked away from Gardner, searching the walls for some map or diagram that might match that block Eric had used. None of them looked like it, so he spun back to the man in the chair. "Or Eric forcing a business meeting with my mother, and grabbing her too? If that's not a conspiracy, then what is?"

His voice echoed around the office. *Wow—I got pulled right into this* bad cop *role.*

Gardner only gazed back at him. "I'm sorry about what you've been through, I honestly am. But we do have a wide range of employees…" He lifted an arm and motioned to some many-branched chart on the wall. "That doesn't make Gardner Development a part of what one ex-employee seems to have done to your family—"

"Our family? Eric never stopped at that either. Just this morning he grabbed an old woman," and Colin leaned in, "demanding to know about *Rayo Spark.*"

They might have been random words, for all the reaction Gardner showed. "Please. If Mr. Rowe had an interest there, I'm afraid I don't understand it. Our company has tried a whole range of different plans—" He gestured around the room, and Colin's gaze followed.

A faint shimmer lurked outside the glass door.

The sunglasses were right before his eyes. All it took was a single thought to draw it out, the hidden halo around Eric. As Eric crept back out of view.

"—for Rayo Hill. Some have been to revitalize the community, but those never seem to take. My father made some effort at industrializing it, and still—"

"This is pointless, letting you lie to us." *Did I keep the shock off my face, can I get us moving in time?* He turned to Hoyle. "If you're not arresting them, we need to go. You've got to get back on Eric's trail, now.*"

Hoyle only frowned. "I thought you wanted to say your piece—"

"I'm leaving, now." Why didn't Hoyle get it?

"Hold on, we owe Mr. Gardner an apology—"

Colin swept out the door, alone.

Only a handful of figures moved in the corridors, no sign of Eric's shape among them. Colin marched down it, gaze darting around. *I should have stayed back, but now if I can just spot him—*

An older man in a pure black suit took a step toward Colin, mouth opening to make him slow down. Colin stepped on past him, but more heads were turning toward them.

He ducked in around a corner, twisted into a conference room. He only needed seconds, if his practice had been enough.

Skein surged out around him and wrapped him in stealth. He slipped back outside.

The corridors up here were wide, with only a few people to notice—Colin had to fight the urge to move past a quiet walk.

Around one white corner, he glimpsed Eric. Walking away.

Colin crept after him. Instead of trusting to the invisibility, he stayed at a distance, keeping one eye on a corner ready to duck out of sight if Eric glanced back. He edged along, shivering in the overcooled air.

Eric turned a corner, faster now. *Where's he going?* Colin slowed.

Something struck his back. He stumbled forward, locked the invisibility down, as the conference room door swung and the harried woman with the armful of papers stared around—

Colin scrambled clear of her. Eric's corner was just ahead.

He peeked around it. Beyond stood a huge man in a blue security uniform, looking right toward him. Colin jerked back from sight.

Heavy footsteps started toward him.

Colin ducked back. He'd stayed invisible, he was sure of it... he edged back down the corridor, crouching behind a huge glass trophy case. And Eric was getting away.

The stealth flickered against him—he clutched his control tighter. Looking sideways through the case's glass, he saw the guard standing at the corner with his hand on a taser baton, staring both ways along the corridor.

Wait, listen... Colin let the few sounds on the floor fill his ears. The guard must have glimpsed him move or heard his footstep, did he *know* about invisibility or did they just want security that alert?

I could pull back and find a way around him—no, I'd lose Eric or blunder right into him.

The guard started toward Colin.

A sound cut the corridors' hush. A single moment's whine of tearing metal.

The guard spun and charged back the way he'd come.

Colin moved after him, eyes picking out cover and turns to duck behind if he needed. But the guard ran straight up the way and through a single door.

Colin peeked in after him. A short row of old filing cabinets stood there, and the guard had one drawer pulled out to peer inside. The metal up on the cabinet's corner hung twisted and cut. The lock on the door was sundered as well.

No bolt-cutters could do this—only Eric's claws.

A *thump* sounded behind him. Colin glanced over and saw the door to the stairs gliding closed, and another footstep rang from further down the stairwell. He scrambled aside before the guard headed for that door, but he could picture Eric leaping down those steps, clearing a floor every couple of seconds.

Colin slipped away, back up the pale corridors, trying to fit together what he'd seen. Eric had *stolen* some records from the Gardners, even dodging around their guard... just like he'd been desperate to learn about Rayo Spark from Jessie. But he'd done it just *now?*

Another turn away, Colin ducked into another conference room and pulled his skein out of sight. He headed back for the old man's office.

Eric made his move after seeing them there... because Gardner would be distracted? Or, just to grab the files for fear someone else could? And yet he was *there* when Colin and Hoyle came by, he was already there...

Then Colin was opening the office door, facing Hoyle and Gardner, and he had to reach for words again. "Sorry I stormed out. I guess I needed to clear my head, and I should have done better."

"I'm sure you had the right," Gardner said. "I may not have understood just how much you've been through before."

The sympathy flowed in his voice, too thick—*he does make it easy to play angry.* "Don't patronize me. Eric has attacked my sister, my mother, and destroyed the building we've looked after for years."

"And I am sorry."

"He's still killing. And the last I heard him, he was looking for your Rayo Spark project." *And I bet I just saw him take it...* one more breath would throw that at Gardner, and see if that "shook anything" from him.

"Again, I wish I could help you. But I'm afraid I don't understand what's going on in Eric Rowe's head. And as I was telling the lieutenant, our lawyers will insist you follow the law when you're hunting a former employee of ours. That would be best for all of us, don't you agree?"

And Hoyle said "Of course it would."

So that was it, Hoyle was backing down?

Colin turned to stare at Gardner again. That wrinkled face had to be hiding something... secrets from them, from Eric...

Josh Gardner lifted his head to smile back. And his neck... twitched.

The smallest spasm, but Colin had seen it in Terri too often: some kind of pain, and the fine, body-wide flutter of effort to keep it hidden. Not that chronic pains were anything rare, important, or suspicious.

Unless it was a pain that Eric had put there. Or if he was offering Gardner a cure.

CHAPTER TEN

CRACKS

When they walked out of the Gardner front door, Colin turned aside to the next office building, and walked around behind that to the next. Some of these vantage points should let him watch if Eric slipped back in…

"You can't keep standing around here." Hoyle began walking faster, pushing them on toward the parking lot. A few voices murmured around them. "If Rowe got his files, he's long gone."

"Didn't Gardner tell you anything? All those ways I said Eric was out of control and they're too close to him, and he didn't give you a thing?"

"It's not that simple. Some of my time with him was just making sure he didn't sue you."

"I guess." Colin eyed the glassy back of the Gardner building, and the thin stream of people moving in and out in the shade between the buildings.

"Nothing slipped out. He didn't ask me for help. And you heard him, his lawyers will keep watching how I work the case." Hoyle's stride pushed a fraction faster. "We have to move on."

Colin slammed to a stop. "Move on to where? Your searches have any luck yet? Eric could start—"

A glance around, two men were passing by too close. When they moved on—

He finished "He could start *killing* again, this minute."

"Alright—killing who?" Hoyle jabbed a finger at him. "He took Jessie Chapman because he thought she knew about Rayo Spark. Could be he already got his answers with those files."

"And Joe Martin? Did he know something, or did Eric just want a body to feed his skein?" *A body... but then, Martin's body hadn't been eaten away, just stabbed...*

"We don't know, yet," Hoyle said. "So that means you want to stand watch here forever?"

"Why not? Till someone gets a better plan, I mean. It's the one spot we do know Eric had ties to—"

"Because, what's the best case if you do? *If* Rowe does come back here," and he held up a finger, *"and* your stakeout spots him..." another finger, "we don't have a plan to bring in the forces to take him down. Certainly not in the middle of downtown. And you'd call in—what?"

"That I... saw an invisible man?"

Colin tried to laugh, but the sound wouldn't form in his chest.

Instead he leaned against the wall, bricks cool where the other buildings kept them out of the sun. "Anyway, Eric smashed my phone."

Hoyle said "About that—"

"Hold on." That was *Dennis Fields* coming around the building's back.

And Fields moved at a quick jog, shooting brief glances around the buildings and shying away when one passer-by glanced toward him—

Colin stepped out and waved him over.

Fields trotted to them, casting one more nervous look around him. "Glad I found you," he said.

"What is it?" Colin said. "Up there, were you trying to warn us about seeing Gardner?"

"Not... warn. More like, 'watch your step,' " Fields said.

Hoyle nodded. "And then you came out after us. That suggests that you know something more, about the company's connection to Rowe. Say, about certain files they kept?"

"Oh." Fields sighed. "No, nothing like that. I was hoping *you* were closer to finding him."

Colin bit down the frustration and offered a smile. "I get it. Eric's a killer, and you really do want your company to be, well, the opposite of that."

"That's right, I do. Thanks for believing that."

Colin edged closer, ahead of Hoyle. *This is my and Bea's friend, not his.* "It's just... I remember Eric telling you that the Gardner partners would approve of his leaning on Zara. Why would he say that?"

Fields lowered his eyes. "Um. Company policy goes way back. We've tried to support the people in town the best we can, but then there have been times we haven't."

"Like Zara and Jessie said this morning. Sometimes you just lose interest in us." Whatever that meant—but it kept him talking.

"That claim stuck with me. And I looked at our company history... I think we might be *less* community-minded than I thought, and it's fairer to say that we have certain upswings in it. And our recent years are only some of those." There was pain etched in his voice.

"Oh. But now..."

"Right now, we're on the right track. And that may have started when Josh Gardner took over. So I *don't know why* Eric would think he's on his side!"

Oh. Colin shook his head—if this Gardner was such a good man, why had Eric said it... what were those files, or was it something else about him like that tremor he'd seen...

He grasped for his last thought: "Does Gardner seem alright to you? I mean, has he been sick, or anything that seems like it?"

"I haven't heard. I suppose I wouldn't... but that's really all I know."

"Thank you, then," Hoyle said. "Now please, be careful. It may be we'll contact you again, but until then try not to draw attention here. In case Rowe or something else *is* in place to notice you."

"I know. I've seen what he can do." Fields took a glance around, then said "Just catch him!" and he rushed away.

Hoyle took a long sigh.

"Well, at least he should be safe," he told Colin. "Come on, I'll have a squad car take you to the hotel."

*　*　*

Colin tried to rest in the car, but his gaze kept turning to search around them. The cop at the wheel brought them through a few twists that must shake off ordinary tails as well. And he never said a word.

I'm getting door-to-door service now. Hoyle was certainly looking after his anti-Eric weapon, no matter what his men thought of all the special treatment.

When he walked into the suite, he found Terri lying with her eyes half-closed, and the TV running a nature channel as a low stream of patter in the background.

"How are you doing?" he asked.

She didn't answer.

He moved closer, eyeing how still she lay in the cushions. "Terri?"

Her eyes blinked sleepily open.

"She's been resting." Zara stepped in from the next room.

"Sorry." He backed away and stepped around to his mother. She moved slowly, and her eyes looked tight, worried.

She said quietly "Are you alright?"

"We learned a few things. But we missed Eric again." His own voice sounded tired. One of those cushioned chairs sat right near him.

"You got a package from the lieutenant. And yes, I called and checked it was him," she smiled, and handed over a small shipping box.

A phone slid out of it, smooth and black and a neat fit in his hand.

Wow. Is this royal treatment what everyone gets when they hunt invisible killers? "I did need a new one," he said.

"Colin... do you have to start searching right now, or practice with the skein or any other part of this? Can we just relax a while before dinner? It's been a long day."

"Sure." He sank down into the chair.

The phone settled in his lap. He pushed the first keys to start setting it up, but then he leaned back. The hotel chair really was a different kind of comfort from the cars he'd sat in, or standing around the Martin crowd...

The TV droned on, too low to tell if it mentioned *waters* or *otters* unless he turned his head to see. Out in the hall he heard the stillness and the random voices of the hotel just starting to fill up for the afternoon. And beyond the yellow-curtained window, he could just make out a low hum of downtown traffic, so much steadier than on the Hillside.

I've tried plan after plan today. I should be able to lie still for now. Save my strength for when it's needed.

Except his thoughts kept going to Eric, and all the people out there that he could be snatching up just to make himself more skein. Colin's eyes couldn't close.

Then there came a single "Hello" at the door, and Bea shuffled in.

That's not how she moves, Colin found himself thinking. *Not such slow, subdued steps.*

"The review's finally done," she announced. "I'm clear."

"About time." The grin spread over his face.

"That *is* a relief," Zara added, warmth swelling in her voice. "From what I heard, it was the other officers who supported you?"

Bea nodded. "A couple testified that Eric was reaching for a weapon."

"And he was," Colin said. "Or that's how it turned out." Though nobody could truly see that when she opened fire.

"More or less. I came through it because of the others' support, more than anyone trusting my judgment."

She says that like it's a bad thing. And it bothered Bea more than she admitted.

"I hear you went to the Gardners?" Her tone was crisp again.

"We did. And right behind our backs, Eric stole some documents they'd been guarding."

"While you were there?" Her eyebrows went up. "You have any reason to think he was already on the site when you got there? Does that mean he was close and he knew where to find them... but he still needed to steal them at all?"

"Same thing I've been wondering." He laughed—why did her guesswork make him laugh?

"Now back up here," she said. "What was your plan with the Gardners—"

"Stop a minute, won't you?" Zara said. "Terri's resting, and Colin's been running all over town. Can this wait a while?"

"It could," Bea nodded. "Or we could step outside."

"Okay."

The word was out of his mouth at once. He moved for the door and followed her out, with only a glance back at Zara.

A few doors down, a trio of children thronged around where a woman fumbled with her key. Bea turned the other way where they had the corridor to themselves.

She whispered "So, about your run at Gardner?"

"Josh Gardner... he does seem like he cares about this town, same as Fields. Said he didn't know about Eric, but right on the same floor they did have those records Eric wanted."

Bea swung open the door to the stairs. They stepped inside and halted on the landing, out of sight of stray guests.

Except, the stairwell would echo. Colin moved closer to Bea, close enough to breathe "Then, then Fields said the company wasn't always as concerned with—"

"Back up—"

He flushed, drew back from her.

"I *mean,*" Bea added, "don't start with what they told you. What was your plan going in there?"

"That I accuse Gardner—since they gave us enough suspicious signs with Eric—and make Hoyle look 'reasonable.' And yes, it was Hoyle's plan."

"I... you're trusting him with a lot," Bea said.

"Yes I'm trusting him. He's the one in charge, and we need some kind of edge here. So far we can't find Eric, or when we do we can't stop him. Look, didn't you say you had Hoyle wrong?"

"You simply decided to bring him in." Bea turned her head away, a small motion made larger by the close quarters. "I asked you to get a handle on fighting with the skein again, not give away what we've learned. Did you tell him about the spell too?"

"No." His hands twitched, wanting to shrug, reach out, something, but the tight space made that unwise—and unfair, when Bea's movements were more contained. "But the cops that hunt Eric could sure use it."

Her eyes locked on his, cold blue ice. "They do that, and then *anyone* who hears the spell, or hears it from them, can start this all over again. If they get one fragment of skein, they can start building it up by feeding people to it."

"I know."

"It's bad enough now, when any minute could be the time that Eric Rowe grabs one more body for—"

"I *know!*"

The word burst out and echoed up and down the stairwell.

Lower this time, he said "You think you're the only one who keeps thinking about that? But the cops need a fighting chance too, or else it means your own people are lining up to be slaughtered! Hoyle's tried to give them bigger guns and a plan—"

And confide in the police commissioner to get an all-out man-hunt—no, I'm trying to keep Bea calm *here—*

"Well, they need some kind of edge," he said again. "We all do."

"What we need is to take Eric down." She said it so calmly.

"Like you shot him, and staked everything you had on that slowing him down. And Hoyle saved you from the cost of that, and you can't even be grateful?" *Why'd I say that? This can't be about either of us, it's about catching Eric.*

"I... I'm grateful," Bea said. "I'm just trying to keep this threat under control the best way I know."

"Control? The way you know? I hope there's more to this than keeping all of it in your own hands. Tell me that's not all you care about."

"Alright."

She seemed to steady herself, and those eyes seemed to grow cooler and more certain.

"Yes, I want to stop Eric Rowe. I want to know how his weapon works and what he's after, so we can shut him down some way that doesn't set off even more nightmares. And everything I learn about it tells me the best answer is me, and you.

"Colin, you say I'm making this about control—but I just accepted you're the one we need to hold onto the skein. Tell me, what do you want?"

Besides you to stop fighting me? "I want Eric gone too!" His fists clenched, useless at his sides. "I want to stop guessing who he'll kill next, and just have us be safe!"

"I'd like to believe we can." Bea sighed. "You didn't tell Hoyle about the spell. What about what you saw at the park?"

"No." *If there was even that much in it. But they might need Hoyle's clout to follow up there—*

"Alright." A smile peeked onto Bea's face, then shrank back to almost nothing. "If you really want to follow a lead, it's getting dark now. This is our chance to look at that park without being seen. Just us," she added.

Colin's mouth opened. His muscles felt hollow and emptied out, his nerves worn to a frazzle trying to hold his fraying bonds with her together. And he'd still only eaten once since breakfast, that should be an eternity to someone with skein...

Bea's eyes were waiting. Of all the smiles he'd coaxed out of her, none had been this small, tentative.

"Let's go."

*　*　*

Neither of them spoke on the drive. Bea kept her eyes on the road, and the fragile peace hung between them. Colin finished the basics of his new phone, and then he let the silence linger by giving Zara just a text:

Checking something with Bea.

Her answer came right back: *I thought you might. How long?*

An hour or two? But... he answered *I wish I knew.*

The drive sped and slowed as the traffic changed. When they neared Cherry Street, the day shift was still letting out from the little factories and plants that were running. And there'd still be hours of summer daylight ahead, nothing like the discreet darkness Bea had promised.

Actually losing track of the time of day and rushing them out here—that was unlike her. He could just see a tension in how her hands gripped the wheel, that had to be embarrassment. She didn't look at him.

They parked in front of the empty plant where Eric had taken his prisoners. The place looked as deserted as ever, now further marked by crime scene tape and broken windows. What few people passed it on the street looked uneasily away.

Still in the car seat, Bea began with "So Eric came looking for something about Rayo Spark. Here."

"Right, he was searching all over the area. He left Jessie here while he ran around—I saw him stop to look at one sign that mentioned it, and when he didn't find what he wanted he was mad enough to almost kill a woman on sight."

"We know Matt Vargas mentioned Rayo Spark." Bea spoke softer now. "And that Spark partnership, including Gardner money, tried rebuilding this neighborhood in this industrial form. After the Beast Killings."

"A sign in the park hinted at that, I think. And when the pavement broke open, I saw what could have been footprints."

"Prints. That were still in the ground, after concrete broke over it?"

I know, I shouldn't believe it either, but I need you to—

She added "And Eric came after this place's secrets, and then some files at Gardner. Let's see."

They stepped from the car and walked out, still only to the far corner of the plant, just far enough to see more of the tiny concrete park without being seen glancing over that way. The chunks of concrete Eric had torn up lay there undisturbed.

First cracks from the earthquake that the town never fixed, now the crime lab missed this too... for once Colin was grateful.

"No closer," Bea said. "How's your invisibility working?"

"Better, at least this afternoon. Maybe you were right and I just needed a meal. Or the chase at Gardner didn't last long enough to wear me out again," he added. "You want me to sneak a closer look?"

"Soon. Let's dig through the data before the pavement." She didn't laugh, but her lips twitched.

They settled back in the car. A few vehicles rolled past them as they waited, a sad, scattered few that were still too many eyes nearby for them to make a move. Two old men moved along the sidewalk and stopped for some kind of fist-shaking argument, almost in front of the park.

Colin started his new phone searching, trying to build on what he knew about the area. Cherry Park was a small part of the general drive to industrialize these streets... Rayo Spark had been a small group that had encouraged the businesses to come...

"Here they are again, Gardner Investments," Colin said. "One of the Rayo Spark backers."

"The only ones still in business. By that name, anyway," Bea answered.

Colin watched her on her phone. Was there really that much they could pull off the net now, or was she killing time to let the evening darken? To cover her mistake in rushing them out here?

He texted Zara: *Still at it. You ok?*

Fine was all she said. Just when he needed to stall.

He tried *Anything Terri wants to say?*

No answer came back. Five seconds, ten...

Then: *Please. Just let us rest.*

That was all, all that Terri and Zara had?

Something cold dug in his gut. Terri had been in a slump all afternoon, and now this? Should she even be out of the hospital at all? Or maybe this was the limit of what the doctors could do for her.

Or what anybody could.

The coldness swelled, swept over him.

The strongest that Terri's shattered body had ever been was when it was wrapped in skein. But the best hope Rayo Hill had was to get rid of Eric and... and somehow bring back the Vargas House and Zara's confidence and...

His hands were shaking. He clenched them tight on the phone, pressed them against his lap.

Out by the park, the old men were still waving their arms in whatever debate kept them rooted there.

Bea stirred in her seat and murmured, "I checked around the patrol desks. No reports since we chased Eric off—I was afraid he'd already be abducting someone else." An ember of relief warmed those words.

"Me too. So when do we..."

The two figures at the park had turned and begun strolling away. Still shaking their fists at each other, but leaving.

"Whenever you're ready," she said.

The street was close to quiet now. Colin squeezed himself down under the dashboard, far enough to be out of casual sight. Bea gave him a nod.

Settling the skein around him was a slower process with his body all folded in around itself. When he finished, he dug his will deep into the mental twist that concealed him, held it tight, and swung the door open. The car stirred when his unseen weight left it, but there was nobody near to see.

Softly and smoothly, he moved down the sidewalk—just a glimmer of light in the evening's haze. He only had to stop twice to slip around a passer-by before he reached the concrete "park."

It was a mere twenty feet of space, squeezed in between one silent building and another's chain fence, just a gathering of old benches around would have been a tiny fountain. Earthquake lines and cracks in the concrete must have lain unrepaired for three years.

Colin stood over the deeper slashes that Eric had carved. Slowly, his invisible hands pushed broken fragments aside.

The last piece rattled away to expose a patch of hard rock. The strike that Colin had deflected into it marred the surface, but that indentation in the stone still looked peculiar.

His finger traced the inside of it. Smooth, unnatural.

The shape… from what was left, it *could* be the heel of a footprint, of a huge man or even larger. Stamped into the rock, or seared.

What am I thinking? It's some fossil print, that's all. Here, ages before the Beast Killings were here.

Why couldn't Bea be next to him, to tell him he was shivering for no reason? It was a fossil, it didn't mean there were prints like this all under the street and this spot was the only place to crack open…

At least he could grab her a picture. He looked around the street, checking if it was clear to bring his phone out from under his skein.

On the opposite rooftop, a shadow moved. A shadow with a halo.

Colin dropped to a crouch. If Eric leaped at him, or if he'd spotted Bea's car up by the crime scene...

But Eric only moved away along the roof without a glance around. He might really have missed them both.

So what was he up to here? Colin watched him move away, then slipped across the street, up beside the wall where Eric would have to look right down to see him. *Now I call Bea—no, I try that and those men up on the sidewalk could see my phone appear.*

Instead he crept forward under the shadow of the wall. He had to reach the building's corner in time to see if Eric moved to the next roof.

But an invisible shape was already dropping up beside that corner. Eric's feet hit the sidewalk behind three workmen there—and one man glanced over at the sound.

Run, get in and save them... but Eric wasn't attacking. The murderer only stood still, and the man turned back and strolled on with his friends.

Colin leaned against the wall and held his invisibility firm until the three workmen had passed by. Eric was moving along in the other direction.

For a moment the street looked empty, empty enough.

Colin pulled his phone out and snapped Bea a text: *look up!!! its E*

And he let himself appear, and waved her forward with a broad swing of his arm. Then he tucked his phone away under the skein and vanished again.

No heads spun toward him, Eric didn't look back, and a block behind him Bea stepped from her car and started toward them.

They'd figure the rest out together. Somehow, they just had to get her in position to ambush Eric, and the spell could finally beat him... when she couldn't see what she was tracking. Why hadn't she taken just a bit of skein to clear her sight?

Eric had drawn further up the street, and Colin kept after him, hanging back to use what cover the few buildings and the wide spaces between them allowed. Some muddle of old chemicals tickled his nose.

A block ahead would be the place Eric had stopped to look at this morning, where he'd almost struck a bystander down. Colin crouched down and brought his phone out of concealment again.

He texted a frantic:

its eric

going to next street on left

again

Only a moment after he sent it, she came back with *Ill get up ahead*

And she ducked around the corner at a run.

That was all the hint she needed, to read what happened and match him? They were *that* well in sync? His hand shook as he tucked the phone away. And he was sending her against Eric with zero protection against those claws... except the spell, and himself keeping Eric busy until she used it. But, this time they might really get that chance.

Colin moved faster now, with Eric further ahead and the street quiet. Once a pair of women walked past him, grumbling about their boss, and he froze and felt his invisibility waver. But he made it hold and they walked on by.

Closer. Closer.

Then Eric turned into an alley just halfway down the block. Too soon.

Colin stared. *Can't lose him*—he scrambled for the alley's corner, gaze sweeping around and up for any sign of a trap. Which way was Eric headed?

He peeked around. The alley lay empty.

He stepped inside it. Eric could have reached the nearest door, or jumped for the roof on either side. Colin looked up to take in both angles above, as he closed in on the door.

Feet thudded down behind him.

"Colin. I saw you…"

Colin dove away. He rolled, spun—*did I go visible?*—and braced for the attack.

Eric didn't lunge. Instead the halo-shape stood in the street by the alley, and he said softly "You chase me, I chase you. It could go on forever, and it doesn't change a thing."

And he glanced back around the street. It must look empty enough—only a few sounds cut through the stillness. He was too close.

Then Eric said "Just one thing. At least tell me, is Terri alright?"

"She's fine," Colin snarled. "Away from you, now."

Eric turned slowly toward him. He'd only *half* faced the alley before, like he couldn't see him right. *And I just gave myself away, again.*

Except, Bea was out there somewhere, his fragile, almost-secret weapon. If Eric would just keep talking.

"Of course you say she's fine," Eric said. "I wish I could believe you."

He closed in—one sudden step, but then he halted.

"Colin… can't you see I'm trying to *save* her? And show you people that this ghost town should never have sucked her in at all?"

Colin gritted his teeth against the lies. His fingers flexed. When the attack came, his skein *had* to be strong enough.

"And still nothing gets through to any of you. All I can do is kill, kill…"

Eric's voice cracked.

"I'm trying to heal her! Just give her enough skein so she has a life again! You let me do that, and you can sit around on this empty hill and tell all the lies you want about your 'home.' *Let me save her!"*

The sound echoed in the alley's stillness.

Colin held his place. Any motion could set Eric off, any word he said might come out as a dare for him to strike. But of course Eric wanted Terri healed, just enough to let him steal her away again.

Eric shimmered into sight. The bare outline of him filled out into a true visible shape of silver-green, and he stretched out his hands:

"Just let me give it to her. That's all I want, not more fighting. Let her take it and cover up how she's got some miracle cure, or go somewhere and start a new life—anything. All this can be over. I can let her go as long as she's okay."

What if he means it...

Across the street, Bea stepped into view.

The next moment she looked right toward them, and took her first stealthy steps toward Eric's back.

Keep him talking. Bea closed in, out of sight of the alley now.

Colin said "We just heal her and sneak away, and that's it? And you, what... you go somewhere else and keep dissolving people to bulk up your power?"

"Colin, why would I *want* more? I've got enough skein to disappear, and I'm stronger than anyone. I can already do anything, anywhere. And I am so sick of killing."

You? You goddamn liar. "Didn't help Joe Martin, did it? You skewered him just last night."

"I..." Eric's head dipped, as if there was still some kind of regret left in him. "He kept trying to yell. I lost my temper, I know. I've been trying to make him the last one, I swear I have!"

Bea had to be near the alley entrance by now.

"So what was Jessie?" he answered. "You'd settle for melting her skin off if you left her alive? Or did you just *have* to ask her about Rayo Spark?"

The project that worked *right here,* that paved that park over the marks in the rock—

Eric said "None of that has to matter, if we can save Terri soon. You really think she's getting better without me, *ever?* Just let save her while we still can!"

"She's fine! Don't you get it?"

Bea stood at the entrance of the alley, behind Eric. She waved toward somewhere out of view, like motioning a pedestrian away—

"Is she healing?" Eric said. "You can't even *ask* Terri if she wants to walk again? Let me tell her, damn you! Take me to her and let me tell her we can end all of this!"

"You really think I'll let you near her, ever?"

"Then call her! No—you go ask her, then you meet me. You want to know why I'm giving up about the Beast Killings?"

Bea charged.

Her hand thrust at Eric's back as she snapped *"Gratshay ko—"*

As the syllables sang, as she closed in, Eric's arm whirled around in a blur. It *cracked* against her arm and knocked it away.

She staggered back with pain across her face.

Eric swung his arm up, ready to sprout claws. Colin charged.

Eric spun away—he was *already* spinning away, to face him.

"Grat—"

Before Bea could gasp the spell out, Eric leaped upward.

He arched up out of reach, and slammed down on the roof.

Colin stepped in front of Bea. Any moment now, any moment, Eric would dive at them...

Eric crouched over to watch them, just ten feet above.

"Just talk to Terri!" he said again. "Then come to the *first* Beast Killing, out on Silverlode Road, before morning. See what you say then."

He shimmered away as he pulled back out of view.

CHAPTER ELEVEN

LOOK OUT

Footsteps sounded on the roof, just a few and then gone. Colin's eyes flicked around for a route to follow Eric, but that would mean fighting him alone.

And Bea stood clutching her arm. The arm Eric had swatted away, all his strength against human flesh, and now her teeth clenched in pain.

"Are you…"

"Let's see." Why were her words so calm? She fumbled to loosen her coat, with her left arm only.

"Here, let me—"

"Don't!"

She twisted away like her wound was some kind of private shame. Her eyes *avoided* his.

He fell back staring, too many things roiling in his stomach. How could she, how could it happen, she'd done everything right and still the one hurt was her…

He slid his skein mask off, and tried to watch her without *watching* her as she eased the coat off her shoulders alone. Her shirt underneath had no blood on the white—her face was just as pale as she felt at her arm, flexed it. Every spasm she tried to hide went grinding through him.

"It's not broken, or dislocated," she said. "We were lucky."

" 'Lucky.' Here, this can help you brace it." He scooped a hunk of skein off of his arm and held it out.

She shook her head. "All of that's yours, to give you any chance against Rowe. But, I can still take enough to *see* him." She pinched off a dollop of green from it.

There she was—practical, capable Bea again, Eric hadn't broken that. Colin heaved out a sigh, then reached for a way to draw that comforting wit out a little further. "Listen. I know we'd never trust Eric's 'deal,' but..."

"But what happened on Silverlode? The 'first Beast Killing'? We need a plan about his offer or how to trap him, and we need to find out what happened there. Or just where on the street it is."

They started back for the car.

She walked too slowly. Her steps looked shaky, her face winced when she thought he wasn't watching. *Damn, damn, how can I ever let her get hurt again?*

Except... this wasn't about *letting* her. And Eric's other words kept coming back: *you can't even ask Terri if she wants to walk again?*

Bea handed him her keys, and he held on tight to the wheel to keep his thoughts on the road back. Bea sat quiet with her bit of skein across her eyes, relentlessly watching the twilight all around them.

* * *

When they reached the hotel, Bea walked in with her old brisk step. Colin pushed himself in as if he was carrying weights that grew every second. He did see the "janitor" spot them and tap out a quick text— their police guards were still alert.

Zara was on her feet when the door opened. "How did it—Bea!"

"It's only a few bruises," she said. "Here, let me clean myself up." She stepped into the bathroom.

Terri lay asleep in her bed.

Zara turned to Colin, and her voice was calmer now. "Are you..."

He forced a smile. "We almost got Eric."

Or had a chance at something else, that they'd been denying…

He slumped in the nearest chair. His phone slid out, ready to start researching Silverlode Road. *Another Beast Killing? And I thought the footprints were a find…*

But his fingers weren't moving. His eyes drifted closed.

—He snapped awake. Terri was still asleep, Zara looking up and turning her laptop away. Bea was nowhere in sight. Had she simply left and he missed it?

Focus. He pulled himself up and stepped over to Terri's bed.

There she lay, unmoving in the nest of cushions. His big sister had *crawled* for a chance to face Eric again, to push back against anyone but her making her choices.

"Hi." His voice quavered.

Terri's eyes stayed closed. She only lay there, frozen except for the shallow movement that was her breathing.

He glanced at the table beside her. That had to be a dozen different medications, all sorted into different rows by Zara's care. *Eric said she'd never get better like this. We have to do something.*

He looked back at Zara. "Has she been awake at all?"

"Of course she has."

But her eyes swung away—not fast enough for a lie, but some other pain she was hiding. Back toward the chair where she'd left her laptop. He stepped back a pace to see around the screen.

The blue logo of a bank website glared at him. He moved closer to spot the words *Loan Application.*

God. Was that what she was struggling with, just to keep Terri going? He spun toward her and gasped a ragged "Zara, you…"

Someone knocked on the door.

"We have to talk. Now," came Hoyle's voice.

Now?

Colin's feet were frozen, his mouth couldn't move. He looked numbly at the door, at Terri.

Zara swept over to the door. The bathroom swung open too, and Bea stepped out, still pale.

Hoyle marched in and headed straight to his detective. His gaze raked over her as if he could deduce every bruise she was hiding.

"The guard said you two went out. Want to explain that?"

Colin cut in "We…" and ran out of words. *Not yet, I have to check with Bea and Terri before we talk to Hoyle.*

But the word did bring Hoyle spinning around to glower at him. "You do know you risked everything by running off alone? You two make one wrong move out there and we lose our only chance to track this cop-killer."

"I know." Of course he knew, it had always been on them.

Bea said "It was my idea." Hoyle swung around to face her, as she went on "We took another look where Rowe had his prisoners. And we ran into him again—looks like he was still looking for signs about what Rayo Spark built there."

Hoyle shook his head. "Rowe *was* there? I suppose you never thought to bring in backup?"

Colin said "No time to think at all. We were tracking an invisible man who moves faster than any of us—not a lot of time for making calls."

And yet for everything they ever did, he ended up defending the choice from someone. *This can't be just me and Bea, but it can't be Hoyle yet…*

"This ends now," the lieutenant snapped. "No more chasing monsters, unless I have a squad to put behind you. Do I have to put you under house arrest until I get my task force cleared? Do I?"

Colin swallowed. Not yet, not yet, why couldn't Hoyle let them think?

He met Bea's eyes, and flicked his gaze toward where Terri lay.

And Bea *got it.* She said to Hoyle "Of course you need more options for hunting Rowe. Like seeing through his invisibility—it's easy," and she held out her bit of skein.

Hoyle's eyes locked on it. Of course it was a distraction, but the bait must be too enticing. She stepped toward him and whispered something, and they moved into the hall.

Colin stared as the door closed. Bea had been the woman who'd rather lie to her own sergeant—and she *trusted* Ed Jordan—than remove her skein. Now she was handing it to Hoyle to buy them some time?

Zara said "Am I missing something, or did you just ask Bea to distract him? With one look?"

"Yeah. I need to talk with Terri."

He moved over to her bedside again, and Zara moved behind him. Terri *still* lay asleep, whether it was from the medications or the stress or something. But he needed her now.

He crouched beside her. "Terri?" He touched her hand.

Her eyes flew open. Cold fright squirmed in them, for one moment until her gaze focused on her family, and her face eased.

Right. She spent three years as Eric's prisoner watching him crack, of course her reflexes are on a hair-trigger. Terri had more reason to hate Eric than all of them put together.

And all that was why it could only be her decision.

"Hi," he said.

"Hi. I'm fine," she added.

That was the first thing she thought to tell them? Colin pushed on "We ran into Eric again."

"And?"

Colin felt Zara leaning in beside him. He went on "Eric said we were keeping you in the dark about something. I mean, he says he can fix you by giving your skein back. We can't trust him, but..."

He leaned closer.

"He says if we let him, he'll stop killing. And stop taking it out on the town, and just let it be over. He says he'll let you go."

"And you believe him?" That hoarse tone had to be fury.

"I can't, of course I can't."

But. The word he didn't say hung between them.

Terri took a slow breath. "But I'd be healed, some. Even if it's all we get. And if he does deliver more..."

"If?" *That* word was like the first crack of a wound tearing open.

Terri's head lolled to the side, away. "Andy Anderson. Leo Tozier. Joe Martin. Four cops. And how many die next, because I don't take gifts from *him?* We forget, a devil only gives deals because the bait really is rich enough."

She whispered a sigh.

"So many dead. Do I have the right to say no?"

"But..." Zara pushed in beside Colin. "You *can't* trust him. If you start thinking like that, you can talk yourself into wanting him back."

"No! Not that, ever. He locked me up for years. Years—"

Terri's voice choked off, too weak for the rage within it. She stopped, breathed, and looked over at Colin.

Softly she said "Any chance you'll catch him?"

"I don't know. That 'meeting' could be our best chance to trap him." Just saying that felt like urging Terri to see it his way. *But why shouldn't I?*

Terri said "I bet he keeps coming after me. But, I'd still be patched up more than this. I'm so tired... every part of me's broken, all I do is lie here..."

Her eyes fluttered shut. She whispered:

"You know, after Eric went mad keeping me? Now part of me's waiting for you to go crazy too, someday. Watching over me."

Colin couldn't speak, couldn't breathe.

Zara gasped "No. Don't you..." Then, slowly, she said "If, if you need to take what he's offering..."

Terri's head rolled toward them. Her eyes swung past them, toward the table behind them.

"With skein, I could pick up my own glass of water. With his 'help,' maybe much more."

She stopped. Her mouth trembled, and the room fell silent.

In that stillness, Hoyle's voice growled outside the door "Enough. The thing isn't working for me."

Colin said "So what this looks like is, you're almost sure to get some healing from Eric, and in the best case it's more than that. And there's the chance that he really would be satisfied, and he'd leave us and everyone alone. Or…"

"Or, he does go," Terri said. "Anywhere he wants. A killer, who's killed on impulse because it's so easy—"

The door rattled open.

Hoyle marched in. They spun around as he declared "Alright, you show me how this stuff works."

Back behind them, Terri breathed "You *get him*. Don't you ever let him escape."

Zara nodded, and wiped back a tear. Colin reached out and stroked his sister's hair.

Softly, Hoyle said "When you're ready…"

Colin turned, saw him holding Bea's bit of skein.

The lieutenant added "You show me how to see through that invisibility. Simms says it should be easy."

Colin stood, tried to shake his thoughts away from Terri's courage. Seeing through the skein was nothing like easy, and Bea should be the first to admit that. She had to be playing games again, maybe to frustrate Hoyle and make him give the skein back…

He shook his head again, pushing all of those away.

"Here's something a bit bigger than that," he said. "Eric offered to meet me tonight, to talk about some deal for healing Terri. It could be our chance to trap him."

The room went silent.

Bea stood at Hoyle's back, utterly still, while Hoyle's gaze darted between her and Colin. Bea had bought them their chance to decide this, and she'd never even had a chance to say how she saw it herself.

Then Hoyle advanced on Colin. "A shot at Rowe, and you're only telling me now?"

"That 'shot' is a deal he offered Terri." Colin glanced back at his silent sister. "That makes her the one I had to ask first."

"Is that what you think? And if she wanted to say yes, you're telling me you'd let the killer go?"

"Yes!" Colin flung back. Just because it was the easy answer—he could already feel the doubts and the anger rising at the thought of backing down. A choice they wouldn't have to face now.

Hoyle turned to Terri. "Ms. da Costa, thank you again. This town owes you a great debt for your support. Now," and his gaze pinned Colin, "when and where is this meeting?"

"When is, Eric said I could come any time tonight. Where... he said on Silverlode Road, where the 'first Beast Killing' was." Colin grimaced. "We never got to narrow that down."

Hoyle's hand rose to shade his eyes. His head bowed, for a long moment deep in some private calculation.

Then he grabbed out his phone and tapped a few keys.

"Hey, Ned. Quick favor—tell me, is there a chance something happened around Silverlode Road, that could have been Beast Killings before the two on Cherry? Yes, Silverlode."

A moment later he looked up at them, cell still at his ear.

"He said *any* time tonight?" Hoyle's words came in a rush, like they were swept along by the sheer weight of the forces in motion. "That gives us time to set more officers around there. Da Costa, we'll need you on the scene—and yes, I'll try to keep him back from the action," he added to Zara.

His fingers tightened on the phone.

"Say again? *Thirty* years before the Killings?"

"Could be," Colin said. "There's already a forty-year gap from those to now." *If something goes that far back, if it's tied to the skein... what has Eric found?*

Hoyle told his phone "Any others it could be? Okay then, I owe you one."

He swung the cell down, and a grin flashed onto his face.

"We've *got* the bastard. The only place is what's now the Moon View Diner on the edge of town. Wide open, and Rowe's open invitation gave us time to surround the whole site."

"The whole site?" Bea said. "Can you do that?"

"It'll take every hand I can get. Wish I had the task force approved, but—" He waved Bea for the door. "Alright, we set this up this step by step."

"And we reinforce the guard back here," Bea added. "It could still be a distraction to get at Terri."

"Of course." He turned back to Colin. "This'll go down long after midnight, if it does at all. We'll come get you, but till then you *stay here.* Understood?"

"Sure. Whatever brings Eric down," he added

"Good. Try to get some sleep. We're going to need your best."

And Hoyle swept out of the suite with Bea in his wake. She never even looked back.

The door thumped shut. The room fell silent, with only the far-off motions around the hotel and out in the street whispering against that sudden stillness.

Zara shook herself. "Sleep? When this whole nightmare might be ending tonight?"

"We have to try," Colin said. "It's part of any battle—"

He froze. *God, did I really say* that? *It's what Dad said, and he never came back.*

Zara's lips moved, without a sound. She coughed, once.

"Please. This time..." She took a step toward him, and her hands reached toward him. "This time I'll just say it: *don't* you go running into danger again. Not now, not when you can stand back and let dozens of police take the risk. The people who've been trained to do this."

"I..."

He looked away from his mother's eyes, over at Terri. His sister said nothing, as if she could let the warning go by with none of it touching her. Even though she'd taken worse risks than any of them.

"I'll try," he said. "With enough cops I'd just get in the way anyhow."

With that, they did their best to settle in.

They called up dinner, mostly liquids for Terri and extra plates for Colin—Bea could be right, eating that afternoon might have helped him control the skein later.

And he tried to study the site. The Moon View Diner was the latest name for the restaurant by the bus station at the edge of town. The pictures he found showed broad spaces and open land, hard to imagine setting a trap for Eric there. Finding seventy-year-old deaths there that might be like the Beast Killings would be harder yet.

A text popped up from Bea:

Careful what you tell H.

Colin blinked, glared at the letters. Was she really going to start this again, now?

He answered *He's making all this happen! Pls dont argue.* It would be easier if she'd called him, and he could work with her voice.

Bea sent back:

I hope it works. But do the math.

He got to the hotel just 20 minutes after us.

So he was on his way before the guard saw us. He already knew.

Her string of steps made some sense—no. Colin sent:

Or he was nearby. Keeping an eye on us?

We need him.

He set this up, and he's working on a bigger task force.

Bea said *So I keep hearing.*

She was still pushing back? He sent:

He took me to test Gardner.

He chased Eric back to save Jessie.

He got me this phone.

The last words made his fingers freeze after he sent them. Sure the phone was Hoyle's, but that didn't mean a thing.

This time it took whole seconds before Bea answered:

Could be I'm just nervous. Try getting that sleep. Sorry.

And that was all she'd say, after he mentioned the phone. Did she really think Hoyle had it tapped?

Colin shivered. Hoyle had been proving himself, but Bea's suspicions just never went away. Except now the idea kept buzzing in his head. The phone in his hands felt colder, and he gave up searching for old clues about the diner.

He said a soft goodnight to his mother and sister, and tried to settle in the second room's bed.

Calm...

There were ways to push himself to sleep. Steady, deep breathing... tensing and relaxing different sets of his muscles, squeezing the worry out of him like toothpaste from a tube. His father had mentioned those too.

What would Dad say here? I've joined up with a professional force to hunt down a deadly threat, but I'm still an outsider. The person I trust most keeps warning me against the one in charge, and she could still be partway right.

And in a few hours this might all be over.

The sounds of the building and the town steadied into evening. It didn't make resting any easier.

The phone lay beside the bed, ready to fill the hours with studying the location and the Beast Killings... but Bea's reaction about that phone kept his fingers away from it.

Sometimes a voice broke the stillness. Often a single low, controlled voice out in the corridor, sometimes a man's or a woman's— those had to be the police. But they only stayed on guard in the hall, instead of coming to pull him out of the waiting.

Colin lay still and breathed, slowly. He thought of further outside, in the parking lot or the street, where other officers might be on watch too.

While Eric... if Eric wasn't eyeing them all here, he *would* be out where the trap was taking shape. *And all I can do is lie here, minute after minute after minute, and keep wrestling the tension out of my body as if I ever could sleep...*

The knock came.

He grabbed up his skein and a last snack and darted to the door, no slowing down to say goodbye. Waiting outside stood two older cops in uniform, who led him off with just a "This way." They passed another cop on guard in the corridor, before they stepped out into the cold night.

The drive set out silently. These two cops were new to him, and they sat in the car with a coiled readiness that all but ignored him.

Colin broke open the orange he'd grabbed. A last bit of nutrition couldn't hurt, if he needed the skein tonight.

The second cop looked back as he worked. "Nervous?" he grinned.

"I guess." Colin held out a slice, but there was no way to offer it to them with the heavy mesh shielding the front seats from him.

The driver said "Orders said, no talking. We save it for at the site."

They drove on, through the dark streets and into the unknown.

When they pulled off the road it was at the fringe of the town, where a ragged mix of buildings broke up the shadows on the way onto a wide, open slope. The three of them climbed out and picked their way through that openness with no lights, and every misstep made Colin start, or the cops struggle to keep their curses down.

The night breeze felt colder with every step.

After half a mile, they reached an outcrop of rock high enough for figures to crouch behind: Hoyle and three other cops. Hoyle had binoculars trained on a handful of lights far down the slope, at the isolated shapes of the bus station and the diner beside the state road's exit.

Hoyle turned to meet them.

"Good. All of you keep your voices low, and your lights hidden from down there." He held up his phone, with what looked like a map of the space below, and he kept it sheltered behind the rock. "The scouts have crawled their way in past this point here, but our suspect could still be anywhere."

Colin nodded along, pressing his arms to his sides to keep still. He could make out one shape by their feet: a bundle of their SWAT rifles wrapped a tarp.

"We know the job," one of the cops muttered, a woman.

"We take this slowly. Those men took more than an hour to crawl close, because they checked every space with their IR scopes. *You remember that*—Rowe has a camo suit that's fooled better officers than us. But these scopes can nail him."

He held up his binoculars, and patted the bundle of rifles.

Colin felt it rising up him, a thrill, a hope. If they *could* see Eric... Bea had her bit of skein, they must have tested this on her...

"We just finish closing the net," Hoyle said. "He's not getting away."

Another, smaller cop said "Lieutenant... how many men have we drawn out here? The brass didn't say—"

"Let me worry about that. Remember, none of you blink. That's how we lost four cops to this animal."

Colin looked at the rifles again, from what he could make out in the shadows. Eric had run from those before, they *had* to have enough punch to hurt him, or knock him around. They had to.

And there were lights on down there. That meant other people in the way of those bullets.

Hoyle crouched down and crawled away to raise the binoculars again. Colin crawled after him.

"So infrared works on this," he said to Hoyle, not quite a question. "And Bea's out there?"

"Yes, and yes. Watching the teams on the other side, of course," Hoyle grunted.

"And everything's still clear back at the hotel?"

Hoyle lowered the binoculars to scowl at him. "It's not going to go smoother with more questions, you know."

I deserve that. "Sorry. I'll wait for where you need me."

He crawled away, flat along the cold earth. When he'd gotten some distance, he slipped out a fragment of skein, and stretched it across his eyes—a gauzy blindfold, what would look like little more than a strip of pale war paint. At this hour the view through the sunglasses would have been solid blackness.

Methodically, he looked up and down the slope for any glimpse of Eric or his halo. The ground sucked more heat from him the longer he lay there, but it was better than bending in a crouch for what might be hours. Bea was out there somewhere, enduring the same thing.

A shadow edged down the slope at once point, and another further to the side—Hoyle's scouts creeping toward the buildings, scopes ready.

So, Eric had to be *in* one of those little structures. At least if he'd actually been waiting there all night... and the longer Colin looked, the more that one doubt gnawed at him.

Scrapings on the ground signaled another cop edging toward him, bald head gleaming faintly in what moonlight they had.

"Is he really down there, you think?" the cop said. "What makes Hoyle so damn sure?"

Because Eric's doing this to save Terri.

Because if he's not down there, he could be breaking her door down right now.

"It's the best chance we'll get," he said.

"For us, or Hoyle's career—"

The cop broke off. He pulled back and crept away, and across the slope Colin saw Hoyle watching them both.

Colin checked his phone, hiding its light with his hand: pushing 3 AM.

And still nothing moved down there except the breeze, and what few cars moved along the state road—ignoring the town's edge except that pretense of a bus station, and the diner that tried to serve it. What lights glowed in there looked all alone in a wide-open night.

A single hushed voice drifted around the slope. Hoyle was motioned the team together behind the outcrop.

"It's time. We've scouted right up to the edge of the lights—if Rowe's there, he's in one of the buildings."

"If," one of the cops grumbled, and a few others breathed something like agreement. Colin scowled.

"We've IDed the cook and the bus clerk in there, so anyone else would be Rowe. Officers, grab your rifles and be ready to close the net. *Make* him surrender, if you can."

The other cop said "We got it already—"

"No you don't!" Colin burst out.

He stepped toward the doubter, the man who thought Eric was beaten, and wrestled his voice to stay low.

"Four. Dead. Cops," he said. "You don't know how *fast* Eric Rowe is. All you'll ever see is one flicker of movement, and that's if you're lucky. He—"

"All right," Hoyle cut in. "Time for you to do your part, Mr. da Costa."

Colin's breath caught. Other voices around him gasped, all watching him, but none of that mattered now. He nodded.

Hoyle went on "It's all set. You go down there, just far enough to see if you can draw Rowe out. Keep the phone on vibrate and I'll signal when you're close enough."

"Boss?" one of the cops gasped. "Okay, good joke on him, but—"

"Move slowly," Hoyle went on. "These officers are precise shots. You'll be in no danger if you keep clear of Rowe. It's our last chance to draw him away from potential hostages."

"What the hell?" That was another cop, right at Colin's back. "You can't send him—"

"Sure he can. And thank you, you and Bea. I think," Colin added with a grin he didn't feel.

Then he started down the slope, setting the phone as he went.

More arguments sounded behind him, with Hoyle keeping the others in line. That trust was the warmest thing in the night.

Coldness was already closing in around him. Eric could be in front of him, and bullets ready behind him—his back prickled at the thought.

I told Zara I'd let them take all the risks, and I still jump right in. But he was still the best chance to stop Eric grabbing those two people or slipping away. The skein under his clothes had to make him safer than anyone else here.

His fists opened, shut, shaking with something more than cold.

The shapes slowly grew up ahead: the tiny, blocky little bus station with its one light on, and the blue neon *Moon View Diner* sign over the little restaurant and gas pumps.

The only sounds were his shoes on the ground, and the night breeze. But Hoyle could be phoning him to halt him at any moment, depending on how closely they could cover the site ahead.

Eric was behind one of those walls. He tried to believe that, and walk with his head high. Bea should be watching him too.

He kept his eyes from looking too squarely at the buildings' lights, to guard some of his night vision. The corner of his vision still caught a figure moving in the diner... but, Hoyle had mentioned a cook in there.

His fingers worked, faster and faster. If Hoyle didn't call soon, he could walk right on inside, stroll through every building there—and probably find Eric was never here.

A haloed shape stepped around from behind the diner.

Colin halted, to let the killer come to him. Eric strode toward him, the same bulked-up figure marching through the darkness as if nothing could harm him. His steps scraped on the pavement.

Eric had no expression to read, with even the mask over it reduced to this hollow outline. Colin tried to keep his own eyes on him, anywhere but on the shadows around them where the snipers would be closing in.

His fists tightened, too tight.

Thirty feet away, twenty. Any moment now, it had to be soon…

A shot screamed through the night. A single gunshot, and a distant curse back up the hill.

Eric only *stood* there—the bullet never touched him at all. Time hung frozen in the air.

Eric whirled and blurred for the diner door. He wrenched it open, and Colin caught a glimpse beyond it of an old man looking up in shock.

The next moment Colin pounded through the door himself.

CHAPTER TWELVE

BLUE MOON

A weathered old face, staring around the diner's walls in search of the gunshot...

Eric barreling through the door—and suddenly visible, the skein folding back from his face to leave him just a man in an odd green hoodie and gloves...

Colin crashing in behind him...

The old man jumping up from beside the counter. The book falling from his hands.

"You're surrounded, Rowe!" Hoyle's megaphone voice battered at the walls. *"We know all your tricks!"*

The diner looked even smaller inside than out. Peeling blue walls only had room for four, five, small tables, nowhere to hide. Not a soul was there except the gray-haired man with the name embroidered across his blue apron: *Phil.*

Eric stood only a few steps from that cook. Colin sidestepped to line up a charge that would shove him away—

"Look out!" *Eric* leveled a finger at Colin. "Look out, he's crazy!"

The words rocked him backward. Eric dared—

Phil's eyes locked on Colin. "You stay back!"

God, is it that easy? Do I look that dangerous now?

Eric drew back and circled behind the cook. Just one motion short of stabbing him in the back.

And the police were closing in. Colin pulled in a deep breath and bellowed out to them "Careful! There's a hostage!"

Phil scooped up a plastic tray from the counter, and brought it up ready to swing at Colin. "Don't you come near me! I won't go down easy."

"Not *me*—" Colin drew back a step, holding up his hands. "That's Eric Rowe behind you, they're after him!"

"You chased *him* in here!"

Eric's eyes burned at Colin. "Right. And you lied—after tonight I'll never believe a word you say again." His voice shook with what felt like real rage, ready to explode.

"Just stay back!" Phil said.

"I'm... not... lying," Colin said. "I'm with the cops out there."

Out beyond the walls, a male voice called "Phil? You okay?"

From the bus station, there'd been a man out there too—

Eric reached toward the blind spot at the back of Phil's neck. His gloved fingertips stretched, sharpened, and waited.

Colin yelled again "I said, he has a hostage! *Look* at him!" he added to Phil, but the cook's gaze stayed locked on Colin.

"Easy, Rowe!" Hoyle shouted. *"Think about what you're doing."*

That sound had to be closer now. Colin looked at the place's small windows—only darkness showed in the glass, no moving lights or any way to tell how close the police were now. How many were out there? What were Hoyle and Bea planning now?

Eric had pulled his claws back in, but he crouched behind Phil, out of reach.

"You *did* lie to me," he snarled at Colin. "I trusted you just once. I gave you a chance to talk. And you, you used that to destroy everything."

Colin raised his hands to protest, but the fists wouldn't stop clenching. Phil glanced back at Eric—now that the claws were gone, of course.

Eric went on "You had a chance to save a dying girl tonight. But you can't let go of your grudge for one second, can you?"

Phil told him "Easy there, you're making him worse. Whatever he did to you, we want him to keep calm, right?" He turned back to Colin.

Eric snapped "No, you did! You tricked me, didn't you?" And his finger flicked out in another blade, over at Phil's back.

He's loving *this...* Colin's teeth clenched, but he forced out "Yes! You came to talk about Terri, and I set you up, I admit it. Just don't hurt him!"

"Selfish bastard," Phil said, and his eyes never left Colin.

"She *is* dying," Eric hissed. "You know she's going to. And all you saw was a chance to come after me. What the hell is wrong with you?"

The words hung in the air. A sound filtered in from outside, the voice they'd heard from the bus station: "Don't shoot, it's not me, they're in there with Phil..." The police were closing in.

Eric said "That makes you a murderer. All I wanted tonight was to save Terri. And," he added, "to talk about the monster in the red corner."

What? Colin stared

But Phil's jaw fell open. He twisted around at Eric. "You heard about that, kid?"

The rage in Eric's voice had retracted like his claws, leaving him with the same smooth tone Colin knew so well. "I heard that a monster killed someone here, long before people remember. If that corner is still here."

Phil knows something... that's why Eric brought me here, why he didn't stay invisible... he's still trying to grab some information before the cops close in... that's why Phil is still alive...

Colin gasped "You can't tell him!"

"You *won't* shut me up!" the old man snapped. "Never. There was a monster, there was, something on two legs with claws that cut up my father. Right there!"

He waved at a corner of the diner, one space where another table could have squeezed in. Instead there was only an empty place, and a picture on the wall.

Colin said "Please, I'm warning you, don't say any more..."

Phil shrank away—*all I'm doing is scaring him.*

Eric's savage grin glittered in the light.

From somewhere beyond the walls came a sound, a hushed command. The police must be closing in.

"You hear what he said?" Eric said. "A monster, and there are still signs of it left. Don't you get it, the truth was always all around us. Anyone could see it if they looked."

And he took a crouching step toward Colin. Out from behind Phil.

"Truth? What truth?" Colin said. *He's* talking *to me now, not taunting me or manipulating Phil, I have to keep him going...*

"Why it's all too late now. You had one chance, one chance, to save the only good thing in this worthless town. And now our time's run out."

He turned back toward Phil.

"You think nobody remembered your monster story—"

"What about Terri?" Colin begged, anything to pull him away from his victim. "Why is it too late? You forced us into this—"

"You did, tonight! I could have helped her!"

Bang!

The shot blasted through the crowded space—it left Eric untouched, untouched where he crouched, but he dove away and landed flat on the floor.

A second shot boomed out as window glass sprayed. Colin leaped forward and dragged Phil down under him. *I've got skein all under my coat, that has to be some protection for us.*

Phil's muffled voice whispered from under him: "Watch yourself! *He* looked like the monster when he came in."

Colin froze. Phil knew, he'd seen Eric's skein when he ran in, and the old bastard had just been playing along with Eric's tricks.

Eric advanced on them, gloved fists out ahead of him, hunched low like some knife-fighter under a low ceiling. His "hood" had flipped up to shield most of his head, leaving only his face below it where his eyes gleamed.

"That 'monster' was here ages ago," he said.

Colin rose to his own crouch, and Phil slid away to the side. Eric's eyes darted toward him.

"I bet the monster was a liar too," Eric growled.

"Lies like holding a girl prisoner for *years?*" Colin spat. "Or saying he gave up killing, and then one nudge sends him right into it again? We all know *you're* the backstabber here—"

Eric struck.

Colin took the first punch on his arm and the skein under his sleeve, and dropped back a step to slip away from the follow-up swings. One crushing blow almost caught his unarmored hand, but he withdrew another step.

Phil had to be watching, but Colin couldn't look away from their enemy.

Another step back—he'd run out of space soon.

Eric paused, grinned.

One chance. A surge of Colin's will brought his skein leaping out from his sleeve and clamping down around his fist. Eric lunged as it settled, but Colin slammed his armored knee up—blocking out the horrified gasp from Phil—and lashed out with the still-forming gauntlet.

Strike, strike, faster, push him back from Phil and out the door to the cops—

Eric caught his balance. One thick-armored arm shrugged off a punch, and the other thrust at his chest.

Colin toppled back and scrabbled to keep his feet. Too strong, nothing he did was standing up to *that much* skein.

Something slammed into Eric's face. The tray, the plastic tray that Phil had caught up from the start, Phil swung it under Eric's hood and caught him in the jaw.

Eric swung out—

claws sprang out—

fingers tore through the blue apron—

Over in a heartbeat, and Phil dropped to the floor.

"No!" Colin flung himself in, forcing power into one strike and another with his bare hand... Eric toppled back, off balance, out the door.

Oh no you don't— Colin charged after him.

Cold night air snapped him back, made him remember. Ten, twenty yards all around he saw figures in the dimness. Ready to shoot.

"There he is!" he yelled.

The green shape was gone. Colin peered through the "wrapping" over his eyes—a halo flashed into view. Running away.

"He's still there! Your scopes, *look!"* he screamed, he waved his arm after their target.

None of them moved. Eric dashed through the night, past the ring of police, up to the tiny stall of the bus station. He leaped, and his feet thunked against its roof and flung him up higher.

"There! Shoot!"

The invisible shape hunched in midair, billowed outward. Skein stretched and spread from his back, arced out, locked in its shape and caught the air. Caught the wind.

Eric sailed away on unseen wings. Still gliding, riding the currents and angling downward as he slid away above the slope, passing over and out of the cops' view, and *none of them looked up.*

"Up there, the scopes! Come on, Hoyle—" Colin yelled it again. He charged across the pavement.

One of the cops stepped in his path. "Hold it!" The rifle wavered, then swung toward him.

"Just point the damn scope down there—"

As Colin pointed down the hill, Eric's wings folded and he dropped to the ground. A moment later he was racing away into the night, leaping with all the power in his skein.

And the cops *missed* it.

Colin spun toward the nearest sneering figure. His fingers tensed, reaching out, it'd be so easy to drag that rifle and scope around and make the cop look—

I touch that gun and they take me down in a heartbeat.

He dragged himself back, gasping for a saner breath. "He's getting away, go, go!" Useless words.

At least the police started to move. A motion, a few sharp words, and they reformed into search teams and spread out. But they moved in all directions.

One pair even headed back into the diner. "Not there, he's long gone!" Colin snapped. None of them listened, of course.

Any trace of Eric in the distance was lost by now, but the police fanned out as if he might still be crouching twenty or fifty yards away in the night.

Hoyle stepped out of the dark to snap orders. Bea moved up from the other side, silent.

Two cops came back from searching the bus station. One, a woman, muttered as she walked past Colin "We'd have got him if you stayed out of the line of fire."

"Got who?" her partner said. "Was Rowe even here?"

Then the cop at the diner door said "We got a body."

"Phil?" The man in the bus jacket's voice broke. "Phil is..."

Colin couldn't look. Not at him, or through the door. Up at the other end, Bea's gaze lingered on the ground.

But *Hoyle* was right there, and Colin stomped toward him. "You! Where were you, all of you? Just a couple of warnings and that's it, and then you start shooting?"

"This is nobody's fault," Hoyle sighed.

"No? Would it have killed you to—"

To tell all these cops what their scopes were really hunting, that their eyes were useless? And I went along with the lie—

It was too late, too late to scream about invisible men. Instead he said "Who took that first shot? Who spooked him?"

"Accidents happen." Hoyle drew his hands from his pockets and advanced to meet him. "But you! Why'd you walk right up to him? I kept buzzing you to stop."

No, no— "My phone never got a thing! Don't lie to me!"

"Don't you think," and Bea looked straight at Colin, "that it's time you stopped shouting?"

His words choked in his throat. He fumbled for the phone, the proof Hoyle was wrong.

She added "We're trying to salvage this search, and you're still in the way."

His hands fell to his sides.

"Must have died instantly," came a voice from the diner. "That's one nasty stab wound."

The bus station man shuffled back and forth at the door, head in his hands. "No no no... How'd this happen? Who did it?"

"Easy, sir," one of the cops said. "Let's step over here and you can give me your side of this..."

Another cop stepped in the doorway, blocking Colin's view. "Ask the genius 'source' here."

Someone else muttered "Or ask the lieutenant who brought him out here. He knows everything." It was only one voice in the dark, but nobody spoke up against it.

Colin stared past the cop in the doorway, at what he could see of where Phil lay. That was one more man that Eric killed, right in front of his eyes. *Could I have stopped him if I'd kept every thought on pushing him away from Phil? If I'd come alone, or taken his deal?*

The night was quieter now, only a few crisp orders from Hoyle and the crunch of feet in the dark. He wanted to sink into the ground and be gone... *Focus.* He wracked his numbed head for something he could *do,* anything to push past thoughts cf what Eric might do next and whose fault it was. Something good from tonight.

The "monster." Phil had died thinking of a skein attack, long ago.

He picked Bea out of the night, her one smaller, stiller figure managing the others in their search. The night would have been *so* different if she had just spotted Eric's invisibility in time—

He walked up to her, past the glaring cops. They had to be one twitch away from dragging him off the scene by now.

Right at Bea's ear, he said "Listen, Eric knew there'd been a 'monster' here—"

She turned away.

Bea walked away and moved off with the other cops, without a word.

He clamped down on a groan, and shoved himself away from that betrayal—slowing down would finish him. Hoyle stood at the other end of the pavement.

This time the police around his "ally" backed away as he approached. He moved in to whisper "Blame me all you want. But Eric and Phil were talking about a 'monster' here once. So there *was* a connection—"

"Could be," Hoyle said. "Any more digging you do has to be under close supervision. If I'm still on this case either," he added.

Colin winced.

"Now, I need to take your statement..." He led him away, well away from the others.

* * *

The sun was rising by the time Colin headed back. The same two cops he'd arrived with walked beside him, and he caught a couple of grunts from them about parking so far back.

Then they were driving through the dull pale morning, and what the officers muttered was a few words about the reports they had ahead. Colin hunkered down behind them, trying not to think how useless that would be when none of them knew why Eric had slipped past them all. And Colin's own report would probably be gibberish when Hoyle was done distorting it.

Then the driver's voice rose. "Here's an easy way. Just put down that our 'expert' walked right into our gunsights, and then his yelling let the suspect escape."

"The thing was all his scene anyway," the other said. "His tip dragged us all out here."

"All of us, up all night for that fiasco. And Hoyle still let him there at all. Did they even once think he could have set the whole thing up?"

"Seriously?" Colin's voice burst out and filled the car. "You really think that's what went down?"

"No." The cop at the wheel sighed. "Da Costa, I think you did what any damn civilian would back there. What I don't get is why you were on the scene, or why Hoyle sent you in closer. The lieutenant has to be too sharp for that."

The other cop added "How about why he rates all those *other* cops watching his safe house? Yeah, I'm putting this right in my report: it was Hoyle's informant, and Hoyle's call. No good hiding who let it happen."

"Hey! Some of us want to keep this job."

And Colin could only sit and listen, gut churning, not knowing who to blame first. Again and again he opened his mouth, ready to ask them to let him out and get themselves back to their regular work, but asking them for anything would only fan the flames.

So he reached the hotel and got out alone.

The early sun glared off the sign. *I'm forgetting something, something I forgot once before...* But he trudged on in, into the quiet and the empty corridors on the way up.

A rushed footstep sounded behind him.

He spun, fists rising in a tangled moment of cursing himself for letting Eric follow him *again*—but the sound was too light, the figure was Bea. Walking toward him, with her eyes not quite meeting his.

Bea. After *that?*

Icy fury clenched through his fingers. His mouth worked, but no words came that were vicious enough. Not *how'd you let that happen* or *I needed you back there* or *where's the bus to throw me under*—

She broke into a run. "Sorry, I'm so sorry—"

She reached him, and her hand clamped over his mouth.

"Sorry—" She stopped.

He couldn't move. Her hand, after the first rush to cut him off, went slack against his mouth. Her skin was cool after the long night, but he felt the palm trembling.

She stood so close. That ruff of pale hair fell a fraction out of line, as if she'd only raked it back into place after crawling around the countryside. But her *eyes... I can't move, I don't dare...*

Bea drew away. Her hand slid back, those shining blue eyes looked aside.

"Hmm—"

Her voice shook.

"Ah, I hated that out there. Every moment, every word they threw at you, and I had to pull back and let them. I *had* to. Don't you see? You have to see it, don't you?"

His face could have been on fire, where she touched it. She had pulled back first, of course she had, but *she did feel it too...*

Numbly he said "See? See what?"

"That whole operation, it looks like your fault. All they saw is your running around in there, and it tearing apart. Hoyle didn't just back off and let you take the blame—he *set you up*, so that if anything went wrong it's on you."

Hoyle... no... He shook his head and one thought fell into it. "But, it's on him too. They're not leaving him out of the blame, they're saying he's the one who brought me in at all. It's all wrong."

"I know! But, he's playing us somehow, I'm sure of it, I just don't know how yet. Please—"

Her eyes went wide. Pleading.

"Please, tell me you see it too."

This time. She didn't say those words, but they burned in her eyes, more than anything she said aloud. That and *Believe me.*

He nodded.

*   *   *

Telling Zara and Terri the basics of what had happened took the last of his strength, but sure enough seeing his own outrage reflected on their faces made it easier to bear. And he skimmed past the worst about Hoyle, to let himself settle in for some sleep.

And then there was the phone.

Hours later they heard Bea outside the suite again. The moment she'd walked in, he gave her the words he'd planned out:

"This is... awkward. When I was walking down toward Eric, I never noticed any calls from him to stop. But..."

He held up the cell. There it was on the call log, right at what had to be the time Eric had appeared: an unanswered call from Hoyle.

"I was sure I had it set up, and sure I'd notice the call. I must have been wrong."

And he moved his head in the slowest, most deliberate *shake* he could. With no sound a phone could pick up.

Bea smiled.

He set the phone on the table. The fake entry on the log meant something in it was compromised, but how much? Could someone hear them speak now, and what about him and Bea earlier?

Bea said "Hoyle's facing an inquiry this morning, about pulling in so many cops last night and still missing the killer. I need to be there."

"Of course you do," Zara said. "If they blame him for that, our safe house would be next on their list to go."

Colin added "With Eric still…" Still deadly, still close to unstoppable.

"I know." She turned back to the door. Colin followed her.

Then he stopped, reached back and grabbed up the phone. If Hoyle *was* tracking the phone, he'd expect it and Colin at the inquiry anyway—better not to give him more signs that they were onto him.

And if he was wrong, Hoyle might need him there.

* * *

The police station looked small, corridors sparsely furnished with gleaming plastic. It had been over a year since community business had brought Colin there, and now he wondered, was that style some cost-cutting plan for struggling Rayo Hill budgets?

And he and Hoyle had tied up more than a dozen police for most of the night, and done nothing but get a man killed.

Most of those cops were crowded into the corridor now. So many black uniforms, faces he'd started to know, and eyes that went cold when the few at the edge began noticing him beside Bea again.

And none of them know what they're really fighting. If I tell them now I'd look like a madman, if Hoyle hasn't cleared the way with his superiors to make them listen.

Or he could show them the skein right now, and Hoyle's secrets be damned.

He stopped short of the front desk, instead of pushing in past all those hostile cop eyes. Bea moved in alone.

They gathered up the corridor outside a single door, in one loose mass of low, tight murmurings.

The door opened and Hoyle stepped out.

"We're ready, boss," one of the cops said, loud enough for Colin to catch.

"Sorry, all of you." Hoyle raised his voice to address them all. "The whole thing's been reshuffled. They'll be calling on a few of you later, that's all, and you can get back to the job. I'll be clearing most of this up right now myself."

Voices rang out, some supporting and some angry. Hoyle moved off deeper into the building, led by a small man Colin thought he'd seen before, some kind of town aide. A couple of cops that tried to follow pulled back when they saw that man.

Too weird. Hoyle was either keeping more secrets or in real trouble... right now...

No more waiting for what Hoyle tells me.

Colin ducked down below the front desk. He had a few seconds out of view—he called the skein out and faded from sight, and left the phone on the floor.

He scrambled along the edge of the wall, just a bit of shimmer sliding over it. He swept past the muttering, scattering crowd—he caught one glimpse of Bea herding an officer away with some question— nobody looked toward him—*please let me keep it controlled now...*

Or if he did wink back into sight, he could explain the truth to all of them right there.

When the crowd fell away behind him, the corridors were almost empty except for Hoyle and his guide ahead. Twice some worker raced into view and rushed on, so hurried they were at more risk of colliding with Colin than noticing him.

The two stopped at a heavy door marked *Commissioner Walters.* The aide walked away, Hoyle stepped inside, and the door... whispered closed.

Colin eyed the door. It wasn't simply thick, he'd glimpsed some kind of foam along the frame. A sound-absorbing door, in a penny-conscious building like this?

He crouched down by the base of the door, and drew out a needle of skein. It sank slowly in through the bottom of the door, to leave a small hole in the wood. One more trick Eric had found first—*and now I'm cutting up town property. But the town owes me something, by now.*

He leaned in to listen.

"—instead you've got another dead, and no killer." The man's voice was a sneer. "You want to explain that?"

"The killer got away, sir. All I can say is, it happens." Hoyle sounded almost calm, against his boss's demands. Was he waiting to make some kind of move?

A rattle of footsteps passed by behind Colin, but then the voices came clear again:

"—borrowed those night scopes too. Now we both look like fools."

"I thought they'd make a difference. I'm afraid it wasn't enough."

"Wasn't... enough, Hoyle? You and your pet project *stripped* the streets of their protection last night, and our overtime fund too. Or maybe you think all these deaths are making Rayo a *calmer* place? What kind of sad, stupid excuse for a cop lets that happen?"

The room was silent.

Hoyle still wasn't giving them the real reason, not with a boss like that. Colin tightened his concealment and waited. He could still barge in himself and prove what they were up against.

Finally Hoyle said "I admit it, I bet everything on catching our cop-killer last night. He still slipped by us, and we're trying to work out just what happened."

"Are you? All that manpower running around the landscape, and somehow Rowe just got away?"

"There's... a lot to dig through," Hoyle said. "It was crazy that night."

"Something's crazy. Starting with the whole tip. Your 'source'?"

"We're trying to be more careful with him. Da Costa has been through a lot—"

What's that mean, that I've taken too many hits to the head? Colin gritted his teeth.

"—and he was right in the middle when we recovered his sister, and the first incident the next night."

"When your detective shot a captured suspect." The commissioner's voice grew darker yet.

"Bea Simms is a solid cop. Of course I support her."

"Support her. Interesting words, Lieutenant."

"The shooting board cleared her. She's always done good work before."

There it was again. Hoyle was defending Bea too, but with the same guarded praise that left her and Colin as the weak links...

"Oh, has she? But it'll take more than that to save your career, the way this is going."

"I know it looks bad. All I can do is my best, for as long as I can."

Colin frowned. Hoyle sounded *resigned...* he was setting both of them up to take the blame, but not defending himself instead? So what was left for him to fight for?

"All you can—"

Walters broke off. Then he started again, slower:

"I'll give you one chance. Nobody's going to say you blew this because I pushed you. You want to say there's one thing that could turn this around, that one thing you just don't have? You want to sit down with the mayor, or the state police? Convince me."

"I wish there was. This case may just be my bad luck—I'll have to ride it out."

No words that wrong should be that soft.

Bad luck? You've been telling me for days you were setting up authorization for your big plan, and you just turned the chance down? Did you ever have *a plan?*

"You know what that means, then," Walters said. "The state police will be all over this soon. And that's if I don't call them."

"You can't! They'd take forever to get up to speed. Please, just... let me run with this while I can."

Now he was nervous? Not about his plan or his career, but about staying in charge a little longer?

"More rope to hang you with, then. Unless I see results soon—"

That sounded like the start of a dismissal. Colin ducked away from the door, and watched Hoyle swing it open and walk out.

The lieutenant's face shook, with spasms of rage trying to get a grip on his features and being forced down. He stood still and heaved out one breath before he walked away.

What if... what if Hoyle was only stalling, telling his bosses anything they needed to hear, to keep the case under his own control? If he'd given up on his "plan" and that bully of a commissioner but not the real chase?

That's still too trusting, after the phone and the rest of Hoyle's tricks. But part of Colin wanted to believe it.

Hoyle drew out his phone.

Softly as he could move, Colin crept up behind him. Hoyle wasn't calling, he was sending a text—

on track, it said.

Nothing more. No answer, nothing familiar in that first glimpse of the number it went to... and fury clenched Colin's breathing, made him pull back before it went harsh and loud. Hoyle walked away.

On track? Hoyle was failing at everything, even his own career, and this was *on track* for someone?

Fists squeezed. Hoyle could have been working with Eric all along.

—Cool shadowy stealth fell away from around him, burned off by his rage. He wrenched at the skein to hide him again. Only a few faces around, nobody staring toward him...

He glided slowly for the exit, stealth steady, breath steady, feet soft and easy on the floorboards.

Still, the text only linked Hoyle with *someone.* And he'd given Colin everything to trap Eric, and to keep Terri hidden. Everything except letting the truth out, and now he was sabotaging him and Bea…

His trap let Eric get away, he has to be with him—

Steady. Slowly, fists opened, thoughts cleared.

Terri had been safe so far—Hoyle could have given her location to Eric any time. And Hoyle *was* watching everything crumble around him, would he really risk that for a deal with someone as unstable as Eric?

Or I'm just wrong.

Or Eric had some kind of hold on him.

Or… *me and Hoyle, meeting Josh Gardner. Hoyle apologizing to the old man alone. Or claiming he was, Bea would say. What* did *they talk about?*

Hoyle could be in Gardner's pocket—or under Eric's claws. Something here wasn't what he knew at all.

Step by step, he worked his way back to Bea.

CHAPTER THIRTEEN

BEHIND THE LIES

Play along with him for now. Easy for Bea to say—"playing along" for her still let her go through the police-work motions of searching for Eric. Colin had to slink back to the hotel, all too aware how little he had to chase their enemy that didn't come from Hoyle. With Hoyle's phone back in his pocket too.

On the walk inside, a cop dressed as a repairman shot him a cold look. That was the support of their protectors slipping away, or the whole police force.

Zara sat by Terri's bedside, both of them bent over her laptop. Colin gazed at them together and wondered if he could break the news to them at all.

"Found a trail." Terri made the words firm even with her weak breath.

Was I staring? Colin moved to their side. "What's that?"

"Phil Balan's father Carl."

As Zara said it, she brought up a screen of a smudgy newspaper article, from decades ago—had she been scrolling through years of simple scans that weren't even searchable?

"Phil said a 'monster' killed his father. There's only one piece on that—"

"Wait, I think I've seen those," Colin broke in.

That lie needed to be enough to lull Hoyle's suspicion, if he picked it up. Colin moved to the other room and its bathroom, and wrapped the phone up within a towel, then a second towel, then closed the door on it. If the thing was bugged, that had to be enough to screen their words out.

And here I thought I could keep the news away from my family... He headed back to the two, and squeezed himself in close between them. "What did you find?"

Zara frowned a moment, then turned back to the screen.

"This does mention an ex-employee being questioned about that attack. Howard Strickland, a laborer, miner, con man. And ages later," and she swung her hand to the keyboard with a magician's flourish and switched over to a new screen, "it was Silas Strickland that died in the Beast Killings. His son."

"So you think the Stricklands... there's that theory that Silas killed his girlfriend himself, and then died." And Eric would track that theory because— "You think he used skein he got from his father?"

"There's not much recorded. All of them were cut up, but I don't know if it was in the same way." Zara shook her head, but a sad smile tugged at her lips as she listed her findings. "What would Bea say? That Silas killed her and then someone killed him, or someone else came after them both and then stopped?"

"She'd say it's too early to make conclusions, but we should be ready for anything." That *was* what Bea would say, he knew that much.

"Whoever it was, the violence did end there. And it was the years after that, when Matt Vargas began placing skein around town."

"Skein passed from... Howard Strickland to Silas Strickland, to Matt Vargas maybe?" Colin ticked them off on his fingers. "Or there's someone else in the history, or Vargas already had his. We just know it went quiet."

Terri added "And it's about when Vargas mentioned the Gardners." She took a slow, shallow breath, and whispered out. "Then the

Gardners put up Rayo Spark buildings. Eric wanted answers there. Now Eric takes some Gardner files. You think his *first* answers about skein were from Gardner data he found at work?"

"That's one of several theories," Zara added.

"That could be it," Colin said. "You never stop surprising me..."

He let his words linger in the air for one warm moment.

Then he leaned in to Terri and waved Zara closer. He whispered "All I found out is, we've got more trouble."

"They took the case away from Hoyle?" Zara said. "But—no, it's about that phone, isn't it?"

"Yeah." Of course they noticed. "Bea always said something about Hoyle was suspicious. I should have listened. And last night, with Eric, I never got a warning from Hoyle—but the phone he gave me said I did."

"His phone," Terri said. "Easy to fake."

After all the pain Eric had caused faking messages from her...

Colin pushed on. "So today I follow him, to a meeting with his boss. He *still* doesn't tell them all what we're hunting, or defend us either. But he sent a secret text to someone: 'on track.' "

"Meaning..." Terri mused.

"Meaning I showed our secret to someone with a hidden agenda, when he and his men are the only ones hiding you here. Hoyle could hand you over to Eric any time, or just *abandon* us if his real goal is something else." His words came out ragged, hard to hold down to a whisper.

Zara's hand closed over his. "We don't know any of that yet. And Eric hasn't come after us here, so that may mean it isn't him that the lieutenant's working with."

"I thought of that too." Colin managed a grin for their matching thoughts.

It only lasted a second.

"But... Eric's winning," he sighed. "Either he does have something on Hoyle, or Hoyle's letting his own games push him out of this manhunt. Either way, that's your hiding place on the line. I don't see a way—"

"Don't."

Terri's word snapped out, more than loud enough to break through his whisper.

"Don't think about letting Eric go. He has to pay for this." Her eyes glared, the only part of her that hadn't shrunken.

"Thanks."

He sighed, and the fury eased from her face.

"But…" It wasn't enough, he still had to ask: "You ever wish you could take his offer, and get his help to get you back on your feet? Of course my skein is yours if we ever finish this, but I'm sure he knows more about how to—"

"Don't."

He dipped his head in a promise.

As he did, something flickered on Zara's face.

"Okay," he said. "We'll find a way."

"From who Hoyle texted?" Terri said. "Or, how you and Bea tracked Eric before? Or the history?"

He chuckled. Terri didn't miss a thing.

Zara stood up. There *was* something in her eyes, as she turned away from Terri…

"I bet we do get him," he said.

Zara walked away to the other room. Colin moved after her, and he saw her step falter as his footsteps drew near.

She stopped in the other room, and turned to face him.

"You can start with—" She halted, and stepped in close to whisper "You're thinking we might be bugged, aren't you? But, you can start with the Gardners. Since the Vargas trail leads through them, their lawyers are still defending Eric, Lieutenant Hoyle wanted to meet them…"

"I think so. But, are you…"

She glanced away, then turned back, *forced* her gaze back to meet his and hold it.

"I never put it together," she said. "Terri's bills were lining up... she must suspect that, and it's eating at her. But she honestly is growing weaker too..."

"Zara?"

Her eyes never wavered. "There *is* no money for what Terri needs. I've looked at savings, friends, training in nursing, everywhere. There was nothing. Except Josh Gardner was... 'concerned.' "

"Wait, *Gardner?*" The word came out louder than he meant.

"He's been talking about paying for Terri. It could have been a fair compromise for us both, if it kept us from suing them about Eric keeping her on their property. But Gardner is the *only one* who'll help.

"And all of this leads through his people... it's only a matter of time before we start seeing strings on his help... I can't see how we can get out of this..."

Her voice faded.

Colin reached an arm around her and drew her in.

He'd thought he could let her lean against him until she steadied. But instead he felt her holding him up, and his own body trembling and shaking until it passed.

*   *   *

Zara went to sit with Terri again, no doubt telling her the news she'd been holding back. Colin stood beside the window, cracking the curtain back just enough to watch a sliver of the streets rolling by.

All that space where their enemy could be, but it always came back to Terri and how trapped she was... and now Hoyle had the key to her safety, and Josh Gardner to her health. Hoyle still *seemed* like he wasn't with Eric, but then Gardner had his marks all over this... and he *could* have some tie to Eric. And if his hooks were in Hoyle too...

Colin stared harder at the street. Looking at those same two shabby shops out there didn't hide how cars still glided by from all over Rayo

Hill. There was a whole town, and all the land around it, and he might have to find an invisible man in it without Hoyle's help.

I barely came to the main town before this, this isn't the Hillside where we know each other. And Eric could be anywhere out there.

Too late now, Eric had said when the police closed in. What that meant, what that left Eric with doing now, Colin's mind couldn't even guess at.

He slumped against the curtain.

I wanted to stop him. I said I'd do anything so nobody else died— and in twenty-four hours I found Joe Martin and then Phil Balan, more of Eric's victims.

When I was alone I thought I could run Eric down myself. Now that I've got the police with me, just the thought of losing them makes it clear how foolish that was.

He clenched a fist, tighter, tighter. He'd just push on to the next step—if he *had* a next step right now.

But then there'd be another step, one more place to try, forever chasing after Eric and watching Terri wither away and Zara crumble…

A glint in the glass caught his eye. A tiny strip of view where he peeked out, but that torn texture should never be someone's face.

The scars never bothered Bea.

The thought flashed out of nowhere.

Bea, standing close, the sheer pain in her eyes when she thought she'd driven him away. Her hand over his mouth, lingering.

Alone? No, it felt like I could do anything when she was with me.

He closed his eyes, just to let that warmth fill him.

And here he was, standing alone in a room instead of telling her…

Tell her? She already knew.

He shook his head, felt a bitter laugh trying to work its way up his throat. Of course, Bea always knew how outmatched the whole fight was, and what adding any more emotions to it would do. If she felt any of this, she'd never admit it.

Or if he had her wrong, she'd still say the same thing.

The laugh spilled out.

* * *

Ten minutes later came her call.

"How soon can you be ready?"

"Any time…" *What else, what else can I say next?*

Bea hung up.

Colin looked at the phone in his hand. The thing *could* be a threat, but leaving it locked away would only put Hoyle on alert. Either way, having to watch their words around it put his teeth on edge.

He worked the skein under his shirt: out over his hand, back under the cuff, out to encase his fist. His control seemed firmer than ever, so far. Ready, then hidden again, faster…

"Ready?" Bea swung the door open.

He stepped toward her, faster than he meant to—

Hoyle stood behind her.

Colin froze. *It's got to be all over my face—no, Hoyle did partly blame me for Eric's escape, I'm allowed to be hostile—*

"Still in charge of the case?" he tried, and his voice came out cold.

"So far."

Hoyle's hands were in his pockets again. Just like a man with secrets.

"We have to hope you can keep control of it," Zara said. "But if something does change, do you know what that might mean? How committed would other police be to keeping us safe?"

Not one quaver in her voice. She could have been asking a plain question, to an honest ally.

"I'm sure you'll be looked after. Though… I can't promise any replacement of mine would make the same effort to keep you hidden away."

"But," added Bea, "having this many 'disguised' guards here risks the secret leaking out anyway. I'm sorry to worry you, but your best defense was always our catching Eric first."

Hoyle said "If you're asking if you need to make your own plans, you might. Rowe talks about using skein to heal you," and he turned to Terri. "You think that's possible?"

Terri said "Sure it's not that simple."

"Then we've got work to do. And I promise, we'll do everything we can to finish this."

Hoyle's smile, his reassuring nod, were all too smooth for a man who had to be lying about something. Colin followed him and Bea out.

In the corridor, Hoyle said "Don't you make me regret letting you try this. Any progress at all and you call me, ASAP."

"Understood," Bea said.

And then they were moving, Hoyle leaving them while Bea and Colin headed out together. Down to her car, and away.

Colin let himself breathe, to just be sheltered from the world in Bea's trim black car again. His head shifted between watching her at the wheel and eyeing the road. There had to be a right way to ease into… into something they could talk about. And Hoyle's phone was still in his pocket, giving the lie to their "time alone."

Finally he thought of his skein, and tried "Can we stop for some food?"

"About what I was thinking."

There it is, when we're just in sync—

She went on "It might make a difference in the search, it might not. That's what I hear. I've never looked for missing homeless before."

Oh, she meant for this search. "Homeless? No surprise there—" he tried to cover with, then he heard the insult he'd said and tried to walk it back. "I mean, the police aren't known for putting the homeless high on their list. If you're looking into one of them missing, you must be sure it's Eric…" He was still babbling, trying to bend himself toward an apology.

"Oh? Tell me, what do you think is going on here?"

"I don't know. I guess this just isn't your responsibility or anything you've trained for. And Rayo Hill just has too many people pushed out, after the quake and everything. Zara's tried to help them, but it's never easy—"

Too many people. His brain finally caught up past his embarrassment. His stomach clenched.

"So many people out there," he breathed. "Untraceable. That's what Eric sees—whole sets of people he can just scoop up for more skein. Easy pickings."

"Yes." Bea's voice was tight and cold, like fingers on a weapon. "It's the last thing we need. Before, he seemed to focus on Joe Martin because he worried about sending the wrong message, or Jessie Chapman to get information. This could mean he's given up on all that, and he'll go after the surest route to all the power he could want. It's what I've been afraid he'd start, ever since we learned how the skein grows."

"I guess you would." How long had she been living with that fear, knowing the fight could go that bad, that easily?

"I had to get involved. We've just got one report, but I have to assume the worst."

"And Hoyle has to let you, he knows the danger too." Right, the lieutenant couldn't just admit he wanted to leave Eric loose… if it was Eric he was scheming with, none of that was clear…

So now this is about how badly *an ally's betrayed us, and how to work behind his back.* The more he thought about that, the more he felt the ground shifting under him. And Hoyle's phone didn't even let him say it aloud.

* * *

Thirty minutes and one snack stop later, Bea looked at the street ahead. "The tents are gone alright."

"Tents?" It could have been a typical back street, but with several times the carpet of trash over the pavement.

"Normally there are a few homeless tents here," she said. "And they picked today to pack them up."

"They might not have gone far. We've got enough actual houses empty, I sometimes wonder why they'd use tents at all. Unless it's to give them a bit of community."

"But now something's changed."

"Try up to the left. Back in the residential blocks."

She swung the car up the street, working their way through the blocks. Colin studied the dirty, beaten-down houses along the sides, looking for signs of anyone squatting there. His fingers tightened on the bag of jerky he'd grabbed, and still felt too guilty to open.

"Two houses back," Bea said. "Someone moved there."

He stole a glance back—if someone was inside *that* battered place with the sagging boards, they had to be hiding from something. Or too poor to afford a few nails.

They pulled over at the end of the block.

Colin tucked the food in his coat and left Hoyle's phone on the seat as they climbed out. Then he waved Bea over, pointed back down at the cell, and leaned in close to whisper "Is *yours* safe?"

She didn't answer.

She only stood there, *inches from him* where he'd leaned in without thinking. Her mouth hung partly open—

"Safe," and she pulled back. Faster than she had to, he thought.

They marched up the street to the ruined house… really just the worst of several on this block. One window in the front was simply broken—not so different from where Eric had kept Terri once.

Bea knocked on the front door. "Hello? Rayo Hill Police, and I've heard you might be in danger—"

She broke off there, in time for them to catch the sound of running feet.

Colin bolted for the back. A bit of skein power around his legs—

The power wavered, he stumbled forward against a toppled trash can. He gasped a breath and flung himself on with his own strength. *Maybe I do need that snack.*

The back door swung open.

Colin lunged in front of it. A tiny man, ragged clothes, ragged beard, pulled up short in the doorway.

Something *squealed.* A white rat—cleaner than the hands that held it—jerked free and skittered back into the house. The squatter whirled after it.

Colin's hand caught his shoulder.

The little man squirmed, reaching after his rat. "Vinnie! You come back!"

"Your pet's fine," Colin said. "You're the one someone's after."

He let him go, and the squatter stumbled away a step. "What? Me?"

"Anyone on the street—or sheltering from it," and Colin waved to the house. "There was a tent group a few blocks away."

"Tents?"

Then he blinked and stared harder.

"You're… Colin, from the Vargas House? How'd you get…"

His eyes locked on the scars over Colin's face. His hand went to his own, undamaged, cheek, and *sympathy* welled in those eyes.

Colin swallowed. "Long story… Wesley, was that it?"

The little man nodded.

"Listen: do you know why those tents are gone? Has anyone heard about… people running scared, or gone missing? Or scars like this?"

Wesley shook his head.

"Nothing I heard. You should ask at the—" He stopped.

"Yeah. At the Vargas House," Colin sighed. It *would* have been the best place to put the word out, if it were still in place.

"Man, I'm sorry. You were good people. Always had something for us, always asking us what we could do to give back too. These days, even the other places are drying up."

Without Zara to pull them together. That couldn't be the whole reason, but it stung at him anyway.

"Maybe this'll help." Colin pulled out the bag of jerky.

As Wesley reached for it, a slow footstep echoed in the house behind them. Bea walked forward with the white rat in her hands.

The next moment the rat squeaked again, and flattened back against Bea's shirt.

It's me. The rat's afraid of my skein, the same as that police dog was when Jessie vanished.

Colin pulled back a step, and tossed the food to Wesley. Another step back, and another.

Wesley squinted at him—what *could* anyone make of a reaction like that? Then he moved over to take his rat from Bea, and back away.

"The tents, yeah," he said. "Haven't talked to anyone from there, but they liked that spot. Maybe something did scare them."

"Thanks. And..."

Colin forced a smile.

"And keep Vinnie with you. If someone else spooks him like I do, run."

* * *

"So yes, I think he's started."

Bea looked straight at Hoyle. The street corner where he'd met them was quiet, but she didn't let his secrecy slow her down.

She went on "That tent community seems to be scattered, and the nearest shelter gave us the same sense as that witness. If Rowe is picking off the homeless, this is exactly how it would look."

"If." Hoyle closed his eyes, and his features twitched as ideas whirled behind them. "This is still rumors and guesswork."

"I know it's all too likely. This is *exactly* why we have to get him, at any cost. Because he can simply *buy* his way to more power, in *bodies.*" She stepped toward Hoyle as she spoke.

Colin struggled to keep a grin off his face. Bea was using the clear-eyed truth of the case to force Hoyle to listen, and her conviction vibrated in the air.

Hoyle snapped "Don't lecture me. If you're right… where do we look?" He waved up the street, at the several blocks and many empty houses just in view there. "Or we warn his targets? There's no proof, and these people don't trust us anyway."

These people, he calls them? Colin thought. *And that's why they don't trust him.*

"So if Rowe's doing this," Hoyle finished, "it's because we can't find him. He could be taking them anywhere."

"You could start with the Gardners' properties," and Colin moved in on Hoyle beside Bea. She was right, they could use the obvious to *make* him act. "Eric already used one to keep Terri. The Gardners have a whole network of spots from abandoned to half-rebuilt—a fugitive's paradise. Start there."

"Start with everything that Gardner Development worked on? They already think we could be wrong about Rowe. I can ask for a search warrant, but that's a big list—hard to get, hard to search through, easy to hide something on."

Hoyle looked down at the pavement.

"We may have to bring Rowe to us. Moving your sister would draw him out."

"My sister as *bait?*" Each word crackled, ready to explode. "My paralyzed, shattered *sister* as *bait?*"

"I didn't say that. Or there's the pattern Rowe showed last night. He's got an interest in places the skein has been seen before."

"I… guess." Colin forced his fists to unclench, to make his thoughts move on. Eric did take Jessie to where he could search for signs of the Beast Killings…

Hold on, did Hoyle just bring up Terri to distract *me? When I mentioned the Gardners?*

Bea's head dipped downward—stealing a look at her hand, and the phone she concealed in it.

"What's that?" Hoyle snapped.

Bea held the phone up, with a faint grin. "A text from Dennis Fields. He wants to meet us about Gardner."

Hoyle flinched, just the smallest motion. Of course he couldn't play that clue down after demanding to see it.

And yet, he'd *wanted* to play it down…

Colin kept his mouth closed. Everything had a lie behind it now—watching these two cops circling each other was like dancing with two mismatched mirrors.

* * *

Fields walked across the parking lot to the three of them, shooting nervous glances around at the few cars that drove by.

"I've just got a few minutes," he said. Worry was stamped on his face, deeper than ever.

"You could have called," Bea said.

He looked away. "Of course. I just… sometimes I think something might be bugged. Panicky, but there it is."

Bugs… Colin kept his eyes locked on Fields, where Hoyle couldn't see his suspicion.

"It depends. Any particular reason you think of that?" she said.

"No. Just—"

Fields stopped, let a car drive out past them. When he started again, his voice was a tight whisper.

"Eric's crazy. He's already killed a teammate of ours, you saw that, I have to believe that was him. But, I keep wondering if the company's really cut ties with him. Not just the lawyers defending their technicalities, I mean… Eric has to be hiding somewhere, and getting food and all. Someone helping him here could explain all that."

"It would," Hoyle said. "If there was a motive to side with a murderer. Like the detective said, is there any evidence?"

No, she asked for suspicions, and Hoyle just raised the bar beyond that.

Fields leaned closer. "No. It's something different. Before all this hit the fan, Eric asked for a meeting with Mr. Gardner. I just heard that now…"

He hesitated. Hoyle only waited, eyeing him until he went on.

"And… you called it before," and Fields nodded to Colin. "This was after the old man took some unexpected time away. You thought it might be about his health?"

"Why is that important?" Hoyle said.

"I don't know! Please don't tell me Eric's keeping him poisoned him to get his protection. That's just too much. And, what gossip I can get is that he's had problems for years."

Josh Gardner, sick. Eric meeting with him. Colin opened his mouth, but Hoyle was already speaking:

"Listen carefully, Mr. Fields. We've been interested in any other properties of yours that Rowe could be using."

"Like for your sister, Colin?" Fields glanced over at him. "I'm so sorry he was able to use us for that."

"What you have to deal with now," Hcyle snapped, dragging that gaze back to himself, "is that all your suspicions are either right or they're wrong.

"And if they're wrong, you can go on with your life and laugh about this someday. If they're right, you still go on with your life, and you keep your head down. Don't go looking for other signs about this—after you send us that list of properties, that is. And you can send that straight to me."

He reached into his coat and handed Fields a phone, that could have been a twin to the one he gave Colin.

"That should be secure. And if you do stumble over anything else, send that to me too. I'm the one in charge of this investigation, and that makes me the one who can send you protection if you need it. If the worst happens, you may not have time to go through anyone else."

In other words, Fields should keep his eyes closed, but make sure that anything he did find only went to Hoyle himself... Did the lieutenant really think they hadn't noticed by now?

"If you say so." Fields pocketed the phone. "I'll send you what I can. And, thanks."

He scurried away. And Colin had to let him go, with Hoyle's eyes right on them all.

"Now," Hoyle told them, "that won't come through for a while. And we need to get to the truth of this history trail Rowe has been on. Ms. da Costa has her books and everything set up. So none of us are leaving there until we get some answers."

"None of us?" Bea said. "There are more abductions out there, you know there are. You ought to be running—"

"You heard me. This is still the best lead we've got, unless something on that Gardner list jumps out at us. I can send a few cars out anyway."

Bea opened her mouth.

"Did you hear me, Simms?"

"Understood."

They turned back to their cars, and Colin could *feel* Hoyle's eyes on them now, herding them along.

He tried to think. Hoyle had always taken charge, but never like this. *Research, about the skein... he wants that, right now? I could still just walk away and hunt Eric on my own, but* where?

Hoyle's phone chimed.

He glanced at it and shot a text back.

Then he scowled. "Be right back," and he stepped away, up the lot, and out of sight behind a parked SUV.

Colin glanced at Bea. She *nodded.*

He crouched down behind the nearest car. In the quiet parking lot, a moment's cover was all he needed—the skein flowed out and settled its invisibility around him. This time it had to hold.

The hard pavement rang under his feet and echoed in the closed space. He edged toward Hoyle's spot—he could just make out the lieutenant speaking now.

"I understand that... yes sir, the media always wants it solved yesterday... no, I didn't mean..."

The steel in Hoyle's voice was gone. Now he only listened and deflected and tried to apologize.

Colin peeped around the SUV to look.

The man's face was *twisted,* struggling against spasms of pure rage. Somehow that clenched throat and flared mouth managed to keep the apologies in the same mild tone:

"Just one more lead... yes, I'll be at the station soon..."

Not his secret partner. Hoyle was talking to his official boss—more like getting another earful from him. The kind of pressure that could push a man to sell out...

Hoyle turned. He looked right at Colin.

My invisibility. It's flickering again.

Colin couldn't move. Hoyle knew, he had to know everything— and those eyes wavered like their shame, their rage, could stab right through anyone who'd seen him...

Hoyle shook himself.

And he said "So paranoid? That's a sad thing to watch. I said we're going to find answers in those records, *now.* "

The words were a promise, but the tone felt more like a threat. Colin could only pull the skein in and walk with him, on to Bea and the road back.

CHAPTER FOURTEEN

ON THE TABLE

A "maintenance man" in the hotel corridor gave them a look, a cop's look checking with his superior, as Hoyle marched Colin and Bea in. One way or another, all of this came down to his control.

The moment Hoyle shut the suite door behind them, he scooped up a chair and thumped it down beside Zara, at Terri's bedside. Colin saw his hands trembling as he moved.

But he pushed right on. "Alright, no more holding back."

"Holding back?" Zara's face was the picture of innocent offense. "Lieutenant?"

"You've been locked up with these books for days. Right now, all of us are going to put together everything we know about what Rowe is up to. Right now."

Colin glanced over at Bea, standing silent. *All the pieces... if only it were that simple, if only they knew where Hoyle himself stood.*

"Why are you here?" Terri asked. "Not out tracking Eric?"

"You're going to help us get the jump on him."

Hoyle turned, to look right at Colin.

"First thing: *you* said Rowe was abducting people to use their bodies. Then you said he picked them to make a statement about the town, or pick Jessie Chapman's brain. Which is it?"

Zara said "Are you implying something? There's nobody, nobody, that Eric has hurt more than this family. Please don't start hinting we're doing anything less than our best to stop him."

"Right." Colin met Hoyle's gaze. Whatever else was going on, he had to hope the cop cared about the victims. "I think Eric's targeting both ways. Look, Joe Martin and Jessie were both on the verge of leaving Rayo Hill—we can't ignore that. And the way Eric talks about the town, we have to look at that as him making sure Terri won't say *he's* scaring people away. Crazy as it sounds."

Then he leaned in to stare at Hoyle's hard, narrowed eyes.

"But there's the other reason we need to stop him. We have to. Because no matter who he'd prefer to grab, anyone can give him more skein and make him unstoppable."

"He's *already* unstoppable," Hoyle sighed. "We're still only guessing SWAT rifles can hurt him, with all the armor he's got now. And last night he skipped right out of your trap like it was nothing."

That was your *trap. You set it up, you let your men sit out there and never told them to watch their scopes while Eric flew right over them...* Colin choked down the surge of outrage.

"Then we'll make the next trap a better one," Zara said.

She looked at Colin, at Bea, and he knew she was weighing a decision.

Then she stood up, and slid a small table over beside her and the bedside. A stack of their journals and her laptop lay on it, and she opened the first book.

"Eric seems to be following the skein's history," she said. "Consider *where* he held Jessie, and where he brought Colin to talk about his deal. If you really think he wanted to talk," she asked Colin.

"He... seemed like he could have." *And I didn't. If I'd come alone, would Phil still be alive?*

Zara swung her computer around to Hoyle. "Look. Here's the one thing we've found on Phil Balan's father's death: Howard Strickland was a suspect. The father of Silas Strickland, who died in the Beast Killings."

"I—"

Hoyle caught himself. As if he'd been about to say *I know*.

Instead he said "Alright, what does that connection mean?"

"Phil Balan compared the skein to the 'monster' that killed his father. Wouldn't the simplest answer be that Howard Strickland did that, and years later his son and that same skein caused the more infamous deaths?"

"It's possible…"

"Sounds like Eric thought so," Terri added.

Zara and her stack of records were drawing Hoyle in, Colin realized. Impressing him, pulling him closer, and also keeping him near Terri to remember Eric's victims.

Bea nudged Colin.

He glanced over. She angled her phone toward him, showing a text she'd gotten—in enlarged, slow-scrolling type for him to make out:

Another homeless man missing. His friend swears he "vanished" in seconds. Like you said Chapman did.

So Eric was raiding the streets. Bea had been certain from the start, and her instincts were right on the money.

"And Rowe's retracing the skein's history?" Hoyle leaned in at Zara's shoulder. "Why? You say he's busy making more of it, but he's looking for something else too? How much more power could he *want?*"

Another text flowed across Bea's screen:

If this is like finding Terri da Costa, keep her brother out. Lawyers are sniffing around.

"What've you got there?"

Hoyle was staring straight at the two of them. Colin fought to keep from flinching away—

"They just confirmed," Bea said calmly, "that Eric has been taking more homeless."

Hoyle grabbed out his own phone and scrolled through it.

When he looked up, Colin said "Look, Zara can keep digging, but we need to get out there. You do know the cops can't even *see* Eric, right? Think about it: you're a police officer, and you know people are being attacked. And instead you want us to stay here. We *have* to get moving!"

But Hoyle's commissioner had been ordering him in too, on that call in the parking lot… for him to stay here, he had to be *desperate* to crack the case, or for something else…

Hoyle shut his eyes, and something wavered across his face.

Then he looked up. "We're finding what Rowe's really after, right here. Where he'd go, what he wants, maybe what else he needs to make more skein. We've got to."

He turned back to the books on Zara's table.

Colin hoped he'd kept his face still. They already knew the spell, everything Eric needed to create skein—and the way Hoyle acted, he was glad they'd kept that last secret hidden.

Terri spoke up, from behind Zara and the books. "This is all we have on its history. The Moon View attack was long before Matt Vargas and his hints—"

She drew in a slow breath. When she went on, her voice was weaker:

"Then he makes one mention of seeing the Gardners, during the Beast Killings. No more notes on that."

"None?" Hoyle said. "You're the historians here."

"Show him…"

Terri stopped, her eyes half-closed where she lay. What was it costing her, to impress Hoyle—or distract him, which was it?

Zara flipped a book open for Hoyle, and leaned in to feel Terri's forehead and her pulse. The way she moved, she looked calmer than Colin felt.

Hoyle turned from the book to his phone again. He tapped a quick message, and Colin saw a badge icon on the screen—at least he was still keeping an eye on the search.

Then Zara leaned back to her chair, and Hoyle pocketed the phone and pushed the book away. "Just one reference. That's nothing."

Zara tapped her finger in the book. "One reference of Vargas's to the Gardners, and another to Rayo Spark, during the Beast Killings— that's where the trails cross. The Gardners, where Eric worked. Eric, who knows the skein's secrets better than any of us. This trail leads from Vargas to the Gardners to Eric, and today Eric stole files from the Gardners too. Or stole more files to complete what he already had."

"It... seems like something." Hoyle said it slowly, almost afraid to say it aloud. "Rayo Spark."

"A redevelopment push, that sprang up after the Beast Killings. It tried to cover that history up. I think that's what Gardner Development has done."

Terri's whisper slid in. "But... how far back?" She leaned out from the pillow. "The Gardners, old family. They go back to selling supplies to the first mining camp... until the fire, from the lightning strike that gave Rayo Hill its name."

"The lightning?" The words slipped out of Colin's mouth, just on their own.

"What? You think the *hilltop's* part of it?" Something flared in Hoyle's eyes.

What had they just given away? They still didn't know whose side Hoyle was on anymore.

Hoyle glanced at his phone again. Only looked, not sending anything...

Finally he said "The Gardners, covering this up? You think that's it?"

"It appears that they did it after the Killings," Zara said. "It could be much wider than that."

As she spoke, Bea edged in behind her, standing ahead of Colin. Something moved behind Bea's back—her phone. Showing him one more text:

The brass is shutting down the hunt for the homeless. And pushing again about you shooting Rowe, and being close to da Costa. Watch your back.

"Rowe stole files from the Gardners," Hoyle was saying, "but their lawyers still protect him. Is that still a cover-up?"

The police, letting Eric's raids on the homeless go… a cover-up…

Terri whispered "The Gardners knew something. Eric had to learn the word *skein* from somewhere…"

Her eyes closed.

Colin twisted around to watch as Zara leaned in to examine her again. Terri looked more pale than ever, and she was barely moving. She couldn't have simply worn herself out, not her…

Zara drew back. Worry lay across her face.

"I called Nurse Setter half an hour ago," she said. "I hope it's nothing more."

Colin let out a breath—or tried, his chest felt too tight.

Hoyle glanced between Zara and Terri, back and forth.

Then he said "Rowe thinks he can heal her. And he keeps trying to make more skein. You think he *could* patch her up?"

Hoyle asked that once before, Colin realized.

"Terri turned him down. Hard." Zara patted her daughter's hand.

Hoyle leaned closer, past the books, to Zara and Terri. Something urgent stirred in his voice. "But *do* you think it's *possible?*"

"Eric had years with her to try," Colin growled. "If that was healing and not just keeping her as a pet. But… he only had so much skein then," he had to add.

"And now he has more? Something changed?" Hoyle's eyes bored into him.

Colin locked his face still, anything to keep the thought off of it: *yes, we let him see the spell for making skein, we know we did.*

Then Bea's voice came from his side, calm and drawing Hoyle's gaze away. "Something must have. Eric started collecting the skein Vargas hid, you know that—that's when we both got involved, when his plan escalated. And he's been gathering information too. Especially from Gardner."

She leaned down, over where Hoyle sat at the table of books.

"You know it all leads through the Gardners. Maybe they're tied in with Rowe beyond simply arguing with the judges. Or they could just be sitting on answers—Rowe thought they had something worth stealing. And Eric Rowe has killed police, and he's *still* grabbing homeless people to feed his power."

Her voice swelled, one small fraction as the words came faster, tighter. Her face flushed. She looked unstoppable.

"And now you're letting someone shut us down about those, because it's street people? Or are you waiting for him to target someone else again? You know our best lead is Gardner Development. Tell me, Lieutenant: *do you have orders for me?*"

"It's... not so simple." Hoyle turned away from her gaze. "It's a whole career... and there's no good way to tell them how deadly this gets..."

Except I heard your boss offer you that chance. But then your career seems like it's already crumbling, and all you've got is your secret partner. And us. Hoyle shook where he sat, staring at the window...

The door rattled open. Nurse Setter walked in.

"Is our patient alright?" She spoke so softly she only rippled the stillness that had settled.

"Okay," Terri's whisper answered.

"L-let me decide that." She walked briskly over to the open side of the bed, slid off her coat, and opened her bag.

Blood pressure tests, then studying Terri's eyes and mouth, testing her slow-moving fingers... Colin looked away, at Hoyle sitting quiet and glancing at his phone. Weighing whatever he saw there against Bea's fiery sweep through the facts.

But Colin's eyes kept turning back to Terri, and Zara's haunted look where she sat opposite the nurse. Any moment, any moment, that woman in white could say one word that changed Terri from an exhausted fighter to the doomed girl that Eric said she was. *And then I'd wish I'd dropped everything and let Eric heal her.*

It hung over him like a rain-soaked coat, that cold certainty of what he would have done.

Then the nurse looked up. "She needs rest. And… the animal that attacked me, he was really after her?"

"Yes." Colin heard a world of frustration in his word.

She looked at the floor. "I'd like to do a few more simple tests here, to track how her system reacts." Her voice came colder now. "Just to be sure."

Terri breathed "We were talking…"

"We can take that up later." A smile wavered on Zara's face.

Hoyle added "We could use a break." He scooped up two books and pulled back to the corner of the room, tinkering with his phone again.

Colin puffed out a breath and stalked to the opposite side. His legs ached to move, to pace up and down in this cage or break out and run. Hoyle was right there, Colin could scream at him to go after the Gardners or the missing homeless.

And Terri… she seemed okay, and he'd do anything to just get out and *do* something again.

Bea pulled out her phone.

Hoyle looked up at the motion, but she brought the cell up to her ear instead of taking some discreet text.

Her eyes went wide.

She tapped the phone onto speaker, and the voice of Dennis Fields whispered through the room.

"—trapped, trapped in the server room, I think it's Eric outside."

The nurse croaked "What—"

"Shhh!" Zara cut in.

"Listen to me." Bea's voice steadied like a lifeline. "Can you stay out of sight?"

"I'm trying!" Fear shook in his words. "I found the lock cut... now someone's here..."

"Can you get to somewhere public?"

"Not if he saw me... I have to hide."

"We're on our way."

Her words broke the spell and freed Colin to move for the door— but Bea herself stood in the way, waiting, glaring a question at Hoyle. *She can't, she* can't *let him stop us now—*

"Go," Hoyle said. "Just—when you get there and it's already over, try not to burn the place down until we have a case."

Tell that to Eric, Colin heard in his head, but he held the words in and followed Bea to the door.

"Here!"

Zara's voice cut through the room, and a paper bag arched through the air into his hands.

It had to be food, fuel for the skein, she must have kept it stocked up... He took one instant to look gratitude back at her and Terri.

Then the door swung open and the two of them raced away.

*   *   *

Bea kept the siren screaming as she drove. Colin fumbled with her phone, watching for any words or text from Fields, but there was nothing. With his other hand he used skein claws to split open the two oranges in Zara's bag, and slurp down every juicy, tangy piece inside. The nutrients might not reach his skein in time to matter, but at least he *felt* stronger.

They had to be in time. To get to Fields, Eric, traces of it, something. He drew his skein out into its "hoodie jogging suit," that would be seconds away from giving him full protection.

Bea pulled up in front of the Gardner building.

"Squad cars should be here already," she muttered. There were no black and whites in sight.

She led the way inside, weaving between the few murmuring figures in the lobby.

Then she thrust her badge at the receptionist behind his counter. "Where's the server room?"

"I… we don't have one anymore…" The man's hand was reaching for a button on the counter.

"Look at me!" Bea snapped, and the hand froze. "Now think. Where would a server room be?"

"Maybe… something still in the basement…"

A tall man in security blue strode up. "Is there a problem?"

"An emergency." Bea moved in with her badge held up, to softly say "You. You're going to take me to the server room, or the basement spot where it used to be. Now."

"Wait, wait, don't you need a warrant—"

Something in the guard's voice, the way he glanced around as if he was trapped between Bea and something else, put Colin on alert. This guard wasn't hesitating, he was *blocking* them, on someone's orders… *Fields can't still be trapped down there, but if…*

Colin dashed back up the lobby.

The guard called "Hey, where are—" but Colin was already dodging between the couple of people there, until he reached a corner behind the layered "model neighborhood" display case the Gardners had set out. He crouched down behind it, out of people's view.

A moment was enough, no matter how they had to explain it afterward. Skein closed over his hands, shoes, head, and he faded from sight.

Then he ran back inside. Twisting steps, light as he could to slide around people, fast as he could to get clear and leave them wondering what shimmer might have swung past them. Bea was still arguing with the guard.

He padded alongside the wall, to the door to the stairway. He yanked it open, and caught one surprised "Who—" behind him before he darted down for the basement.

The footsteps echoed along the stairwell, and he caught at the railing and forced himself to slow. If Fields and Eric *were* somehow still there, if this was more than covering up a crime scene, making noise now could shatter that last hope.

He could hold his feet back, but not his pounding heartbeat.

The "basement" looked like a run of half-empty corridors, jumbled with tables and supplies and shapes lined up along the walls, all blurred in the low light. Half of Gardner's history could be down here, from days when they did more than buy and sell properties through others. Colin crept down them, studying the doors.

The AC coolness seemed to thicken as he neared the second door—then he saw the precise sheer mark through its lock. Just as Fields had said.

Colin put his ear to the door. If Eric was in there, he was silent.

He pushed it open.

This had to be wrong. The room was another *storage* space, with bulky shapes stacked against the walls or left in piles near them... still, that rack along the back could have been computers once.

He stepped softly inside.

That step brought one outline into view, slumping half over a table in the dimness. Those uneven, bunched-up lines used to be a man.

Dennis Fields lay there where he must have fallen. Eyes staring blindly, darkness spattering the objects around, sharp with the smell of blood.

No...

One more, murdered...

Colin snatched his hand back where it had been reaching toward the body. Thoughts jolted awake again—he swept a look around, for halos or just figures lurking in the clutter.

No Eric.

No sound, except the distant hum of air conditioners.

Nothing more, nothing standing out...

One shape glinted in the dimness. A bit of pale plastic, tucked against the dark column of computers; Fields had called this the *server room.* And his phone stood propped up against one of the machines.

Colin reached toward it. There were other oddities about that one machine in the stack, more cables on it and some metal-housed device at its back. But the phone's camera... was recording.

He halted it, set the video to replay.

Dennis Fields's face loomed on the screen, quavering in fear while his hands stretched past the picture's edges to set the phone in place. Then he crouched down, back behind the table, out of view. The camera's angle caught the front of the room, but just missed the door.

So it was only after a few steps into the room that Josh Gardner came into view.

The old man had his own phone at his ear. He swept a glare around the room, and growled "Enough! What are you playing at in my basement?"

Then his eyes went wide. Even through the camera's angle, and with the phone covering part of his face, he looked *eager.*

"Now? It's ready? Yes, yes, of course I can get to the hilltop."

He pocketed the phone and walked out. The room went still.

Still, until Fields raised his head into the frame. Peering up from behind the same table where...

Colin watched the image move, in the motionless room where the man was about to be... *don't you move, stay down!* he wanted to scream, but all that shape could do was step into its destiny.

Dennis Fields looked around—

The sharp metal cough of a suppressed gunshot sounded. Fields dropped. He fell below the screen, only an arm and a glimpse of his head left held in view by the table, like some abandoned doll.

Then, stillness. Nothing but that one view left stuck on that figure, and footsteps fading outside, until even those were gone. The frozen image hung in place, uncaring.

Eric... wasn't even here? Josh Gardner *was, and* he *must have killed him?*

But it had to be Eric that cut the door open earlier, that called Gardner away. To the "hilltop"—and Rayo Hill only had one of those worth the name. To something so urgent he'd shoot a man to get there...

Outside the motionless screen, footsteps clattered up.

The door opened. Guards in blue stared, stared at him in that frozen moment—

"He's dead!"

"The same masked bastard—"

The moment shattered. The two guards grabbed for their batons, and Colin ducked behind a crate near the wall and wrenched up the invisibility he'd *let drop.*

One guard moved slowly into the room, the other recoiled and stared... then Colin slipped past the first and darted by the second into the corridor.

The guards were here alone, came the thought that stirred awake. Then where was Bea—

Another set of guards tromped into view, with Bea in their midst.

"Murder!"

"Where'd he go?"

Colin flattened himself between two boxes along the wall as they rushed by. He watched Bea pass and struggled to think, *can I go visible and walk up to her or not...* but there were too many guards, and Gardner was *getting away.*

Bea stopped in the room's doorway and looked back around.

As if she knew he'd be there. He blinked into sight just long enough to beckon to her.

She bellowed into the room "Nobody touch a thing!"

"But you—"

"Nobody!" And she stepped back from the crime scene, out toward where she'd glimpsed him. She stopped right in front of where he stood.

"Gardner shot him!" he whispered. "And then he got called 'to the hilltop.' "

Back in the room someone said "He had a mask. All shiny green, like—"

"Go!" Bea hissed, and she held out her keys.

He grabbed them, and handed her Fields's cell. She took it easily— *oh, I left it outside my skein and "floating in midair," anyone could have seen it!*

"Watch yourself," he said. As if that could ever be enough.

He tucked the keys away and slipped up the stairs.

Up, one quick, shaking step at a time. Silently on past the faces along the entrance, still unseen.

On outside.

Finally he slid into Bea's car and pulled the mask back to let himself reappear. His hands fumbled to start the engine, his foot to nudge him out into the street at some safe, steady pace.

Dennis Fields was really dead. Bea was alone with the crime scene and the Gardner security—*please let her be alright. They already saw me walk in half-covered in skein, like the shape they saw at the...*

Murder. And Gardner's eager voice.

Those clawed at him, pulled him up through the late-afternoon streets up the hill.

"The hilltop" could only be one place. Terri had said the Gardners began by selling to the original Rayo Hill miners—and the hill crest itself where the mining camp fire had been, it fit too well. It fit for Eric too, if he was tracing their history. He might even have his prisoners there too, like he kept Jessie.

There had to be something up there. Colin's fingers clenched on the wheel. At least Bea had the phone, and solid evidence about the real killer.

A squad car stood beside the road ahead. Two cops were out talking to a woman in street-tattered clothes and a street-gaunt face.

Colin slid the car up beside them and lowered the far window to call out "Officers!"

"What's the problem, sir?"

"Just listen. I'm working with Detective Simms, you can check that." He held up his phone ready to call her. "Let me guess, you're looking into any more missing homeless?"

The nearer cop's eyes narrowed, interested. "We were. What's this about?"

"How many missing—no, hold on. We need your help."

"We?"

The other cop cut in "Just a minute." And she waved her partner back from the curb.

The two of them leaned in together and muttered. Crackles came from their radios, low-tuned fragments of words and police codes... Every second they delayed deepened the chill rising through him.

"Can you step out of the car, sir?" the woman said.

"Please. She told me to go, just check with her—" *Why can't I stop rambling—*

"Please, step out here." She moved closer, and her partner was walking toward the front of the car.

"Just call Detective Simms!" He was shouting now. "Call Lieutenant Hoyle! I'm not the problem here."

"Please, just get out of—"

She reached the window.

Colin grabbed for the window switch. He fumbled, trying to find it on an unfamiliar car—no time. He yanked at the gearshift and lurched the car back from between the cops.

Another twist swung the wheels over, ready to pull away—

One word came through the open window, "homicide"—

He roared into the street, rattled by the engine roar and the thought of *oh god oh god they saw my skein suit, they do think I killed Fields...*

The car whined and skidded between what cars were on the street. A blue light flashed behind him in the mirror.

Bea could clear this up. Or she was in trouble too—*why'd I ever leave her back there?*

Josh Gardner still had to be up ahead.

He shoved the pedal down and raced on. Around one car, past another, but the squad car was gaining. Every twist of steering and brakes and acceleration squirmed against his control, too new to his touch. Like the car needed Bea back too.

The police drew closer in the mirror, smooth and unhurried, too good at the chase.

He willed the skein out over his hands again, and slipped his phone away under it. *How'd it all go* this *bad, this fast...* He squealed to a stop.

Mask over the head. Shimmer from sight. Yank the door open and leap out.

The police were still slowing down behind him, and he dashed away up the sidewalk. What people were out—on this quiet Hillside neighborhood—gawked at the motionless car. The police closed in around it.

Colin jogged on. Skein pistoned around his legs and let him almost *ride* it as it did the work. The cool shroud of invisibility hung around him, with his focus clenched around not letting that slip again.

Half the Hillside must already be behind him. He weaved around a few people on the sidewalk, slowing only to watch for cars as he darted across streets. A siren screamed past him once, but he held the stealth in place. And block by block, the Hillside homes fell away at his rear.

Just think of what's up ahead. The original mining site, lost in the Rayo Hill fire. That had been Terri's insight... and Bea's help had gotten him this far... to chase down Eric's and Gardner's kills, one step at a time...

Another police car roared past him—up the rough old track. So they'd search for him all the way into the wilds?

Reddish boulders and mounds loomed around him, twisting the gravel road between them. This was the last stretch, too rough to settle, where the miners had led their mules between the first buildings below and the camps above. Dust stung at his nose. Another turn or two and he'd get a view of the highest hill where the camp had been.

A police car stood beside the trail.

Colin swung in among the rocks, sideways and away from them. No need for skein to carry his weight now that he was close, so he crept along with his own strength and kept his attention on stealth. He weaved his way through the thinnest patches of scrub where their rustling would be softest. Little slopes and ridges of rock kept his feet alert.

When at last he came in sight of the hill's crest, more police stood silhouetted at the top. Waiting.

Or were they hunting Gardner too? Had *Bea* sent them?

He crouched lower and crept up the rise toward them. Two cops stood around, watching for something. They could be talking, if he could get closer...

His foot skidded on rock. One cop looked up at the sound, started toward him, peering around.

Colin drew back, keeping low. He was just a haze of afternoon light, nothing to see... he pulled back below the hill's rim.

The footsteps above drew closer. Following up *one* scraping sound on rock in the open air.

Soft as he could move, Colin slipped around behind a rusty outcropping—let them look down and try to spot the glimmer of the one hand or leg that it didn't totally block.

Those police were waiting. Waiting, ready for someone as stealthy as him. *But only Bea knew I was up here. How'd it go this wrong? What happened to her?*

He dug out his phone. *Please, let these be Bea's reinforcements...*

"You see da Costa?"

"Shhh."

A shape moved above the edge of the crest. A police rifle, heavy with an infrared scope.

As it began searching, Colin had one moment to dive away down the rock, phone still in his hand. *Hoyle's phone, it's the only thing that shows it's me here and not Eric, and those are Hoyle's guns. He was never on our side.*

CHAPTER FIFTEEN

COVERED UP

He scrabbled away down slopes and over rocks with all the speed he had… each scrape of his foot had to carry in the air, each puff of dust he kicked up was a marker that could draw the cops' eyes.

Still, no shots came, and the silhouettes on that hilltop stayed in place. *I shook their gaze off… or they're not leaving their post.*

Because of Lieutenant Hoyle? Was that what his secret text and all his tricks and his rigged phone really lead to?

Colin ducked down behind a clump of boulders. The skein on his fingertips stretched out into claw-slivers as sharp as his rage, and he twisted the phone's stubborn casing open and yanked out its battery and its card. Just one squeeze of his grip would shatter them… but he pocketed them instead.

The crest had other, steeper ways up. Colin worked his way sideways over rocks and scrub for long minutes, and started up the slope.

The skein clamped his fingers tight on the rocks. But ten feet up that grip began shaking and it grew harder and harder to rouse the skein's strength to pull him along.

Wonderful. He dug his fingers in and hauled with his own muscle. *Save what power it's got left for stealth and for when I reach them.* At least it should still protect him, but not against those rifles.

He dragged himself up by his feet and hands. The slope began to round off to its top, enough to see the cops along the summit. Still standing around, watching, talking too low to hear. No sign of Eric or Gardner, or even Hoyle up there, but there were a total of four officers...

A shriek split the air.

The sound was agony, *urgent* agony to get that pain out—a moment later something choked it off.

The cops' quick footsteps pattered in its absence. They stared *around,* finally looking away down the far bank where it had come.

"Hell no! Come on!" and one tall cop started toward it, rifle ready.

"Hold on—"

A radio squawked.

"Sir?"

The first cop stared at his radio. Then he and another cop tromped forward, and took up places above that side of the hill. They simply watched the hill below...

Colin's fingers trembled on the rock. What kind of people's protector could *ever* leave a sound like that alone?

The far side of the summit. The mine entrance—it would be wide open along the slope, and right in those two sentries' sights.

Colin stared at them, just standing there around the summit. *So I run to them, I* beg *them to look past the lies and just answer that call...* Everything in him ached to charge out and pull it all together.

Except he'd seen how well they listened to reason now.

Another cop looked around in his direction, and began lifting the scoped rifle. Colin had to clamber back out of sight, down the side.

No help. No strength. And one sound had escaped from what had to be Eric slowly melting his homeless prisoners into skein—*and I can't stop him.*

I should have taken Eric's deal. Help Terri, maybe get Eric away from killing people... would he even listen now?

Somehow he made it back down the slope, and stumbled behind a clump of brush thick enough to screen him from those scopes.

Eric was winning. No, he and Gardner and Hoyle were winning.

Hoyle. Back with Zara and Terri.

With shaking fingers he fitted the phone together. He was reaching to call Zara before he remembered Hoyle might be right in the room. A simple text was all he could risk: *u okay?*

Seconds, ages, pulsed by on that damn silent screen.

At last an answering line popped up: *Sure. Is Eric coming after us?*

Of course she'd think of that. *Don't know. But*

—he froze. This was still Hoyle's phone...

He tried: *be careful. You two alone?*

And she answered *Lt. Hoyle's still here. You be safe too.*

His fingertip trembled. Just a few words, they were just a few lines and a screen away, but he couldn't even warn his family. One hint, one sign, might tip Hoyle off. He dragged his hand back from the phone and clamped it over his mouth.

No way to warn them, or help the prisoners, or...

His fingers darted down in a sad joke: *Wish we'd taken Eric's deal now?*

It was one blind grab for reassurance, one piece still untouched by just whether they could make a move.

She answered: *I'd ask Terri. But she's still asleep.*

Colin groaned.

Finally the stillness and separation were too much. He sent: *Gotta go.*

Her answer was: *Alright. Bye.*

He managed to pull the phone apart again without snapping it. And no police had stormed down to chase him—maybe they weren't watching for every blip of use Hoyle's phone got.

On shuffling feet he started around toward the mine's side of the hill. At least it was closer than heading all the way back to town—and trying to guard his family as Terri only grew weaker. The mine was near, but the slope was just too wide open to get past the cops above. A third cop sat outside the entrance, with his rifle's scope right up against his eye.

If he could just slip by… maybe some kind of decoy, maybe the phone, and then he could at least try to get to Eric…

An engine hummed in the open air.

Slowly a jeep crested the trail and made for the cops' position at the top—with four more police on it, and more rifles. Another of the cops on the hill was already climbing down toward the guard at the mine. And another car was moving, somewhere in the hills.

Colin slumped, slammed a fist against rock. *Does Hoyle have the whole police force out just to stop me?*

They'd heard the scream—they *had* to want to check, he could still come beg them to do their jobs.

His eyes locked on the entrance. Still far away, but he could lunge for it, try to slip past them and their scopes.

Feet gathered under him. Just one run, either get past them or tell them the truth, anything to get inside… face the bullets, or bring Eric back to Terri, anything to just let him *move*…

Footsteps scraped on rock behind him.

He twisted away to the side. *No, why now?* His flailing will tightened around the stealth shield as he dodged away, away from where the cop must have seen him.

A chunk of reddish rock waited ahead, and he dove behind it, out of their sight.

Footsteps moved in the scrub. Still coming toward him.

He gathered himself. He'd try to slip away again—no, that cop could have a rifle scope on him, all he could do was bolt and dodge… *please, something has to work*…

"Colin?"

Bea's voice.

The rush of relief left him shaking, barely strong enough to look around the rock and savor the sight of her.

She strode toward him, brushing her wisp of seeing-skein from her eyes. The motion looked almost like wiping away tears—but he was the one staring, fighting for words, tumbling with thoughts of *how did you* or *are you alright.*

He shut his mouth. None of that mattered, when she was *here.*

"What's the situation?"

Simple Bea words... but she'd lost seconds staring at him too, hadn't she?

"Screaming." The first word helped him focus. "One scream, from down in the main mine shaft. But the cops out there are still just guarding its entrance, on someone's orders, and they've got their IR rifles out. It has to be Hoyle in charge, I guess working with Gardner and Eric to cover their 'meeting.' "

"I see." She sighed. "I saw a car on the roadside—Gardner could be already in there. But Hoyle too... I knew it was complicated. And you simply had to be seen standing by a body, after you walked in wearing a skein 'hoodie,' didn't you?"

"Hoyle set us up—yes, you were right all along," he added. "How'd you get out of there?"

"Self-control. I *didn't* punch the people who said you were a killer. Or a boyfriend."

Her slight grin turned to a grimace at the last one. Even in the thick of this.

Then she said "If Hoyle's in on it, are Zara and Terri alright?"

"So far. I sent them a quick text before I disabled Hoyle's phone. But I couldn't *warn* them, that's the hell of it."

Bea nodded. Then a smile slowly spread over her face.

"We can do more than that," she said. "Hoyle may have made his last mistake. First of all, I know he can't trace this phone," and she dug out her own cell.

She brought up a text screen, and Colin stepped in beside her and watched her send to Zara: *Can you chat now?*

Time crawled by. Zara could be busy... no, taking this long had to mean Hoyle was watching, or worse...

Then: *Yes. If you're quick.*

Bea's fingers flew over the screen. *Hoyle's in on it. He just stationed six cops to guard the middle of nowhere, and made them ignore a scream for help.*

She paused, glanced at Colin—to check the facts, he realized. He nodded, and she followed with:

That's on top of how he's holding you there. He's sticking his neck way out. You think enough of your friends could make Commis. Walters listen, NOW?

All of Zara's contacts turned loose on Hoyle… Colin felt a grin spreading on his face.

But, the sun was already lower in the sky—how was Zara going to contact anyone at this hour? Right under Hoyle's nose?

Zara's answer came: *I'll try.*

The words glared at him. If "try" was the most confidence Zara could raise, she had to be feeling the weight of all this too.

Bea ended it with *Thanks.*

Then she looked up at him. Standing there bent over the same small screen, so close.

He heard himself saying "Did I mention how glad I am to have you here?"

She froze.

He tried to think, tried to laugh it away—

"Better if you didn't," she said. But he saw it, that crack of a smile at the corner of her mouth.

"So you… you just gave Zara her way out, and blew the lid off of Hoyle. Maybe. If she can sneak messages out in time." If anyone could squirm out of Hoyle's grip.

"It's your family at risk," she said. "I commandeered a car to get here. You could drive it straight back to them."

"I…" *Trust Zara, dammit.* "There's no time. There were *screams* here—Eric could be killing his prisoners, and every minute gets him even more skein."

"In the mine, you said. Are they watching all the mine shafts?"

"Don't you know——"

Colin caught himself. Not everyone grew up in Rayo Hill, or in a historian's house.

"There were different shafts around here, when different miners scrabbled around after the silver rumors. All of the mines would be separate, and they all gave up except one. And that shut down anyway, after the lightning and the wildfire that wiped out the mining camp up there—or that could just be an early skein attack, for all we know."

He shook his head.

"Look, I heard the scream from the main shaft, and that's what they're guarding. I still don't get how cops could just sit outside when they hear that."

"Not all of them would." Bea frowned. "Hoyle has his cronies, and if he's dirty they could be too. I just have to get through to the ones that aren't. Or distract them and let you get by."

She turned toward the hill.

He caught at her arm. "Distract them? How is that safe?"

"Safe?" Those blue eyes met his. "I'm a cop, and someone's being killed by inches—I *need* to be up there. And I've got a few ideas. Are you sure *you* want to risk yourself?"

Colin could only grin back.

They worked their way around the slope, swinging wide along the rocks to approach from the far side of the mine. Colin stayed well ahead, blurred from sight and watching for sentries above and the next ridge or boulder that could work as cover. Bea darted from one spot to the next behind him, never losing sight of his shimmer.

Partway up, they reached a black gap in the hillside—another mine opening, sealed off by two boulders and a rusty iron grid. Colin glared at it, wishing separate shafts like this could work as a back way in. He glanced up to study the slope above.

Bea moved up beside him. "You never did answer me. *Are* you sure you want the risk?"

"Sure, I..."

Anything's better than sitting here with my strength fading—no, that sounds all wrong. But with the conspiracy all around them, and Terri slipping away and...

A scream burst free, ripping across the countryside and whispering in the shaft and then gone, gone, choked off by what had to be some brutal hand—

"You get it now?" he said.

"You'll need this." And she passed over her flashlight.

Of course she had it ready.

That does it. We get out of this and I'm sitting Bea down and talking out everything she knows about planning and preparation. And everything else between us.

Bea headed up the slope with new urgency, ahead of him, crouching between rocks and brush but climbing faster, making him wince with every low scrape of her shoes.

He edged along behind her. She had a plan, she had a plan...

Then she neared the top, and leaned out around one boulder and whispered "Evans!"

Colin lay flat, just a shimmer of light on rock, and crawled to peep over the crest.

A cop, young, pale, moved slowly toward Bea. Most of the others had shifted toward the far side, toward the mine below, and "Evans" didn't make a sound. Instead he edged toward her and where the jeep sat, until it screened him from the other cops' eyes. His rifle lay still in his hands.

"Simms? You're here?" Evans murmured.

Colin grinned. Like she said, what mattered was finding the cop who'd listen.

"Was that a scream?" she said. "And you're just *sitting* here?"

"They said it's under control." Evans strolled toward her, five steps away, four. "Looking for something down there. I think they've got da Costa trapped."

"Da Costa?" It could have been just any name, the way she said it.

"For the murders. And holding his sister, and the rest. And *you've* been—" He raised the rifle toward her.

Bea's wrist twisted. A spray of dirt flew at the cop's eyes, he yelped, and Bea lunged in past his weapon—a quick punch, a twist, and Evans slammed to the ground.

"The hell—"

Uniforms all around the hilltop spun toward her. Three, four cops, most of them with rifles—

She dove into the jeep. It roared to life and she raced it away, *down* the hill, away down what had to be the shallowest side of it but still one jolt away from breaking her neck—

he heard the engine falter, then rumble again—

Cops stared, dashed after her.

Colin charged along the crest, invisible, eager, watching them all move from their posts.

But half of them rushed *away,* down the slope toward the mine. Bea had only drawn a few of them off.

That left nothing but... but moving fast, trying to take them all out before they could turn and focus on a barely-visible enemy—and all the bullets and broken cop bones that could risk...

Or...

The sound.

He'd heard it, one whisper during the second scream, one whisper coming *through*...

Colin spun and leaped into space.

Skein strength flung him out over the drop he'd climbed. He arced down, down, as the rock rushed up. *I'm worried about bullets and I jump off a cliff—I'm crazier than Bea—*

Feet crashed down and kicked him forward, tumbling, spinning the world into dizzy madness. He slapped a hand out, then another.

And slowed, steadied, clattered to a stop—and not even an ache in him. The skein's protective magic even soaked up momentum, enough to handle a dozen scattered impacts and leave him untouched inside it.

The other mine shaft lay right above him.

He rushed to it and thrust out claws.

The skein moved stiffly on his fingertips, resisting his command. He forced the talons into shape and sawed their tips at the rusty bars over the shaft.

Some of the scream had echoed through here, so it must connect to the main shaft after all—all those stories of miners digging separately had to be wrong. It *had* to be, and the skein had to work.

The last bar gave way. He squirmed over the boulders and on in.

The ceiling loomed low and forced him down to a crouch… and some bump in the floor caught his foot. He fell, and bounced to his feet without feeling one scrape.

He dug out Bea's light. Darkness pooled ahead of him, with the little flashlight only *thinning* it enough to see the tight walls, barely a door's width between them, but that was enough. One branch swung away right, another moved left. He headed up that way with the easy jog of a body that rock couldn't bruise.

The ceiling was still low. The walls were straight, ragged-scraped stone, that looked all the rougher in the faint light and through the skein across his eyes. The air was *clear,* or at least what musty, earthy smell it had was drier and thinner than all the other weighed-upon senses here.

The tunnel's end formed out of the darkness. One half-hewn face of rock, and this path simply stopped.

Wrong way. Colin spun around with a chuckle. He must have cleared this in under a minute, easy.

Shots burst outside. Sharp, vicious rhythms, hunting their prey.

Bea.

He dashed forward, slipped, skidded up from the ground and raced on. Please, please…

The light from the entrance broke off, as Bea slid inside.

Someone laughed weakly, and Colin realized it was him. He walked up and waved her toward the second tunnel. Her features twisted a moment; was that embarrassment?

Hoyle's men could be right behind her. Colin jogged up the path, but he felt his heartbeat already settling back toward normal. She was safe.

He glanced back. Bea was only picking her way along, without skein padding or even the light—*I forgot those.*

He handed the flashlight back to her. "What happened out there?"

"Those were warning shots. I think," she added. "What are you doing in here?"

"The scream. I heard it come out through here, so I'm following it."

"You would." Something tinged her voice—was that annoyance or affection? Her face was a blur of shadows above the light.

Colin moved on again. Slowly at first, then faster, pushed on by Bea's light behind him no matter how its bobbing shadows left him stumbling.

Something moved among those echoes. No voices, but those sounds could be Hoyle's men moving in... or just their own feet. At least he saw no lights at their back.

The shaft narrowed. A sheet of paler, rougher rock lay ahead with only a ragged slit hacked through it—but the way still had to lead on to that scream. Bea's light showed it widening out into shadow, some eight, ten feet beyond.

"I can slip through," he said. "You could be safe back here if they don't catch you with me—"

"You're joking, right?"

He turned sideways and squeezed in.

The rock caught at his shoulders, more harmless scrapes and pressures that the skein let him slide through. One step, two—

A bit of rock caught at his ribs and wedged him to a stop.

What were these miners, men tinier than Eric was under his skein? Colin slid back a step and twisted a hand up to feel around the wall. That projection had to be right about... fingers closed over a rough knob, and he forced the skein out into claws that cut it loose and let him inch by.

Then the tunnel relaxed to its old, four-foot width. He stepped clear, and Bea slid neatly through—easy for her size.

This isn't so bad. Colin heaved a sigh and moved on. They had to be most of the way to where those screams were by now. Or at least nearing the main mine shaft at the front of the hill... if this tunnel even led toward it. In this dim world, they could be all turned around.

They crept on, just dim light and the scratch of their feet in the silence. No sounds behind them; maybe the police couldn't hear them at all, or they'd given up.

Eric had to be close. Colin's fist squeezed—just getting through that tight spot, his skein had struggled to form claws, and he'd had no *strength,* but he'd still crashed down a cliffside unhurt. Eric had so much more power... but they had the spell, and Bea to use it... He glanced back at her face. There was no fear there.

Ahead, the tunnel broke into an opening. The stone formed some kind of wider space, with a shallow grade up and down on both sides and a great jumble of rough-looking rocks below. A shadowy spot at the far end marked where the narrow mine shaft continued.

Cavers must have a name for this kind of basin, whatever it was.

He glanced along the side, back at Bea. Then he set out on a path upward and along it, where the smoothest stretch looped across at some fifteen feet above those rocks.

The sideways slope made him edge along with one knee bent and one foot higher than the other, picking his way by Bea's light with her behind him.

Eric *had* to be near. Those screams were real. Eric could have brought his victims here, and called Gardner up to see it. It had a certain logic... his memory fumbled at the history as his feet worked over the ground. All the mines above the town site that had never really paid out, and the merchants and rumors that had exploited them. *I can believe people like the Gardners robbed them, maybe even burned the last mining camp and blamed it on lightning to hide that there was never anything here...*

Halfway across. He looked back at Bea.

A rock broke away under her foot. It clattered down the side, and more rocks came loose around it.

She was tensing to leap clear of the crumbling. He scrabbled backward to give her room, waved her up—

Under his leap, the ground turned.

He tried to stagger clear, glimpsed the shadows of pebbles and head-sized rocks and larger shapes cascading loose—the rockfall spreading all along the slope and upward, the whole place thundering down...

To drag us down, trample us the whole way down. Across is too far—

His shout vanished in the earth's roar. He stepped over and slid down the side, waving Bea after him as he stumbled down. And she *followed,* she moved her poor fragile body down in a climb and a headlong run.

The motion gathered—some wave of darkness sliding behind the single light, and crashing against his ears. But he reached the bottom and she dropped into his arms and he dragged them down to throw his armored body over hers as the world rumbled down on them.

Again, again again again... a stream of blows that dazed and rattled off of him—he locked his eyes shut and flung all his focus into keeping his skein tough. Some other world somewhere was all deafening noise, where this was endless battering motion.

Reach my arms a little wider, screen off more space from the vulnerable flesh below... no, hold her tighter, can't leave any gaps...

But the landslide only crashed down harder, harder, *please just stop, why'd I ever let Bea into here... just let the armor hold...*

Far, far away, the sound petered out to some lingering clatters. The impacts were

gone

and left him gasping and pinned under so, so many weights.

His eyes opened to leave the same blackness lying around him. Dust choked his breathing.

Under him in the dark, Bea's body lay still.

No no no, how can she be hurt, the landslide never touched her— how would I know—

He flailed in the dark, shrugging and rolling and flinging rocks away. His arms ached to hurl them so they shattered against the sides, but his nerves shivered every time a toss roused more rumblings and crashings, and he thrashed and flailed with the skein for the strength to pull free.

Light glimmered. Somewhere in his struggles he'd uncovered her flashlight below him, and it still shone.

And Bea stared up at him.

Her eyes focused. Her face moved. That was dust darkening her cheeks, not blood. She was awake, alive, stirring to life, and looking up at him.

He couldn't move.

She was *there,* right there, such a small gap between their faces... *it should be gone...*

And there was no gap.

The kiss was soft, gentle, afraid to disturb a thing. Only the miracle of those lips, warm and giving and real. Alive, together.

Heat swelled in his face, pounding, roaring inside him, *but I can't ever move...*

Breathing forced them apart in the end. He pulled back, feeling dust still clogging the air. He should be coughing, but his mouth felt as if no dirt could ever touch it again. And the skein—he didn't even remember willing the skein back away from his face, but he knew he had.

They clambered to their feet, rocks clattering aside.

"Come... on," Bea gasped.

Of course she would. Even in that husky, shaken voice, she'd be the first to push them along.

He swayed for his balance, where the light touched the rocks.

Green glinted under them.

"Wha—"

Peeping between the rocks, between a space he must have started clearing away, he picked out the hints of a shape.

Long, lean, from the glimpses that showed through the rubble. A sinewy form that was no mammal. Bones, thin dry bones of wings peeping through patches where the skein over them was gone.

He whispered,

"Not 'skein'... it's *skin*. Dragonskin."

CHAPTER SIXTEEN

ALL MINE

Colin stared, up and down the tumble of rocks, for more glimpses of the silvery green that would mark the size of the remains. Would there be footprints burned into the rock floor, like the ones covered up in the Cherry Street park?

It had to be. It all came from here.

"Is that... skein?" Bea said.

"Of course. Think of it—they took it from here. Matt Vargas used dragon paintings to mark his own work, but he never made a trail back to here. To the mine where they find all this. If it was ever a mine at all."

And once they dug this up, a century and a half of hiding... Hiding the hide... A chuckle slid from his mouth and grew. *I have to say that when I tell Zara...*

"Then this is what Eric was searching for," Bea said. "And if he's up in that tunnel, that rockslide finished any chance of surprising him."

"Oh. Oh God!"

He grabbed at a chunk of rock and shoved it over the nearest exposed patch. Then another, more.

"We have to hide it," he panted. "If he finds out it's down here, if *anyone* ever guesses—"

He stopped.

"I... I mean, we have to," he said. "We have to beat him without this, or else he finds out about it and we get carnage worse than anything we've seen." *This is how Bea always was, about keeping it all secret.* "But, we *could* try to use it..."

"Just come on. Before he finds us here." Bea turned toward the far tunnel, and began picking her way over the rubble.

Then she stopped, and reached down between several heaped-up stones. When she drew it back, "skein" clumped around her fingers and slid back at her command to form a glove.

"Eric won't notice this much more. And to you, I'm sorry." She bowed her head to the buried creature, and softly laid a rock over the opening she'd used. Onto its cairn.

Uneasy footing clattered with every step, a nightmare of slow, loud movement when they hoped to cut Eric off. But the end of the basin and the climb to the opposite tunnel were close enough now.

Colin led the way in through it again, fast as he could march through the narrow shaft. He'd have to catch Eric first, take the attack on his skein, let Bea grab him and use the spell—it was their only chance against him, but it always had been. *Don't think about that skein burning her hand when she does.*

The close-set walls flung his footsteps out ahead of him, for what that mattered. As long as he slowed down enough to have some of Bea's light...

A gap opened on the tunnel's side, another tunnel branching back. He froze; this was no time to stalk Eric all through some miner's maze.

Another light glimmered against the rock ahead.

Alright then. Colin advanced, slower now. He kept an eye on the branch behind him for any tricks—until Bea's light winked out, and he could pick his way forward and watch her silhouette behind him just by the faint glow from up ahead.

Now.

He crept forward, by touch and the growing light in the tunnel ahead. Another branch passed behind him, he rounded a turn—

Eric loomed out of the dimness. A haloed shape like some huge, startled ghost.

The moment broke. Colin charged, slammed into Eric with one fist and a shoulder and he felt a surge of strength from his skein sweep them up and bulldoze Eric back. They swept down the tunnel with Eric grinding along the wall as hard as he could force him.

Eric wrenched away, sent him stumbling clear.

A wider space stretched around them—maybe room for one miner to pass another—with the lamps he'd followed making it almost clear. And on the ground...

Bodies. No, living prisoners, chained and gagged and squirming in pain. One almost at Colin's feet was half *covered* in skein and still stirring, with the face of a woman just visible above, lost in her own world of suffering. Then another woman, skein wrapped over her throat. And Wesley, with his own patch of the hungry stuff. All in the battered clothes of Eric's homeless prisoners. His skein's *food*.

Josh Gardner stood back behind the farthest one, Wesley, staring at their clash.

Colin wrenched his gaze away and flung all his outrage into a punch. But the skein went slack, and simple arm muscle only rocked Eric back a step.

Eric's fist swept around.

The blow lifted Colin up—crashed, slid, against something behind him, unhurt but head spinning—

He ducked away from the wall, as a punch burst into it and sent rock dust flying.

At Colin's back, a figure crept forward in the dimness. Bea, almost in reach for the spell.

Colin charged. *Strike fast, twist, anything to get him off balance.* Eric blocked and drew back, and his glove stretched into a foot-long piercing claw.

The thrust blurred in. Colin twisted, felt something tear.

Eric hopped back a step and watched, and Colin clutched at the slash along his arm. Sure, the best thing to force through skein's protection was more skein power, and Eric was bloated with that.

But Bea could—

"Stop there!"

The dry *command* in that voice yanked his gaze away from Eric, on to Gardner standing there with a pistol, pointing the useless silencer-tipped shape at him and all his armor.

No, past him. At Bea.

Colin froze. His heart hammered.

Bea raised her hands. She slowly crouched down and laid her gun on the tunnel floor. Something had to be wrong with the light, how could she look so calm when she should be furious at being their weak link?

Gardner said "You actually made it inside." The old man's smug tone set his teeth on edge.

He flung back "Of course we did! You're snatching people off the street, *torturing* them for…"

Words choked, and he could only wave at the chained figures lying along the tunnel.

Gardner's gun twitched—gesturing with its silencer end at Bea, warning her in place. And Colin's gesture had inched him to the side and nearer to shielding her. He held still.

Eric shook his masked head. "Always the same thing. You two getting in my way."

"No…"

Colin swallowed, gulped down the bile he could shout at them, and looked at the prisoners again. Their gags must have slipped before to let them scream, but now they couldn't even do that.

He'd have to speak. Anything, that would save them, and Bea.

He forced out "You don't need them. You want to heal Terri, so let's just do it. Stop this—" he waved at the victims again— "and I'll take you to her. Use your skein, mine… I *need* you to show us how to make her better. Think, you can walk away from all of this, and finally save her."

"Oh, now you make that offer?" Eric leveled a finger at him. "Now that you need to save yourselves?"

Ourselves? Is he blind? "Will you *listen* to me? You always say you're fighting for Terri—but this destruction is just what she hates. What's your plan, keep killing until the sheer number of bodies makes her forgive you?" He waved at the nearest, most-consumed prisoner beside him.

Bea's feet shifted at his rear.

"I said stop there, both of you," Gardner snapped.

Eric pulled back, back another step from them. "More tricks."

"I'm giving you a chance to stop this!" Colin threw the words against the threat to Bea, but the plea kept building on its own. "I'm trying to save you from… yourself, I guess. Are you still the man trying to save my sister, or just a rabid dog? Is there really someone you hate more than you want to help her—is it these people? The town? Me?"

"You think you've got it all figured out." Eric's face had to be a smug grin under that mask.

Bea added "Or are you still in charge, Eric? It's your skein, your secrets, all of it. But *could* you stop this if you wanted?"

Gardner's chuckle was a soft and controlled sound. "You seem to think Eric and I have some disagreement in this. We don't—I'll be glad to help Terri, as soon as we have enough skein to do the job."

His eyes flicked in the lamplight. One glance at Wesley at his feet and then back up to watch them.

There's a whole dragon of skein buried back there!

For one instant those words bubbled behind Colin's lips, anything to interrupt the horrors here. Instead he focused on Eric. "I can *take you* to Terri, right now—oh."

The thought crashed through him.

"You already knew where Terri is, because Gardner has Hoyle in his pocket. How long have you known?"

Gardner smiled. "I think I've been a useful ally."

"So you've been helping Eric hide…"

Colin broke off, as the rest of it tumbled into place in his head. How long *had* Gardner known, and had he told Eric at all? Eric had still tried to bargain with them, he'd said they were running out of time to save Terri before "worse things" happened, and now—

A moan, a ragged, gag-choked moan, came from the woman on the ground ahead.

The sound tugged at his feet. Colin found himself beside her.

"Don't you move—" Gardner said, but Bea was already in motion. Her quick footstep settled into place behind him.

Gardner fired.

Don't move, don't move…

Colin held his place and stared down *the gun,* when the gunshot had kicked against his chest and cracked away along the tunnel wall. The echoing whoosh of air from the "silencer" faded. But the skein had stopped the bullet, kept it clear of Bea.

He heard her kneel down by the prisoner behind him. He squatted to match that motion and keep her sheltered.

Gardner stepped back and forth, trying to angle the gun around him. "Stop her! We need these tests, you know we do!"

A gasp of pain, from Bea. A throttled cry from the other woman.

Eric didn't move. "You can't fix her anyway. Even if you removed the skein, by now the bleeding would kill her."

"Like when you tore it off of Terri?" Colin snarled. *"Do* you care about her at all, or are you just another bully?"

Eric's stare slammed against him, even covered by the skein mask.

Bea sucked in a breath, and her footsteps stumbled backward.

The victim's groans faded to a whimper.

"That's what this woman needed." Bea croaked the words as if she'd been screaming herself. "Once the skein stops feeding, it's a perfect bandage."

Gardner peered at them, gun drooping in his hand, forgotten. Because they'd just *shown* him, one more way that skein could be controlled with a touch and enough focus. They'd saved a life, but...

Bea's voice was calm, measured. "It's the medical uses you're after, isn't it, Gardner? You're sick, and you'll take any risk for a chance at a treatment—even bribing cops, or kidnapping. You must be desperate."

" 'Desperate' is for a man without hope," Gardner smiled. "I seem to be getting everything I need."

"You mean you're *taking* everything." Her voice tightened as outrage slipped in. "All these people, and Eric's other crimes, just so you can live."

"Easy words, for someone young and healthy." Gardner brought the gun up again.

"How long has it been?" Colin burst out, anything to hold his attention. "How long have the Gardners been keeping an eye on the skein? Your family knew what was behind the Beast Killings, so you tried to wipe out our memory by erasing that neighborhood?"

Gardner frowned at him.

He's curious. He wants to know what I know—fine, anything to stall and let another opening happen—

"Did Matt Vargas work with you people about those, until something went bad between you? I bet he got Silas Strickland's skein, and some of Vargas's notes ended up with you."

He motioned to Gardner.

"And then Eric—" he swung his hand back to the killer— "guessed you had those when he worked for you, and he took those. But you never let him have them all did you? He still had to steal the rest from his... *useful ally,* you said?" He tried to laugh, but all he made was a mocking snort.

Gardner eyed him. "And you think the family has spent ages trying to control this power?"

"Not *control.* The rest of you covered it up, every time. You never used it, the Gardners saw how dangerous it is. Because of the temptation to start *that!"* He glared at the two figures ahead of him, still quivering in muffled pain. "But you, you don't care, do you?"

"Cover it up?"

And Josh Gardner did laugh.

"We did more than that. If we weren't here, this town would have dried up ages ago. *We* spent those years making offers, promises, anything to bring people with a few dollars to this place, so it seemed like a real town. Better than anyone coming to a ghost town and looking into why it had started at all. And now that it's my turn in charge, I deserve something for all our effort.

"So I know something about negotiation, Mr. da Costa." He sneered, and swung the gun toward Bea again. "My company trained Eric, and we understand each other. You think an *assistant historian* can drive a wedge between us?"

He laughed again.

"He's got you there," Eric added. "You don't even know all of that history, if you think this place could ever survive."

Colin winced. But Gardner was looking down at the prisoners again, so he shot back a distraction:

"What I *know* is that all of you Gardners spent generations keeping this skein hidden. But I guess all that only lasts until you, *you,* want it yourself."

"But you do know more than that." Gardner looked up. "Perhaps much more. I should ask the real researcher in your family."

Zara, he's going after Zara... but, she's out there looking for a chance to bring the police down on Hoyle... she needs time!

Colin forced confidence into his voice. "You think it's that hard to figure out? This 'assistant' historian *did* trace it all."

All the way back to the dragon—that much he could keep to himself.

"I could ask your mother," Gardner said. "But you see, that might take a while."

He pulled out his phone.

The sight of the tiny cell, deep within the mine, kicked Colin into a moment's absurd laugh. "You think you'll get reception down here?"

"Look." Gardner held the screen up.

The screen glinted in the lamp's twilight—whole paces away, too small to see well. Except, the image filled the screen: a close-up of what had to be a face, a head slumped against a table. The camera moved to play over different angles, from Zara's hair to the toppled coffee mug beside her.

Colin squinted, but he knew what he saw. Zara, lying still and unconscious. Zara, and that meant Terri too, helpless under Hoyle's thumb.

Gardner said "It's that simple, for a nurse to slip her something to make her sleep." He grinned at Colin and Bea. "Once a person's frightened it's simple to reach them again."

Nurse Setter too, he just used *her terror... Gardner just keeps tightening his grip...*

"And then I have the lieutenant's help as well. You know he can arrange to point most of these crimes at the two of you? You were the ones who 'found' Terri, and you're the only witness to Phil Balan's death. That's enough for Eric to walk free."

Bea shook her head. "You know that will never stand up."

"No? Because of a rogue cop like you? Hoyle had to fight to keep you *out* of jail—now he only needs to back away. But..." The dark humor smoothed from Gardner's voice and left something colder in its place. "So much of that depends on keeping Zara da Costa silent afterward."

"No!" Colin roared, stared around at Eric. "You can't let him— Terri would never forgive you!"

"There, you see?" Josh Gardner's face split in a broad grin. "You were calling me desperate, but look at you now—I think you know how it feels to have someone in need. Still, you were right," he added.

Colin stared. "What?"

"I don't have phone reception down here. That video was recorded earlier, so I'll need to move closer to the mine entrance every hour. Where I can tell Hoyle not to finish her off yet."

Colin fought for a breath, clawed for words, anything—

Bea's voice cut through the silence. "You have a hostage, then. And what is it you want?" Something steadied her voice—was that familiarity?

"What I want. There's a common language, between business and detectives, isn't there?" Gardner held up the phone. "What I want first, Detective Simms, is for you to step forward."

And he beckoned with that hand, for her to move up past Colin. In-to his line of fire.

"Not a chance." Colin edged sideways to keep her shielded. "Then you get two hostages?"

"Once someone has one hostage," Bea said, "then to some people, any more can be redundant."

And her feet shuffled sideways, she *moved around him* and up to-ward their enemies, with empty and bare hands spread outward. Eric pulled back to Gardner's side. She was wide open to the gun.

Redundant? What kind of cop logic is that? Colin felt his hands trembling, helpless.

"Now…" Gardner's voice tensed in eagerness. "What is the pro-cess to make the skein feed?"

Eric glanced around toward him. "We had an agreement. You don't need to know that."

"I asked a question. What starts it growing?" Gardner trained his silencer-long gun squarely at Bea's face.

"No." And Bea calmly, slowly, began relaxing her arms down, inward. *Daring* him to shoot. "You're dangerous enough as it is, Mr. Gardner."

Gardner said "I wasn't asking you." He twitched the gun on her again. "Mr. da Costa?"

"You can't!" A useless word—cold shock flooded through Colin. *I should have known he would...*

"In fact, it's only now that I *can,*" Gardner said. "Hostages are redundant? Only in that now I have Ms. da Costa for later, and Ms. Simms for the next ten seconds.

"Now, how do you grow the skein? Ten..."

"No!" But all Colin could do was yell denials. He locked his eyes on the gun. Too far, and he couldn't even trust the skein to give him speed—

"Nine. Eight." That same damn voice counting. Bea never flinched.

"He'll use Terri next!" he gasped at Eric. "You know he will, she's right there trapped beside Zara!"

"Seven. Six."

"Please..." Or his mouth moved, but the sound was swallowed in his heart's pounding.

"No use." Bea's steady voice was clear. "Mr. Gardner only cares about one thing, himself." Her arms settled in at waist level, stretching toward her enemy.

Within her hand, something shimmered.

Her clump of skein appeared—tucked within her palm and peeling back to show the muzzle of a deadly little holdout pistol, leveled right at Gardner.

When did she draw that... she had him trapped all along...

Gardner scowled. "Put that thing away, or you're dead."

"I'm a trained shot, and I'm in better health than you are. I like the odds."

"I'm already dying. If I don't contact Hoyle, you still lose Zara—"

"You still lose *you,*" Bea said. "To you, that makes all the rest of this redundant."

Her voice—under the steel, that was a *tremor,* fear roused to fury. She could, she *wanted* to shoot him now.

Colin snapped "This is crazy! You can't pull some standoff—you'll kill each other!"

"They won't," Eric smirked. "She's right, Gardner won't risk it."

"So you grab her!" Gardner said. "You have to, you need me!"

Colin heard the threat coming behind that sneer, and he cut in "So next is when you threaten Terri, right? It's just that easy for you." He glared at Eric. "Great friends you've got."

"Shut up," Eric said. "Let them make their threats, it won't matter."

"Won't it?" *No, no*—Colin could only keep hammering at one hope. "I said it's *Terri* on the line too! You don't care about Bea or Zara, but are you going to let Gardner's schemes drag her down? Or is this what you want—give up on her and let everyone rip each other apart, and you knock down whatever's left and tell yourself it was already gone?"

"Shut. Up."

Colin watched that green-coated figure, the tension in his half-bent arms, his balance, on the edge of *something*—

A soft beep came from Gardner's phone.

"Th-that's my timer," the old man breathed. "Two minutes left, while I can still tell Hoyle to hold off. If we want to continue this, I have to move out to where I can signal him."

"To save Zara, or Terri?" Colin growled.

Gardner didn't answer. Instead he shuffled back, back, his weapon never wavering from Bea. She followed, and Eric paced along at his "partner's" side.

Colin tromped behind them on heavy feet. Bea was right, all Gardner cared about was his own life and the strings he could pull to keep it. And his control of Hoyle and the nurse might have outsmarted them all.

Step by careful step they moved through the dimness. The light of the lamp fell away behind them, and another, ruddier glow stretched from up ahead. They were nearing the mine entrance, but any cops still outside would be under Hoyle's orders to stay clear...

The light had just swelled to twilight when Gardner looked at his phone again, and halted to bring it to his face.

He kept his voice just loud enough for them to follow. "It's me. You can hold off on them for another..."

He paused, showed them his smile.

"Let's say ten minutes... *what?*"

The smile vanished.

He stared at the phone, face pale in the light.

"Listen—you need me—there are charges already in place against your son—"

Eric struck.

Colin was just closing in when Eric blurred to life. One brutal hand ripped the gun from Gardner's fingers, the other clamped over his mouth and swept him backward.

Colin slammed to a stop beside Bea.

Eric yanked Gardner around as his shield. Pain showed on the face above that armored grip—Gardner's own fingers looked twisted where he'd lost the gun.

The phone fell from his other hand, and clattered on the stone.

Eric kicked it over. It slid only a few feet toward them before it caught on rock, and Colin had to step forward to scoop it up.

On the other end was a voice he knew better than his own. "Mr. Gardner? Are you there?"

"Zara? You're alright?"

"Colin? The lieutenant thought they had me fooled—I let them think I drank their coffee, and they turned their backs..."

"Of course they did..." A laugh came leaping up, cutting off the rest, but his family was *safe.*

"Them."

Eric's harsher, clenched voice cut through:

"Hold off on *them,* you said. So you did aim at Terri too."

Eric dropped Gardner's gun and swung his hand around. Claws dug into his victim's side.

Gardner moaned—even the hand over his mouth couldn't muffle all that pain.

Eric added "Oh, and we have the cops ignoring screams, don't we?"

Bea stepped around Colin toward the two.

"Back off!" Eric snapped.

His talons stirred against Gardner's jaw.

"One question," and he leaned in against his prisoner. "Where are the rest of your files on me? There's the disconnected old server you linked to your office computer... *so* private and secure," he smirked. "And?"

The old server—where Fields and then Gardner tracked him to—

Eric's fingers peeled back to free Gardner's mouth. The old man's face gleamed with pale terror. "That's... all... please don't..."

"Might even be true," Eric said. "You said you were dying, didn't you? Not fast enough."

The claws sank in. The man's throat... fell apart.

"I should thank you," Eric said. He was looking up, past the sagging form in his grasp, at Colin.

"Thank me?" His throat didn't want to work.

"Like you said." A sharp, feral *satisfaction* rang in Eric's words. "Everything I had is gone. So I either hold onto the pieces, or it's time to show you all what that loss means."

Bea jolted into motion and lunged at him. *"Gratshay ko—"*

Eric flung Gardner's body at her. The shape crashed into her, sent her staggering back.

Colin was leaping in, flinging himself between them, at the instant Eric followed up. That thought-sudden rush slammed into him, his block turned the claws away. He thudded off the wall behind him and braced for the next attack.

But Eric had twisted away. He raced away, outward up the tunnel and toward the light—footsteps already fading.

Colin spun toward Bea. "You alright?"

She stumbled up. "I could've reached him... started too late..."

"But you're *okay.*" *We beat him, we chased him off.*

Away beyond the tunnel, a voice shouted "Hey! Hold it—"

And cut off. *Cut* off—he could almost hear the dying gurgle.

Eric, loose among the cops outside.

And—

Colin felt the horror opening up inside him as the picture came clear. He stepped forward, readied himself, waiting for what had to come next.

Eric came hurtling back down the tunnel at them.

Two steps—Colin shifted to head that charge off from Bea.

Eric twisted and leaped aside, on past them. Colin lashed out and felt his fist strike home.

Eric tumbled off balance. Cracked against the wall.

Bea rushed in.

Eric rolled away, kept moving, out of her reach and tumbling away down the tunnel into the dark. Bea glanced back, Colin moved to her side.

Lights moved behind them.

Voices were barking out commands—two voices, three, more, all closing in. Somewhere in the tumult, Colin made out "keep your scopes ready" and "da Costa must be—"

Of course they think it's me. Hoyle was staging all of that... but Zara had...

He reached for Bea's arm. "Come on—"

She stepped away.

"My fault, I was slow," she said. "And the victims, someone has to show the police—"

Show them? "Don't! They could—"

She moved in, brushed a clumsy kiss against his cheek. Light and brief against the skein across it.

Her hands pushed something into his. Her skein, and the flashlight.

Then she shoved him away, on up the tunnel, and turned down to walk toward the gathering footsteps, hands raised.

Eric's footsteps were already fading.

Colin tore his gaze from her and spun away.

Into the dark he ran. Hunching in the shaft, ricocheting off the walls and cradling the flashlight that let him click on brief glimpses of the tunnel, the path, the last echoes of Eric's path through the mine and on through the dark.

*****

Colin's adventures continue in:

Taking Wing

from TAKING WING

Each blind step clattered in the darkness, catching and shifting to save his balance again and again over the tricks of the mine's footing. Only the sheath of skein over Colin's body blocked out the impacts and let his guiding fingers scrape along the shaft's side unharmed.

Eric's footsteps had dwindled in the blackness ahead—he had to catch him. But those sounds were swallowed by Colin's own steps, and the harsh shouts of the police behind him.

Even with Bea staying behind to explain. But Eric's latest victim was lying there, and the police already blamed them for one murder already.

A muffled moan sounded in the darkness ahead. Colin risked flicking Bea's flashlight on.

Two women and a man lay in the tunnel. Their homeless clothes looked as worn as the rocks now, where they showed through the heavy chains around them... and the smears of silver-green skein Eric had laid over them. Two were still straining in agony as the stuff slowly consumed more of their flesh to grow.

Then Colin was crouching down beside those two, saying "Help's coming" and laying his hands on their skein before he wondered if he could control it.

Let them go, stop, rest, now... His thoughts pounded at the greenness with all the strength he could throw at it—it *had* to work.

Somehow their gagged grunts softened. They breathed easier, as the skein's feeding ended.

Colin forced himself to turn away and step past them. Eric would do this or worse if he'd been told where Colin's mother and sister were hiding, and Terri was already too weak. He could only leave these three to Bea and the cops. His feet dragged as he pulled away.

With the light off again, only his fingers told him when the tunnel's side turned. He clicked it on—the shaft branched left and right, but which side had he come up here from? Nothing looked the same from this end.

Light moved behind him. The police closing in.

Colin plunged into the left path. He clicked his flashlight off and willed his skein to cover it, to *twist* at light and wrap him in cooling invisibility. But in the narrow shaft, the cops wouldn't miss the faint mirage-outline he'd still leave... or the infrared scopes they carried would pick him out easily. With those scopes in the dark, they'd be more invisible than him.

He pushed on, trying to keep his breathing steady. He still had enough focus to work the skein's stealth, but he could barely make the stuff move with the better-than-human strength that could be flinging him along. *And I think I can fight Eric and all the power he's wrapped in?*

Every step ground away more doubt, more of his excuses. The next time they met, he'd have to use the spell that would turn Eric's skein to feed on him like Eric had done with his prisoners—*and wake the stuff I'm wearing too. Or else I take mine off when I attack, and try to survive getting past him to deliver the spell's touch.*

One more reason he needed Bea, her striking once he blocked Eric. Instead Bea was stuck back with the police explaining the corpse of Gardner Development's CEO, when their own Lieutenant Hoyle had ordered them to leave Gardner and the tunnels alone.

Eric's sounds were long gone. He might be all the way through the mine by now, and heading for Terri.

The voices of the police behind Colin had gone still too. He tried not to think how IR-sighted cops could come into view of him at any moment, unseen.

A quick flash of his light ahead caught the tunnel giving way to larger shadows.

He stopped at the rim of the strange cave basin, that this shaft and the opposite one both reached to. Down at the bottom lay the pile of rocks and the new stones he and Bea had dislodged when they came through here.

And under that...

He needed an edge against Eric, and here it was. They'd left it there before to keep its secret. But now he was alone and Terri needed him...

Or Eric could be watching right now. Colin played the light around the cave, but he saw no glimpse of his enemy, and even the gauze-thin skein over his eyes didn't reveal the halo-shape of an invisible figure. And he was losing time.

Colin trotted and slide down the basin's side. It was still hard to believe, that under those rocks was the source of their fight with Eric, and incidents going generations back—maybe why the doomed mine had been dug at all.

He slid a rock aside, and another. Until he saw it.

Glinting in his light, a hint of green. Clinging to what they'd seen were long, winged bones of a dead thing that had to be a dragon.

Colin reached into the rocks. *Bea had apologized to the beast when she'd taken a bit...* Now he strained and pulled at a whole armful of the dragonskin they'd been calling "skein."

It didn't stir. He pulled and willed it to come loose and join him, and the great fleshy mass of it lay unmoved.

Colin clenched his fingers, focused his need. Disturbing this creature wasn't right, but he needed its strength or Eric would only keep killing...

I'm worn out. I can't even make my own thin sheathe carry me, and I want to make this mountain of it respond?

Focus. He dug at his desperation and forced the doubts and the aches out of his mind. There was only clear, cold purpose, and everything he'd learned controlling the skein and facing down Eric... and he needed it now, his strength had to be enough... but the skein only clung in place...

Footsteps. Quick, guarded footsteps spilled through his concentration from what had to be the tunnel behind him. The police.

Colin let the skein go, defeated. All he could do was choose to fall back and protect Eric's targets, and not let the cops slow him down. Softly he set rocks back over the gaps in the cairn.

Two quick flashes of his light let him pick his way up the far slope, to the opposite tunnel. His feet on the stones had to be too loud.

He scrambled into the shaft, part of him bracing for some crushing punch out of the darkness—it would be just like Eric to stop and catch him at a secret again. Instead he heard a low *come on* back where the cops closed in. Colin flicked his light on and headed away, anything to draw them on past the rocks.

One step after another, rushing on through the narrow tunnel. There'd be so many steps ahead just to get back to town. And Eric would only be pulling farther ahead.

Colin jogged on. *Think of Terri—my sister's broken body survived for* years *in Eric's captivity, while he tried using skein to heal her.* She'd never lost her defiance, and now Eric could be going to take her back.

And Zara—*my mother's turned all the tireless inspiration that's held the neighborhood together, to getting help for Terri.* And they were alone with the corrupt Lieutenant Hoyle, them and Terri's nurse, and even she'd been part of Josh Gardner's conspiracy to control Eric.

Now Eric had killed Gardner, and he sounded more unpredictable than ever.

More footsteps echoed behind him, farther back now. Had Bea's explanations and the skein-mangled prisoners slowed the cops down at all?

The shaft pinched in ahead, the narrow stretch he remembered. He slid and scraped through it, the skein saving him from losing skin. *Skein, skin—how could we not guess that was the key?*

Then he stepped out into the open air.

A cooling breeze flowed over the hillside, with the sound of birds drifting in it somewhere. Still evening, still the long summer evening, when the time in the mine felt like years.

And down the hill, the whole long way down to the roads and the town.

ABOUT THE AUTHOR

"Whispered spells for breathless suspense."

Ken Hughes dreams of dark alleys and the twenty-seven ways people
with different psychic gifts might maneuver around each corner. He
grew up on comics and adventures before discovering Stephen King
and Joss Whedon, and he's written for Mars mission proposals and
medical devices, making him an honorary rocket scientist and brain
surgeon. Ken is a Global Ebook Award-nominated urban fantasy
novelist, creator of the Shadowed Steps series, the Spellkeeper Flight,
the Mirrorman, and many more series of supernatural thrills.
Don't get him started on puns.
Find more books and join the Overview newsletter at:
KenHughesAuthor.com.